I0629047

DEAD SURE

ALSO BY HERBERT BREAN

Wilders Walk Away
The Darker the Night
Hardly a Man is Now Alive
The Clock Strikes Thirteen
Dead Sure (also published as *A Matter of Fact*)
The Traces of Brillhart
The Traces of Merrilee

DEAD SURE

HERBERT BREAN

Also published as
A MATTER OF FACT

WILDSIDE PRESS

For Dorothy—all by herself.

Copyright © 1956 by Herbert Brean

Published by Wildside Press LLC.
www.wildsidebooks.com

PART ONE: THE C-NOTE

CHAPTER 1

The Double Tail

Shadowy darkness and cold filled the street, the sudden bone-penetrating cold of early November that sends a man indoors and holds him there. Darkness was appropriate to this street as a black garment to a nocturnal thief, for it was a mean, shabby thoroughfare, walled in on either side by rows of high brownstone houses that frowned down on passers-by by day and menaced them by night, obscurely but perceptibly. Before the houses stood unbroken rows of automobiles, illegally parked as though their owners had left them there only long enough to snatch a few hours' sleep before driving away forever from this glowering neighborhood.

Meanwhile the night-black windows of houses and cars reflected back the street lamps' murky light at either end of the block. Only an occasional rectangle of orange showed where someone still sat up, mesmerized by television or solitaire, or absorbed in the evening paper or a wrangle with the old woman. On the sidewalk dusty cans of ashes awaited next morning's sanitation truck, and in the middle of the block a small bulb burned over the *Night Bell* sign beside a garage's door.

A tall man swung into the street from the Third Avenue end, moving with the long, confident strides of the hard-muscled. As he passed under the street light it showed him lean and high-shouldered, wearing a peaked cap like a hunter's and a heavy jacket of checkered wool. In his right hand he carried a brown paper sack that clunked in heavy rhythm to the crunch of his shoes. The street light spread a lengthening, writhing shadow of himself before him that merged with the other darkness and, as he progressed, finally vanished.

When this man was midway down the block a second man appeared at the Third Avenue end. He snapped a quick glance after the first that was like a silent pistol shot and, having seen what he wanted, continued on across the lighted intersection, looking straight ahead without turning into the dark side street. When he reached the opposite curb, he turned quickly on silent feet and began paralleling the first man from the opposite sidewalk.

He walked rapidly and carefully, putting his weight on rubber heels so that he would not be heard above the faint, endless grinding that is the sound of Manhattan an hour before midnight. As he did he strained his eyes after the first man, for he knew there was a good chance that he was being ambushed. You were taught to guard against things like that in the police academy, and the second man, whose name was O'Neill Ryan and who was a probationary-detective, had completed his course there only two weeks before.

But if the man in the wool jacket knew that he was being followed, he disguised it very convincingly. Three quarters of the way down the block he turned unhurriedly, a flicker of black in the larger darkness, into one of the brownstones and took the tall steps two at a time. He whistled a snatch of jukebox song, opened the door into an ill-lit hall, and Ryan, moving almost soundlessly along the opposite sidewalk, caught the diminuendo of boots on a rugless stair before the door swung shut.

Then the street was silent again. Ryan paused behind a parked station wagon.

He was uncertain and scared. He looked back along the way he had come for his partner, who was the senior member of the detective team. For the last fifteen minutes they had been double-tailing the man who had gone into the house. In double-tailing a detective follows a suspect while a second detective follows the first detective, out of sight of the quarry. After an agreed-on number of blocks or minutes the second moves up into the lead position while the first detective drops back and follows the second. It is complicated, requiring quick and cooperative intelligences, but a subject who is on guard against being followed is much less likely to notice this kind of tail.

What bothered Ryan was that he wanted to let his partner, who was not yet in sight, know where their quarry had gone, which meant staying where he was. But he also knew that if the quarry had observed the tail he might have entered the house only to walk through it quickly and escape out the back. Logic indicated he should go to the rear, but that meant missing Jablonski, his partner. A rookie's agony of eagerness and uncertainty seized Ryan.

A wedge-shaped silhouette appeared at the end of the street. Ryan relaxed. That was Jablonski—thick, routine-minded, unimaginative, but solid and knowing. And in command.

Jablonski did just what Ryan had done. He crossed the intersection and then turned into the dark street, coming along softly, watchfully. Ryan whistled from the station wagon's shadow.

"Where is he?" Jablonski whispered back.

"There. Where the light is in the hall."

"Did he make us?"

"I didn't see him look back. But what can you see in this damned street?"

"It don't figure," said Jablonski. His mouth made chewing movements as though he were rolling a cigar between his lips.

"Maybe it's a hideout."

"Hideout nothing! It don't figure. He's shakin' us. I'll hit the back."

He moved hurriedly out from between parked cars.

"What about help?" Ryan whispered hoarsely into the darkness after him.

Jablonski only waved a hand in irritation behind him and went on across the street, a bulky, grizzled, worried man of fifty-three. Jablonski really did not want help. It would have been absurd for anyone to consider him brave for feeling that way, and Jablonski would have been the first to laugh at such an idea. He did not greatly venerate courage, regarding it as a quality usually reserved for rookies and saps. But Jablonski had personal, hardheaded reasons for not wanting, for very much not wanting, any help on this arrest.

That is why he walked quickly up to the door of a passageway between the two houses across the street, pushed it open and stepped into the dark passage which, he knew after years of working neighborhoods like this, would take him into whatever backyard or court lay behind the houses. He was lucky it was there—but it would be a hell of a place to meet Derby.

After a minute he flashed his light down the black passage. He saw only twin walls of eroded old brick, chalked with children's scribbling. He clicked out the flashlight and walked down the passage in cold darkness. Doing that he comforted himself with the somewhat specious reasoning that if Derby, a cop-hater, three-time loser and now a killer—if Derby had spotted them, he was already out the back of this building and was gone. If not, then they had him. And at that Jablonski sucked in his breath, audibly, hopefully.

He reached the end of the passage. It opened into a small yard, faintly starlit and surrounded by the high old garden wall of another era. Above him a window suddenly rasped open, and his hand dove under his overcoat's left lapel. There came a harsh, strangling sound; someone spat out the window, and did not close it.

Presently Jablonski moved across the yard to the wall. On top of it his exploring hands encountered pieces of broken glass, a futile deterrent to juvenile marauders. He picked the glass off, placing the pieces carefully on the ground, then took out his gun and, holding it, drew himself up and over the wall. He eased down into the yard of the house where Derby was. No light showed from the windows. Jablonski waited a few minutes to let his arms recover their strength so his hands would be steady if he needed them to be. As he did this his eyes adjusted to the yard's darkness, and he thought he saw a back porch with a door, and below the porch another door leading into the cellar.

Jablonski stole across the yard, went almost silently down some steps and tried the cellar door. He revolved the knob several times while he leaned his weight against it to see if the door was locked. Doing that he knew he was an unmissable target for anyone standing with a gun on the other side of the door. Nothing happened. Jablonski cautiously climbed the steps and tried the porch door in the same way with the same result. Then his thick, pursed lips relaxed in a complacent smile.

They had him.

For if Derby had spotted the tail and simply walked through the house to escape them he would have been in a hurry. He would not have bothered to lock any doors behind him. He was inside then and didn't know they were there at all. It was perfect!

Ryan and Jablonski had picked up Derby only twenty minutes before on Third Avenue, just as he had gone into a delicatessen to buy some beer, and Jablonski surmised that Derby planned to sit up for a while, drinking it. That was perfect, too. *It's eleven-thirty now. Give him until one o'clock. The beer will make him sleepy.*

Jablonski returned to the wall, wrapped his overcoat around himself and sat down in the shadow. He could assume Ryan would interpret no news as good news and would continue to watch the front. All they had to do now was to wait, and the only thing that could go wrong would be for Ryan somehow to manage to send back for help. Good strategy demanded that they call in for reinforcements, but Jablonski for urgent personal reasons wanted to make this arrest himself. He settled himself in his overcoat and wished for one of the cigars he had been about to buy when they had spotted Derby.

Time passed. No lights appeared in the house's rear windows. An ambulance whined down Second Avenue. Jablonski waited. He rolled an imaginary cigar in his mouth and thought of Derby, sipping beer out of a can, getting heavy-eyed, sleepy, dull of wit…

That's what Jablonski was waiting for. He was good at waiting.

Time passed.

* * * *

Ryan stood beside the station wagon where Jablonski had left him, hunched over for warmth and concealment, eyes never leaving the front door across the street for more than a fleeting second. A feeling of imminent triumph filled him; Jablonski's silence was the best news in the world.

Yet Ryan was jittery. He was not afraid of Derby, even though Derby was the hottest guy in town tonight, a three-time loser who would get life at best but who far more likely was going to the chair. Ryan would never have become a cop and stayed a cop if he did not believe innately that he was smarter, faster and tougher than anyone he would ever go up against.

What worried him was that through his own inexperience or overeagerness he would wreck the delicate, dangerous strategy that he and Jablonski had decided on earlier that night, casually and almost jokingly.

For as the evening wore on they had felt the mounting pressure—on them and on the department of which they were but a unit. It wasn't merely the big type on the tabloids' early editions, nor the thick, indignant anger in the lieutenant's voice when they checked in at the precinct. Nor the unwonted quiet there or the knowledge that the commissioner had ordered direct reports to be telephoned to his home throughout the night. No, it was some deeper, policeman's instinct, born of experience and a feeling for the rhythm of the city's emotions, that told them both the Connors murder would be a heavy one. That was what had been in Jablonski's mind as their plain black sedan idled up one East Side street and down another. That was why he had casually remarked that if they happened to stumble on any trace of Derby, it sure wouldn't do them any harm to work it out on their own.

Ryan had braked the car gently to a stop for a red light at Madison Avenue and looked through the windshield. He had a boyish face and dark, round, long-lashed eyes that held a thoughtfully mischievous expression which women found attractive. It sure *wouldn't* do them any harm, Ryan had agreed.

He did not look at Jablonski; he did not have to. In that instant the pact was made, and they both understood it.

Edmund Aloysius Jablonski was retiring in less than two weeks after a career of twenty-eight years in the police department. As his rank of Detective Third Grade suggested, Jablonski's had been a quiet, lackluster career. He was an uninspired man who had begun to realize as retirement neared that somewhere along the trail he must have missed opportunities. That was bitter, helpless knowledge.

And now Harry Derby represented the greatest opportunity of them all.

Derby was a bright chance for Ryan also. For four years Ryan had walked a beat to get this tryout as a detective. He had been paired with the older man, in accordance with departmental custom, to gain experience and also to be observed. He had been disappointed in the man he was paired with, recognizing Jablonski as plodding, tired and inept. But tonight Jabby was acting and sounding like an eager kid. It made Ryan feel hopeful, because to arrest someone like Derby would do him more good...

And then—it had seemed incredible, for Ryan was new at this end of the business—then he had seen something.

Swinging down Third, walking fast but not furtively, bathed briefly in the colors of the neon signs that he passed, a lean, hard-muscled man with a cold eye and a curt sneer—that was Derby.

Since their car was not a Radio Motor Patrol car and had no two-way radio, departmental routine dictated that they split up, one telephoning in for help while the other tailed Derby to wherever he was going and whomever he was meeting, for there had been an indication this afternoon that he had had an accomplice.

But Ryan and Jablonski had already made their decision. They would bring him in themselves. That dangerous decision was what was in Ryan's mind now as he stood minute after minute, feeling the cold creep up through the soles of his shoes and an ache grow in the small of his back. If it came to shooting and he shot recklessly or held his fire when—*Stop that!* The hall light across the way blinked out.

Was he coming out?

Ryan's right hand dove under overcoat and suit coat and gripped the warm, snub-nosed .38 holstered under his left arm. But no one came out of the house. Ryan concluded it was just the janitor turning out the lights.

A car turned into the street. Ryan hoped it was not an RMP car for then he could have no reason for not asking for help. It was not an RMP car and he felt relieved, and was pleased at his own relief.

But why the hell didn't Jablonski—!

Ryan arched his back and reminded himself that Jablonski was doing the same thing. His watch showed five minutes of one. They had him trapped.

All they had to do was take him cleanly.

CHAPTER 2

The China Chip

Some ten hours earlier a thin sixty-three-year-old woman named Thelma Connors had left the small gloomy apartment she shared with her daughter Elaine on East Sixty-first Street and walked to a branch bank on Lexington Avenue a few blocks away. There she drew out one hundred and twenty dollars from their joint savings account, leaving only twelve dollars to keep the account alive. A white-haired, pathetically proper woman with a slight limp that expensive surgery could have repaired, she confided to the teller that she and Elaine were leaving by interstate bus that night for Chicago and a visit with her son, and she specifically asked for a hundred dollar bill to pin to her clothing for safekeeping.

Later, under the deluge of probing questions by detectives, the teller recalled that a tall man whom he did not remember ever seeing in the bank before, a man in some kind of wool jacket or shirt, had stood in the line with several others waiting for Mrs. Connors to complete her garrulous transaction. The teller could not recall definitely whether or not the man had come up to the window. If he had it had been only to get a bill changed.

Mrs. Connors stopped at a nearby grocery for some sandwich meat and then walked home in crystal November sunshine, a happily excited wisp of woman in a decent black cloth coat. A neighbor, one Mrs. Anders, who was sitting on the steps of a dingy apartment building, spoke to Mrs. Connors. A moment later Mrs. Anders saw a man walk up the steps and go into the vestibule. He seemed to study the mailboxes, and when she asked who he was looking for, he did not reply or look at her but went into the building. It was his incivility more than anything else that made her remember him later: a tall, thin man with a bitter face and wearing a checkered woolen jacket.

The wife of the building janitor, a Mrs. Lombardi, also glimpsed him. She was coming down from the fourth floor when she saw him standing before Mrs. Connors' apartment on the second. She heard him say something like, "I'm from the office, ma'am," when the door opened and she saw him step quickly in.

She went on downstairs, noticed Mrs. Anders outside and paused to smoke a cigarette with her. They were *tête-à-tête* over a match when the first outcry came. They looked at each other over the burning match.

"Did you hear that?"

"A kid maybe?"

They paused, uneasily sensing something wrong yet unwilling to accept that anyone near them could be in such fearful distress as was expressed by that quick yell of terror.

There came a weaker cry and the faint vibrating sound of something falling and then a last, loud cry that was punctuated by a shot.

"My God!" Mrs. Anders' hand went guiltily to her mouth. They knew they should have taken the meaning of the earlier scream and gone to someone's assistance.

They ran into the hall together and saw a tall, rangy man running toward the back door. Mrs. Lombardi yelled, "Stop thief!" and the man turned a snarling face at them as he ran. He shouted something which neither of them could even begin to describe later, and which might have been directed at someone ahead of him, a confederate perhaps. The door banged behind him.

The man was seen by someone else. A telephone company employee named Betty Leonard, who shared an apartment with another telephone operator on the second floor, had been preparing to leave for work. Hearing the scream and shot, she apprehensively opened her door a slit and saw the man in the wool jacket gallop downstairs.

She went to the Connors' door and called. Getting no reply and hearing Mrs. Lombardi's hail from below, she pushed her way, frightened, into the living room. It was darkly gloomy but one light bulb was shining oddly up at her from the carpet.

Then she saw the rest of it and she too screamed.

* * * *

The usual RMP car got there first. Its crew found Mrs. Connors lying face up near the living-room table, a bloody laceration on the right side of her forehead and blood running into her sightless eyes. The remains of a table lamp which apparently had been used as a bludgeon lay beside her, its cheap pottery base smashed into a thousand fragments, its bulb incongruously alight. In the right side of her head above the ear, black-haloing the thin silvery hair, was a bullet hole.

One of the RMP men called the precinct and the routine notifications began. The precinct sent two detective teams at once; one of them was

Ryan and Jablonski, who when the call came in had been looking over the post condition on the bulletin board in the East Fifty-first Street station before starting the afternoon trick.

The radio car was still double-parked in front of the apartment when they got there. Going up the steps they took out gold, blue-centered badges and pinned them to their coats so cops from other squads and bureaus would know they were policemen and not reporters or the ever-present curious.

The deputy chief inspector who was commanding officer of Manhattan East detectives was already there, and his early presence was enormously significant. For several weeks there had been a mounting wave of assaults and muggings throughout Manhattan and Brooklyn; the newspapers had begun to get sharply critical. Ryan and Jablonski went into the apartment briefly to take a look and tacitly let the deputy chief know they were there. He gave them an angry look as though this somehow was their fault, and they went back into the hall to await orders and not clutter up the place. That was all routine.

The RMP man on the door repeated to them what the women had told him and his partner. The deputy inspector, a heavy-faced man with hair like springy black wire, looked out the door.

"Seventeenth Squad, sir," said Jablonski.

"Start on the tenants. The guy who did it was seen. It was a clumsy job—he may have been an amateur. Ask about relatives. There's a daughter and we've sent down for her. She's at work."

"Yes, sir."

The Medical Examiner and his assistant came up the stairway, laden and puffing.

In thirty minutes Jablonski and Ryan and one of the other teams that arrived after them talked to all the tenants who were at home, learned who knew the Connors, and had located who had heard or seen anything of the intruder. Meanwhile the Medical Examiner reached a preliminary verdict: death by bullet wound, which had occurred at the time the other witnesses heard the shot. The men from the Picture Gallery made photographs, and then two serious-looking lab men took over, opened a heavy black kit and began dusting for fingerprints, making preliminary blood stain tests and examining the dead woman's clothing, hands and fingernails. It was routine.

But the crime wasn't. They all felt that. One of the picture men, packing away his camera and tripod, paused to study the slender figure crumpled on the floor like a dropped handkerchief and said, "Jeez," softly.

"Yeah," said a detective next to him. "This was a real son of a bitch."

"I can't wait to read the *Telegram* tonight," said the picture man sarcastically.

This was a heavy one. It had to be cleaned up fast, and whether it was depended on themselves—on their pooled skills and brains, courage and tenacity, on the clues they found and how assiduously they ran them down, on the empirical soundness of the conclusions they drew, on the leads they developed and the patience with which those leads were proven and disproven.

The precinct relayed word that the team that had gone down for the daughter reported she said her mother had been going to the bank that day. Lieutenant Bauer who had come over from the precinct growled an order and two detectives ran downstairs and hurried to the bank. Jablonski in response to another order assembled the three principal witnesses in Miss Leonard's chintz-decorated apartment. When they had seated themselves expectantly, Jablonski began to talk earnestly, while Ryan leaned against the door and felt useless.

"My name's Jablonski," Jablonski began. "This is my partner, Detective Ryan. A very serious crime was committed here an hour ago, ladies. A man followed your neighbor Mrs. Connors home from the bank, tried to rob her and hit her with a lamp. When that failed to…ah, render her unconscious, he killed her. You ladies saw him. You're the only persons who did."

They listened to what they already knew with hypnotized interest.

"It's likely," Jablonski went on, "that, the killer was a known criminal, known to the police, that is. So if you ladies will cooperate, it may be possible for us to find out who he is right away and effect an arrest, ah, immediately."

Confronted with an audience, Jablonski used phrases he hardly knew were in his lexicon.

"What do you want us to do?" asked Miss Leonard.

"We'd like to drive you down to police headquarters," said Jablonski, "and show you some pictures of muggers and robbers who answer this guy's description. It won't take long. All you do is look at the pictures and if you recognize him, tell us. We'll drive you back, of course. Okay, girls?"

Eagerness made Jablonski grow too friendly, Ryan recognized. That made the women suspicious.

"I've got a switchboard to get to," said Miss Leonard determinedly. "I'm late as it is."

"I'll call your supervisor for you, miss, and explain how things are," Ryan offered politely. He smiled diffidently at her, as though he thought she was pretty nice-looking.

She smiled back. He was nice-looking himself, she thought. "Well, if you did that, Mr. Ryan," she said more cordially.

"Yeah," said Mrs. Lombardi in another tone. "But supposing we pick out this guy's picture and then his friends come looking for us, huh? How about that, mister?"

Mrs. Anders looked frightened as the meaning struck her. "Yes— how about that? It's all right for you policemen—"

"Look, girls," said Jablonski anxiously. "Is this too much to ask for the sake of your neighbor, Mrs. Connors, lying dead in there? Aren't you willing to even—" He gestured helplessly.

The women looked rebellious.

Ryan moved from the door.

"Look, ladies," he said. "All you do is drive downtown with us and look at some pictures. If you recognize one, just point. Nobody knows who picked it out or anything else." His glance deliberately engaged Betty Leonard's. "Won't you please help us?" he said gently, and he knew that he had her.

He looked at the two older women. "It's just a matter of our getting our hands on the man who did this before he can come back here or attack some other helpless woman in a building like this. Won't you please help do that?"

It was an appeal Mrs. Lombardi could not resist. She rose. "C'mon, Mary," she said.

Jablonski looked at his partner in surprised approval.

* * * *

The rite in the Bureau of Criminal Identification did not take long, and to the women it even seemed rather casual. Each of them was handed a deck of small photographs and asked to leaf through them slowly. For a few minutes there was absorbed silence, broken by an occasional mutter from Mrs. Lombardi, while Ryan, Jablonski and a BCI man watched them. It was Mrs. Anders who first said. "Well, this *looks* like him, I must say."

The BCI man took the picture and when she had finished with her stack of pictures, re-inserted it in a different position and gave the stack to Mrs. Lombardi. Minutes later she cried out, "Oh, that's him! I'm sure that was him."

It was the same picture.

Now the stack went to Miss Leonard. She had had the best look at the man. They watched her narrowly while pretending not to, and when suddenly she emitted a little frightened cry, Ryan and the BCI man breathed a sigh of relief. They knew what that meant.

The BCI man showed the women other pictures of the suspect, and those confirmed the identification. Then he took his record from a file:

Harry Derby, 37 years old, male, white. Brown eyes; light brown hair; 6 feet 1½ inches; 163 pounds. Longshoreman; North River and Brooklyn docks and bars.

Under "Distinctive Marks" it said: jagged scar on right shin, pockmarks on left shoulder and left neck, almost invisible knife scar leading from outer corner of left eye. The list of Derby's arrests took two cards clipped together; they were mostly for felonious assaults, carrying concealed weapons and robbery or suspicion of robbery.

Minutes later the news that Harry Derby was wanted for murder and his description were being teletyped into the hundred and more New York City precinct stations as well as the police headquarters and state police barracks of thirteen Eastern seaboard states. The bulletin ended: "Approach with caution. He is known to be armed."

Ryan and Jablonski drove the three women home through the clear, cold November twilight and the endless traffic jam of 5:30 p.m.

* * * *

The cluster of photographers and reporters that had been held downstairs in the apartment building's front hall was gone but there was still a uniformed man on the door.

"Anyone up there?" Jablonski asked.

"Ed Furtig," the uniformed man said. "He's carrying it."

It was a curiously expressive bit of police slang, Ryan thought, not for the first time. He's *carrying* it. The homicide men, the lab men, the identification and picture gallery men all would do what their specialties demanded in avenging the murder of Thelma Connors. But it had been assigned especially to one man, a detective in the precinct in which the crime occurred. It was primarily his responsibility, his burden to carry until the murderer was brought to trial—next week, next month, next year.

Ed Furtig sat on the arm of a deep upholstered chair near the window, arms folded, hat pushed back, smoke spiraling from the cigarette in the corner of his mouth.

"Hi, Jab. The desk said you guys should hit the street."

"Okay. All yours, huh?"

"All mine," said Furtig. His lean flexible face grew sardonic. "Naturally. I was starting a forty-eight at midnight." Furtig used the old police expression, even though the department "week end" was now fifty-six hours.

"They get any prints?"

Furtig shook his head. "Too early to tell. One of the boys thought he got a couple partials."

While Ryan listened, his eyes ranged over the room. This, was his first good look at it. A few cheap framed pictures decorated the walls, and immaculate doilies the tables and chairbacks. A large crucifix hung on one wall, a yellowed sprig of palm thrust behind it.

"The daughter have anything?"

"God, no. She flipped. A doctor's with her now, down in the janitor's apartment. One thing she did say—the old lady had some cuff links she wore with a shirtwaist. One was lying near her, but the other wasn't anywhere around. The killer may have carried it away unknowingly, if it caught in his clothes."

Jablonski said nothing. It was something to be remembered, but it would probably never turn up. Things did not happen that conveniently in real life. Ryan, listening, continued looking around.

There were little bursts of fingerprint powder, black and light gray, in unlikely places around doors and table edges. The smashed lamp was gone, taken to the lab for minute examination. The only real sign of violence left in this plain sitting room was their own presence—uninvited strangers who would not be here at all had an old woman's life been permitted to continue its even way.

No—there was one other sign of violence. Behind a chair leg there was a small yellow chip of china from the shattered lamp base. Ryan knew that it was no longer of evidential value, so he picked it up, studied it and then, reminding himself that this was the first murder in his four years on the force in which he had an active, investigative part he dropped it in his coat pocket on the universal impulse of the souvenir hunter.

"Well…here's hopin', Ed," said Jablonski.

"Thanks."

"We better roll, Neill."

They filed out. As he turned to close the door behind them Ryan saw Furtig still sitting hunched forward, smoke drifting up past squinting, unseeing eyes as he pondered what had happened, and the nature of the man who had caused it, and how he might best be overtaken. It was his to carry.

CHAPTER 3

The Walk-In

One o'clock, the deadline that he had set himself, came and went but Jablonski did not move. Let it get late, he thought with Polish stolidity. The later the better. Then, the quiet location of Derby's room, the sudden break-in, the quick pinioning and blinding light, the quick hand under the pillow for a gun…

It was a familiar operation to Jablonski. Meanwhile he thought about a cozy little bar and grill near the New Haven Railroad station in New Rochelle in which he had a chance to buy a half-interest. It had a jukebox and a Puerto Rican chef who made hamburgers with onions and sour cream, the best you ever tasted, and a steady clientele. If they got Derby—*if,* nothing!—it might help swing the deal. Publicity wouldn't do him a bit of harm. People like a joint run by a guy with some background—a fighter, or a former ball player, or a cop. Jablonski saw himself lounging behind the bar, chatting with the respectful customers and buying a drink every now and then. "I mind the time we were looking for the Actor," he was telling his audience. Or, "The D.A.? Well, I tell you how we always had to handle the D.A.'s office. The time I put a collar on Derby, for example…"

That warm vision comforted Jablonski. It made the barbed remarks of superiors over the years, the times he was passed over for promotion, the envy and the failures, recede into their own limbo. The time passed quickly, even though he sat in darkness on cold ground and knew this might bring on another attack of rheumatism.

But at twenty minutes after one Jablonski decided it was time. Derby had had well over two hours in which to drink his beer, and besides if an RMP came through he was not sure Ryan might not hail it despite their agreement. Jablonski rose, stretched his legs a moment and went back over the wall. For one of his bulk he moved with surprising quietness.

He was halfway down the silent, pitch-black passageway on his return to the street when the alley door at the far end opened. A man was silhouetted against the dull light from the street.

Jablonski froze and took out his gun. He heard a scuffling noise and then a flashlight flooded the passage, blinding him and Ryan whispered, "Jabby!"

"Put out that damned light!" He walked forward in blackness until he touched Ryan. "What's going on?"

"Nothing. I just began to wonder, for Pete's sake—"

"Never mind. You didn't send word back?"

"It's been quiet as a tomb."

Jablonski led the way to the street and then walked down it, out of range of the house's silent windows. The nocturnal wind was rising. It was getting colder.

"He's in there," he said. "There's two back doors. Both are locked."

"Good."

"Yeah." Again Jablonski wished for a cigar. Now the time had come, he felt nervous. It seemed all he had read in the last few years had been newspaper stories about cops killed on the eve of their retirement. Then he heard the blare of the jukebox in that bar, the hamburgers sizzling in onion sauce, saw the fat black bottles...

"What do you think, Neill?" he said. He wanted to hear how Ryan might sound. He looked sidelong at him.

"Let's hit it," said Ryan. "He must be sleeping by now. A guy can't take this long to drink four cans of beer."

That eagerness was what Jablonski wanted to hear. "Okay," he said. "Let's go. It'll be a nice break for you, kid."

Ryan recognized the hypocrisy but he disregarded it. His mind was on the job ahead. For if something went wrong or Derby got away from them...the mere possibility of it gave him a cold shiver.

Jablonski grabbed his arm and pulled him to a halt. "Just one thing, Neill," he said. "Don't forget who Derby is. Don't be afraid to shoot. Nobody cares if *he* gets hurt. But if we do, or if he gets away—"

Ryan tapped Jabby's restraining arm, heavy with fatty muscle. "Right," he said. "Let's go." He sounded confident.

They went quietly along the sidewalk. The cold night stretched far and wide over them and over all the city; the stars' reflections glittered in the oil-shiny water of its rivers and bays. Deep in subway tunnels the infrequent trains screeched wheel flanges against the cold satin rails, and in fetid nightclubs trumpets squawked to drum thumps. In skyscrapers' remote corridors old women flung gray mops across silent floors and in bright newspaper buildings, molten lead and electric teletype bubbled and clicked against deadlines, telling the latest news of the hunt for Harry Derby. In apartments young mothers rose from warm beds for the two o'clock feeding. But in flophouse or penthouse, most of the city slept. Ryan and Jablonski walked up the steps of what once had been a mansion and was now a musty rooming house.

There was a row of battered letter boxes, most of whose little metal doors hung askew and nameless. Mail did not mean much here. There was no bell or sign marked superintendent. That was bad.

"I think I heard him go up or down the stairs," said Ryan.

Jablonski pushed the door open, and they stepped into a high-ceilinged old hall heavy with the scent of cooking and rotting plaster. Jablonski flashed his light around. There was a massive, sagging stair-case of dark wood at the end of the hall. He pulled a dangling string and the feeble hall light came on.

"You stay here. I'll try the basement."

"Isn't that light liable—"

"Anyone comin' in late could have turned it on," said Jablonski patiently. "Now remember, them back doors are locked on the inside. If he breaks, they will slow him a few seconds when he tries to get out. We may need those seconds, so remember." He tiptoed to the back stairs and descended them.

It was cold in the house, a damp, unhealthy cold more chilling than the street's fresh gusts. Ryan's chest began to feel tight again. It was all right as long as they were moving or acting—! Suddenly he realized that he could smoke in here. He lit a cigarette.

Jablonski reappeared at the top of the stairs, listened at two doors in the back of the hall and came forward. He looked troubled. "There's one sort of room downstairs, but I don't think nobody's in it. Not a sound. Gimme one of your cheroots, will you?"

Ryan handed him the pack and flicked his lighter. Jablonski bent over it, holding the cigarette awkwardly to unaccustomed lips. "I'm goin' to try the second floor."

"Let me take the second floor."

"Me," said Jablonski. He continued smoking hurriedly in silence for a few minutes. "Wish you'd carry cigars, Neill," he grinned, then ground the stub under his heel and started up the stairs.

In a minute he was back. "The super is on the second floor," he whispered. "There's a sign. And I can hear someone threshing around in there. No lights." His breath was flavored with the knackwurst he had had for supper.

"You think he's in there?"

"Either he is or he ain't. If he ain't the super tells us what room he's in. And if that's how it is he might well have made for here after the job. It was a sudden job. He probably didn't have no hideout planned. Huh?"

Ryan nodded. "Let's go," he said. This was the finale. Suddenly he felt good, not nervous or anxious or tight in the chest, but clear, sure, quick. It was the feeling of being in danger and knowing you could handle it. It was wonderful.

Jablonski led the way to the big staircase. "Me first," he whispered. "If we go up together the stairs may creak."

Again Ryan nodded. He waited until Jablonski's portly back disappeared in the blackness above, then followed him. Little light filtered up here from the weak bulb below. Their feet made soft, sandy sounds in the grit of the hall's unswept floor. Jablonski stopped at a door near the end of the hall and leaned over the knob.

After a time he twisted his bulky body close to Ryan for quiet communication. "It ain't locked!"

"Good. How do you want to do it?"

"I'll swing the door open and you go in fast with your light. Keep low and get well into the room before you turn it on. I'll cover you from the door—so for Christ's sake, keep down."

"Right."

"And. Neill—"

"Yeah?"

"Remember, we don't know who's in there and we're going to surprise them. So whatever they do, don't start shooting until you're sure it's Derby."

"Yeah."

Ryan held his flashlight in his left hand, his revolver in his right. He could feel the heavy throb of his heart. The back of his neck was cold. Jablonski swung the door back. It creaked.

Crouching, Ryan moved quickly through the doorway, took three steps into the room's blackness and then one to the right. His thumb solidly found the flashlight button and clicked it. The first beam showed him the foot of an old iron bed, the white enamel generously chipped, then the frightened face of a middle-aged woman, red, puffy and framed by short, frizzled hair.

"What's that?" She blinked in the light.

"Someone's in bed with her," warned Jablonski from the darkness.

Ryan flashed the light around.

"Who the hell is it?" the woman demanded again, frightened.

Jablonski advanced into the room. Ryan's beam had caught a string with a little doll tied to it dangling from the ceiling. Jablonski pulled it and an ancient chandelier spread light around the frowsy bedroom. Beside the woman another figure lay in the bed, blankets pulled up tightly around its head. Jablonski stood over it. Ryan took his place on the other side of the bed.

"We're cops," he said. "Who's that next to you?"

Hate and fear burned in her look. "Get out of here."

Jablonski dug his gun into the blanket cocoon, felt under its pillow, then spoke to the woman. "Look," he said. "Tell your boy friend to open up. If he's not a guy named Derby he has nothing to worry about—we don't care what else is going on here. Get me?"

There was a second of immobile silence.

Jablonski dug harder with the gun. "If that's Derby," he said more loudly, "he either opens up or he gets a bullet in the guts. If it ain't, he gets the bullet anyway if he don't show his face. One…"

The woman reached over and seized the bedclothes. Two fine, thin hands appeared from beneath them and grabbed them desperately.

"…two," said Jablonski.

A man's high forehead appeared, then a face, big-eyed, frightened, then a mustache that was like a hyphen over tight, pale lips. Ryan relaxed.

"Now will you get outta here?" the woman cried.

"Shuddap!" said Jablonski savagely. They had made a mistake, but what was worse, they had made too much noise. That worried him.

For the second time Ryan stepped in to the older man's rescue. He said, "Look, lady. We're looking for a man named Derby—Harry Derby."

"The guy they had on the radio tonight—who killed the old lady?"

"That's the guy."

"Well, there ain't nobody named Derby in this house. So you two crapheads—"

"Harry Derby," Ryan repeated patiently. "Better listen, lady. I'd rather not have to take you in. But I will if you make me do it. We know he's in this house—right now. He's tall. Thin. Brown-haired. Wearing a checked jacket. Might have moved in here this afternoon." His tone changed to angry urgency. "Now where is he?—and talk low!"

The man was listening owlishly, only his head visible over the bedclothes.

"For God's sake, Maud, tell 'em what they want to know," he said.

The woman deliberately pulled covers over her wrinkled nightgown. On a chair beside her were cigarettes, glasses and a whisky bottle. She lit a cigarette. "I don't think I remember anyone like that," she said.

Jablonski reached across the man and grabbed her bare shoulder. His fingers tightened until the knuckles stood out and he shook her so hard the smoldering cigarette fell from her fingers. Then he threw her back on the bed. There were little red arcs on her shoulder where his thick nails had dug in. They looked at each other.

"We're in a hurry," said Jablonski.

She retrieved the cigarette.

"For God's sake, Maud," the man said again.

When the woman spoke it was as though every word hurt her. "That'll be Mr. Quinn," she said. "In thirty-three. The room just above this. Came in today."

Jablonski continued looking at her. "I hope that's right," he said. "Because if he gets away now, you go up for harboring, common adultery and breaking every housing ordinance in the book."

"Did anyone else come in with him?" asked Ryan.

"No."

"Did he meet anyone here, or ask about someone?"

"No."

That took care of the accomplice, if there had been one.

"Let's go," said Jablonski.

"Wait a minute," said Ryan. He had been studying the tall, old-fashioned door to the room. "All your doors like this?"

"Why not?" said the woman.

Ryan pushed his hat back on his forehead. It revealed, that his black hair was threaded with a little premature gray. He looked boyish and serious. "If he's locked in behind a door like that," he said, "we're going to have to blast him out. They *built* these places. A door like that won't give with one heave."

Jablonski said, "Yeah," dismayed. "That'll sure give him time to go for his gun."

The man in bed whimpered, "Oh, God."

Jablonski grinned humorlessly. "I know what we'll do," he said. "C'mon, Maud. You'll get him to open the door."

"You know what you can do," she said, and told him.

Ryan looked at her. "You're the landlady," he said mildly. "We're police officers making an arrest. You wouldn't want to obstruct justice, would you?" It wasn't really a question.

The woman slowly swung gnarled legs out of the bed and took a dressing gown that hung from an old gas jet on the wall. She put it on leisurely and fluffed out her bobbed locks with both hands.

"Atta girl, Maud," said the man in bed.

She looked behind at him. "You better not be here when I get back," she said. "You know what I mean. Don't be here."

They went quietly out into the hall. Its air was fresh and sweet; now Ryan remembered that when they broke into the room he had smelled the scent of stale powder.

"Not so fast," Jablonski said. "We ain't barefoot like you."

On the third floor she found a light and they gathered silently before a door bearing a card with 33 on it. And as they did from behind the door came the unmistakable sound of a beer can being punctured.

"Holy Mike," said Jablonski.

There came the lesser sound of the opener's wedge making the second puncture.

Suddenly Ryan was scared.

Jablonski had his gun out. He waved it between the woman and the door. "Make him open it," he whispered. "I don't care how—but get goin'."

Ryan found his own revolver in his hand without knowing he had drawn it. He wondered if this wasn't a mistake. They could still wait— But it was too late. The woman's fingers beat a light tattoo on the door.

From the other side of the door came a silence they could feel.

The woman rapped again. She smiled with an unexpected girlishness. She was playing a part, so that when she called. "Mr. Quinn, honey?" anyone could tell by the soft tone that she was smiling invitingly.

A voice behind the door said, "Who's that?"

"It's just me, honey. Mrs. Daniels, the landlady. How's about that beer you mentioned when you came in? I can't seem to get to sleep tonight. Are you having trouble, too?"

There was a pause. "Who?"

"Mrs. Daniels, honey. *You* know."

The voice said, "Wait a minute," and the doorknob twisted and a key turned with a loud switching sound.

Ryan grabbed Mrs. Daniels by the shoulders and flung her powerfully back and to one side. The door opened and a tall man peered out. The first things he saw were the short barrels of two police revolvers.

The long lean face looked surprised and a little stupid.

"All right, Derby," said Jablonski. "Don't jump or we'll blow your guts out."

CHAPTER 4

Derby's Dance

Harry derby's hair was silkily long, the color of brown wrapping paper, and it came to a deep widow's peak on his pallid forehead. His gimlet eyes were fierce, uncomprehending appraisers of what he turned them on, his mouth a hard twist of petulance. Only the jaw, long and clean in its sweep, suggested something worthy.

He said, "Who the hell—" out of a mouth still wet with beer.

Mrs. Daniels began walking away from them toward the staircase, not hurrying, not looking back.

"Put the hands up," said Jablonski.

Derby looked at him a full moment. Then he dropped the beer can in his right hand. It clunked on the floor and rolled, purling beer. He raised his arms, then recognized Jablonski and said, "Hi, cop."

"Over against the wall," said Jablonski. "Hands against it and keep your head down."

When Derby had taken his position, back to them, hands flattened against the paint-blistered wall, he said, "What's all this about?"

Ryan saw Jablonski dart quick glances around the room. Across one corner of it a piece of faded blue cloth had been tacked to make a kind of closet. It could conceal a man.

"What's behind that curtain?" said Jablonski.

Ryan approached it, keeping his gun on it and taking care not to get between Jablonski and Derby. He tore the cloth aside. There were a few coat hangers suspended from wire hooks.

Jablonski said, "Clean him. Watch his pants legs. He may have a shiv."

"What's this all about?" Derby asked again, but he did not sound as though he expected any answer.

Ryan ran his hands roughly over the taller man, watching Derby's shoulder for the muscle-tightening that would signal he was about to try something.

"No gun," he said. "No nothing."

"What'd you do with it?" asked Jablonski.

Derby's reply was two monosyllables.

Ryan emptied Derby's pockets, then went through the checkered jacket that was hanging on a chair. He strewed everything he found on a small wooden table that already held a pipe, a tobacco can and a half-played game of solitaire. The wallet held a small sheaf of greasy business cards bearing many names, a driver's license in Derby's name and a chauffeur's license made out to Harry Durward, and a membership card in the International Longshoreman's Union. There was a meal ticket with four ten-cent punches left. And there was a crisp, neatly folded one hundred dollar bill.

"Got anything?" said Jablonski.

Derby said, "How about me turning around?"

Jablonski gave him the same monosyllables.

Ryan was comparing the bill's serial number with a page in his notebook. "I'll say I got something," he said. "Here's the C-note. And the numbers check."

"Hah!" yelled Jablonski. "Now you can turn around! Want to see what's gonna send you up?"

Derby turned, straightening. He rubbed his long, thin-fingered hands nervously, like a pianist before sitting down to play. Ryan held up the bill.

"Farragut will have a tough time explaining that one for you," said Jablonski. Farragut was the first-class criminal lawyer occasionally retained by the union.

"He's also got nine dollars and twenty-four cents," Ryan said. "Book of matches. Tie clip. Couple pipe cleaners."

Jablonski nodded. "It figures perfectly," he said. "He was almost broke. Eh, Harry? So he clips the old lady. That gives him a hundred and twenty. He buys the beer and maybe got some food before that. That leaves one ten-buck bill to be accounted—Oh, the room rent. That's it! He rented the room. Give him a few dimes to begin with and it just figures. Eh, Harry?"

"You're nuts," said Derby. But his eyes moved jerkily in his head like a defective doll's. He said, "On the level you're wrong. I borrowed that dough."

"Who from?"

"A shark. Guy on the dock."

"Which one?"

"I don't remember his name. I just see him around. I'll remember it."

"What'd you need a hundred bucks for?"

"I was broke," said Derby. "Like you said."

"When you remember the guy's name," said Jablonski with ponderous politeness, "you let me know. And you know how much good it'll do you. This is a chair rap."

"Let's call in," said Ryan.

But Derby was looking at Jablonski like a man in a trance, spellbound, waiting for the word that would enable him to move again. As he did his face grew red and his arms and hands, clenched in tight fists, began to tremble. A little scar that ran thin as a knife blade from his left eye began to show oddly white.

"Chair rap."

Ryan had a sense of something happening inside Derby.

"The old lady ain't dead," Derby breathed. "You don't mean that."

"She's dead," said Jablonski. "What's the matter?—Haven't you seen a paper?"

Derby looked down at the floor. When he raised his head again, his face was a putty mask etched with despair. Only the eyes were alive, glittering, hopeless. Ryan incongruously remembered something he had heard a sergeant say long before: "They can be tough as hell—I don't care how tough. But when you've finally got them, and they know you've got them—something happens. You can see it happen in their faces."

It was happening to Derby. Ryan did not feel sorry for Derby; he hated him with a deep, contemptuous hate. But in Derby's bent head and fallen shoulder, in the low voice and limp arms, he caught a glimpse of the ultimate human defeat, of the prey's realization that it at last has been run to earth.

When Jablonski spoke, his voice was unexpectedly free of rancor. "Where you made your big mistake was in letting yourself be seen, Harry. Three dames made you right away. And the bank teller will too." After a moment he corrected himself. "That was your second big mistake. Your first one was using the gun on an old lady sixty years! Hardboiled Harry Derby—wow!"

"Look—you don't understand," said Derby. He began speaking fast and earnestly, heedless of what he was saying, only hoping to convince them by sheer flood of words and emotion. "You guys don't understand at all. It ain't like that at all. Honest. I didn't kill her. You gotta realize that. I didn't kill her. I know it looks bad—I admit that. But you gotta realize—Sure, I needed a little dough, but this afternoon I ran into this guy and—"

"Where?" said Jablonski.

"Where? Oh…yeah. It was…ah…near the Java Street pier in Brooklyn."

"What time?"

"What time? Oh, well, I guess it might have been around noon."

"Might have been, eh? And where were you around three twenty this afternoon?"

Derby stopped talking, and he looked like a man who did not want to talk.

"Where were you shortly before the banks closed?" Derby was silent.

Ryan began to grow annoyed. He wanted to take Derby in; this bear-baiting bothered him. He looked to the half-open door.

That made him say, *"Jesus!"*

"What's the matter?" said Jablonski.

"Look." Ryan reached up on the inside of the door frame. Hanging from a nail by its trigger ring, and exactly in the position where a tall man opening the door might naturally rest his hand was a .38 revolver. The hammer was cocked.

'There's the gun," said Ryan. He could feel something in the pit of his stomach. That was how close it could be. "Right caliber too."

"Good thing we didn't give this mother-raper a chance," said Jablonski feelingly. "Take it down, Neill. Think Farragut can explain that, Derby—especially after it checks with the slug? And how about the C-note? Still want to tell us it wasn't like that at all?"

Derby said, "I don't know nothin' about no C-note. But you could take it. And get a couple more tomorrow besides."

Jablonski reached over dangerously close to Derby and slapped him across the face as hard as he could. It made an astonishingly loud crack.

Tears jolted to Derby's eyes. "What'd you say, Harry?" asked Jablonski.

Derby began to curse Jablonski, meaningless obscenity gushing from his mouth like vomit.

Jablonski drew his hand back.

"Don't mark him," warned Ryan.

Jablonski took a backward step like a man getting control of himself. "Go call in, Neill. Tell them we got him."

"Wait. Put cuffs on him. I'll cover you. And give me one of your cheroots before you do."

Ryan did. But when he had handcuffed Derby and reached the door he could not help pausing a second to look back. It was like picking up the little china chip. This was his first heavy one, and he and Jabby had pulled it off—alone. This meant promotion and acclaim, but more than that it was what you lived for if you were a cop. He could not get enough of the feel of it.

Not hearing the door close behind him, Jablonski looked around, puffing the cigarette. "Hey—what's the matter?"

"Nothing. Back in a minute."

As he pulled the door shut, he heard Derby say, "Hey, cop, how about a smoke?"

* * * *

Mrs. Daniels answered his light knock wearing a house dress. Ryan said, "You have a phone in this building?"

"You got him, eh?" she said.

"We got him. Where's the phone?"

"Well, I just want you to understand I don't know nothing about him. Not a thing. In fact, I never, seen him—before today."

"When'd you see him today?"

"This afternoon. He checked in around four."

Then he came here almost directly from the job.

"He went out again for a little while. Who's the woman he killed?"

"An old lady. It's in the papers. How long'd he rent for?"

"A week."

"Pay in advance?"

"Everyone does. That room was ten bucks. C'mon in." She stepped back from the door and gestured toward the whisky bottle on the chair. "Have a jolt."

"I can't now. You go ahead."

She poured a shot glass full.

"So he paid you ten bucks in advance. With a ten dollar bill, eh?"

Too late she realized the direction of these casual questions. She indignantly put the glass down untasted on the bureau. From overhead came the sound of someone walking.

"I didn't say it was a ten."

"Let's see it."

"I didn't say I still had it."

"Then who's got it?"

She looked a quick calculation at him. "I loaned it to a friend who was going to Chicago."

"Where was he going in Chicago? What's his name?"

She said, "I dunno," looked at him covertly and stopped.

"Look, lady. That bill is evidence in a murder case—murder, get it? I won't take any malarkey about Chicago. Get it out."

Her face grew sullen. The man upstairs walked back again fast across the floor. It registered only subconsciously with Ryan.

"He rented the room," she said doggedly. "I got a right to it."

"You could get it back."

"Yeah!"

"You could if it wasn't stolen. But first it will have to be used as evidence. Come on—I haven't got all day."

She walked to the bureau in broken shoes, a resentful, helpless, middle-aged little girl. She took a small purse from a drawer, drew a bill from it and looked at the bill. Then she picked up the whisky, drank it effortlessly and extended the money to Ryan.

"That was going to buy me a new dress." Her eyes never left the bill.

Ryan thought of how his sister was with a new dress or skirt. That's how it would have been with Mrs. Daniels.

He took an envelope from his wallet, placed the ten dollar bill in it and replaced it carefully. Then he took out two fives of his own money. He defended himself to himself on the ground that he was tired and that it was late, and that it was better to keep the witnesses friendly.

"Look," he said. "Long as you need this dough, I'll replace it out of my own pocket, see? This isn't exactly regulation, but after the trial when you may get the bill back I'll drop by and pick it up from you. Otherwise you owe me ten bucks. Okay?"

It embarrassed him the way her face softened and unsuspected dimples appeared in her crepe-skinned cheeks. "Well now, that's nice of you, it really is. Though of course why the God—the cops…police, I mean—"

"Okay, okay. Now where's the phone?"

The hoarse, enraged shout that came from the floor above was sheer guttural but he knew at once it was Jablonski's. There came a scurry of feet and a thump.

Ryan leaped for the door, grabbed his gun and ran recklessly up the stairs. The door to Derby's room was still closed. He flung it open cautiously and stepped backward out of reach.

Then he looked into the room.

Derby, his back to the wall again, seemed to be doing a kind of dance, while Jablonski stood in front of him, gun in hand, aiming deliberate kicks at his shins and thighs whenever opportunity presented. Then he realized that Derby's dance was an effort to avoid the kicks. At the same time a gurgle broke from Derby, and Ryan with horrible foreboding recognized that Derby was convulsed with laughter.

Ryan ran in and pulled Jablonski back.

But laughter made Derby helpless. No longer having to defend himself, he leaned against the wall, his gaunt face wrinkled weirdly, tears wetting his cheeks, high tremolos welling up from within him.

"For God's sake!" gasped Ryan.

Rage made Jablonski's face black. "The son of a bitch," he began. "The dirty, sow-headed son of a bitch—have you called in?"

"Not yet. I was talking to the landlady. But what—"

Derby's laugh became a snicker.

"The son of a bitch burned up that C-note," cried Jablonski, frenzied, and Derby went off into a new convulsion.

He must be crazy, was the first thing Ryan thought. Derby was still handcuffed. *They've both gone nuts.* But he turned toward the table.

The hundred dollar bill was gone.

So was Derby's pipe. That lay on the floor and near it was a still-smoking dottle of tobacco. Then he understood.

"How do you…like your murder case now, cop…copper?" Derby struggled with laughter.

Jablonski did not look at Ryan. Ryan did not say anything.

"After you left he asked me for a cigarette," Jablonski said.

"He knew you didn't have any. You'd bummed one from me."

"So he said could he get his pipe on the table. I thought, what the hell? He was cuffed. Why shouldn't the slob smoke? I backed away and let him walk over to the table. He must have picked up the C-note with the pipe."

"And stuffed it in with the tobacco and lit it."

"Yeah. I noticed it sort of flared, but he'd had trouble packing it with the cuffs on and—"

Derby whooped and started to laugh again.

"It wasn't until I went over to get a chair and set down that I look at the table and seen the bill was gone. At first I couldn't figure it. Then I thought of the pipe. I pulled it outta his mouth—" He made an impotent gesture with his hand.

Ryan picked up the tobacco dottle. It was hopeless. Perhaps the lab men could prove scientifically that some flakes of the ash had originally been government banknote paper. But as evidence that Harry Derby had possessed the identical bill of which Mrs. Connors had been robbed, it was useless. Derby had outwitted Jablonski even with Jablonski gloatingly watching over him. Ryan felt a hot surge of hatred for Jablonski, and for Derby.

Derby watched him with the wise air of an old fox. "Still gonna send me up?" he chuckled.

"There's plenty of evidence." Ryan wouldn't flinch in the sight of the enemy. "Plenty of evidence. You're in the chair right now, Derby." He wanted to jar Derby, to beat him down with naked fists, to make him feel the cold discouragement that was beginning to hurt himself. After all this…all they had done… Derby had beaten them.

"There's three dames made you this afternoon," he said with deliberate cruelty. "They're the ones that will give you the chair. That C-note was just contributory evidence. You're dead, Derby."

But there was discouragement in the air. Everyone felt it and none more than Derby. Ryan took out his cigarettes. There were three left. He offered one to Jabby.

"How about a smoke for me?" asked Derby impudently.

Jablonski walked over and kicked Derby's thin buttocks. Derby continued standing against the wall. He grinned determinedly but he did not laugh any more. The time for laughter was over. Now they were up to the next move.

Jablonski thumbed Ryan over toward the door and followed him. "We're in trouble," he muttered. Ryan knew this was really Jablonski's trouble, but there was no point in thinking about that now.

He said, "Well, we still got a case."

Jablonski looked old and tired, and it wasn't just the gray stubble sprouting from his jowls. "Like hell we got a case."

"There's the gun."

"Maybe it checks and maybe not. The slug may have been smashed inside her head."

"Well, there's the women—"

"Those women won't be worth a damn by the time this guy goes to trial," growled Jablonski. "Wait'll his friends start calling them up nights. Or dropping around and making cracks about their husbands and kids. They won't be nearly so sure as they were downtown."

"But jeez, Jabby—" Ryan had to try to keep his voice low.

"And he'll have an alibi a yard long. Half the longshoremen in New York will swear he was playing cards with them all afternoon. *We* know what he was doing. But who the hell will believe *us?*"

"There's the bank clerk," said Ryan. "And just now I got one of the tens."

Jablonski exploded. "Banks don't keep no record of regular ten dollar bills! Ain't you ever been in a bank? And as for the teller—he wasn't even sure the guy came up to the cage. What kind of identification will that make?"

He was silent a moment and when he spoke again it was with the wistfulness of acknowledged defeat. "We've lost him, kid. We can take him in—and he'll go to trial. Least, if the D.A. is willing to take any kind of chance at all. But he'll never in God's world go up. And you can blame it on me—all on me! Because I'm a dumb—"

The rest was bitter self-denunciation. But there were tears in Jablonski's eyes.

Derby could not hear what they said but he could understand their postures. "What's 'a matter?" he mocked. "Something wrong? Didn't I smack down the old dame? Huh? Ain't you got no case after all this? Huh? Hey, squarehead—listen! I killed the broad. You hear that? You got a confession, Polack! What you gonna do with it? Let's see you prove I said it! Still wanna try to beat Farragut?"

Jablonski turned, bent on destruction.

And he paused. His sullen and morose face grew suddenly crafty. "Hey," he said, looking around. "Neill, what was that you picked up in that apartment this afternoon?" Ryan flushed. He hadn't realized Jabby had noticed it.

"A little piece of the lamp?" Jablonski insisted. "Huh?"

"Yeah. I guess it was that."

"Still got it?"

"Ah...yes."

"Give it to me," said Jablonski. "Come on. Come *on!* I got an idea."

CHAPTER 5

You Can Be Thinking of Me

Jablonski pulled Ryan's head close to his own and whispered in husky, meat-flavored whispers. As he did, Ryan's expression lengthened.

"But that's—well, manufacturing evidence," he said.

"Sure it is." Jablonski spoke airily but he was watching Ryan.

"It's—well, it's like framing the guy." Ryan didn't like it. Fairness and respect for the letter of the law were implicit in him.

"Framing!" Jablonski's scorn was boisterous. "Framing a guy like Derby? You checked the numbers on that bill yourself, Neill. You heard him admit he killed her, didn't you? Framing, for God's sake! All we're doing is proving what we know. It ain't as if he was innocent."

"I know it's not as if he was innocent," Ryan muttered. "It's just—that tampering with evidence…"

He felt weary and oddly numb. It was getting on towards three a.m.; this had been a tough night. It was no time to debate the subtler shades of justice. Still, he didn't like it.

"Look, Neill," Jablonski said. "He killed her—we know that. And when he hit her with the lamp he could have got a little of the dust on his jacket. So all we do now is—well, just make sure he did."

"Sure, but…"

"Look, Neill." For Jablonski necessity had become the mother of eloquence. "I want this collar bad—so do you. You know what it can do for both of us. And you know what happens to my retirement if it gets back to the desk that I let him burn that C-note. If we bring Derby in and then lose the case against him—"

"Sure," said Ryan uncomfortably. "Sure. I know. But when he rumbles that he was framed—then where are you?"

Jablonski snorted. "Who the hell will believe him? Look, Neill. We got a case against him now—of sorts. What we need is the clincher. That's what the hundred dollar bill was until we—until I let him burn it. That's what your little piece of pottery will be, especially the way I'll do it. Jeez, can you imagine him getting on the stand and claiming that I—well, you can see for yourself."

Ryan nodded. What Jablonski proposed doing was fantastic. That's what made it safe.

Derby, straining his ears, sensed something going wrong. He chanced a quick squint over his shoulder. He did not like what he saw.

"We don't have anything to worry about." In reassuring Ryan, Jablonski was also reassuring himself. "Matter of fact, our only real trouble would come from telling the truth." He saw that this was the wrong tack. "Look, Neill, do you think you have any right to let this guy go free? What about all the women who are out nights working? What'll you say if he's turned loose and knocks off another dame? All you're doing is what you promised to do the day you took your oath."

He was right, of course. A more experienced cop wouldn't give it a second thought, Ryan thought, not when a guy like Derby was involved. It was just the idea of someone going to the chair, even when he was guilty, on the basis of manufactured evidence. But what was the alternative—giving him a good chance to go free? They couldn't do that.

"Okay," he heard himself say. "Go ahead. Here it is."

Jablonski took the little yellow-glazed button of china.

Ryan lit his last cigarette. Derby frowned suspiciously at the baseboard. Jablonski walked to the door, grinning craftily.

There was a crumpled brown paper sack in the wastebasket near it. Jablonski smoothed it out on the table and placed the little chip on it. He set a beer can on it and pressed down hard, grunting. The little fragment of china crumbled with a grating noise.

Derby's mouth was a tight apprehensive slit. Something was going wrong.

Jablonski pressed the can on the china fragments again, grinding them down. Then he rolled the can on them like a rolling pin, reducing them to powder. He rolled steadily, looking up once to grin at Ryan. "Get his jacket on him," he said.

"I'll have to take off the cuffs."

"Just unlock one of them."

Ryan did and threw Derby his jacket. "Put it on."

"Where we goin'?" asked Derby.

"Out," said Ryan. "And we're not coming back." Derby put on the jacket.

Jablonski folded the brown paper bag to make a trough of it, and poured the fine, whitish-yellow dust into his left hand. He walked over to Derby. "Cover me, Neill," he said.

"You get the hell away from me," said Derby.

Ryan took out his gun.

"Turn around," Jablonski told Derby.

"Go to hell," said Derby.

Jablonski pushed his foot against the back of Derby's knee. Derby buckled, partly turning, and Jablonski swung him around, half-falling, still farther. Then carefully, deliberately, he blew the powder in his left hand over the front of Derby's wool jacket. Derby swung a flailing blow at Jablonski's hand but it was more a gesture of protest than of attack. Jablonski laughed.

"What the hell is this?" asked Derby, and began dusting himself off ineffectually.

"That fixes you," said Jablonski.

That fixed him. *You always try to find any possible trace of the criminal at the scene*, Ryan had been taught at the police academy. *And you always try to find some trace of the scene or victim on the criminal. Either one can convict; getting both is ideal.*

"What *is* that?" Derby was saying anxiously, over and over. "What was that? Was that junk? What was that?"

"That," said Jablonski, "was a little piece of plaster from the lamp you hit the old lady with, Harry. And now it's all over you, and it places you at the scene—even better'n the C-note. And all the Farraguts in the world can't explain that dust in your jacket. You can't cross-examine a spectroscope, Harry."

As Derby frowned in concentration, his hands slowed their dusting movements. He had no idea of what a spectroscope was, but he had a sure sense of evidence and an animal's quick instinct for the moves of the enemy. He looked at the two of them. The older one was smiling sarcastically. The other bastard was wooden-faced, giving nothing to nobody. But he didn't have to. Derby got the general idea. They were framing him.

Frustration had always produced only one reaction in Derby. Jablonski saw it coming in the swelling of his shoulders, but before his mouth could begin a warning, Derby charged, head down, fists hooking, one of them flapping a handcuff.

Jablonski had just reached his revolver when one knotty fist caught the side of his head and knocked him off balance and backward. Derby leaped after him and Ryan saw Derby's long bony knee drive up and catch Jablonski in the stomach. Jablonski uttered a loud wordless cry and his revolver slipped out from his coat and skittered across the floor toward Ryan.

For a second Ryan could not shoot; they were too close together. Jablonski swayed forward on unhinged legs, holding his stomach, his face ghastly. Derby stepped back to bring a roundhouse punch up from the floor. Ryan fired.

The shot missed Derby, but it stopped him because it reminded him of Ryan. With hardly a lost motion he wheeled, took a quick boxer's shuffle forward and swung at Ryan. Jablonski began sagging to the floor.

Ryan stepped backward; he had seen the punch coming, but the force of it spun Derby half around. Ryan coldly thumbed the hammer of his gun. The quiet click ended Derby's outbreak. He knew what it meant—and the revolver just three feet away was pointed directly into his stomach. Ryan was looking at him.

"Start swinging again," he said. "Come on. Give me an excuse."

They looked at each other while the tension went out of Derby. "Face to the wall and hands up against it," said Ryan, and Derby obeyed. Ryan picked up Jablonski's gun.

From Jablonski came a soft sigh.

"How is it, Jabby?"

"'M okay…all right in a minute. He…got me with his knee…"

Ryan had played football; he knew how long it would hurt and how much. Jablonski groaned, trying not to.

There was a knock and the door swung open timidly. Mrs. Daniels stood in the doorway, and behind her a stringy individual in gallus-draped pants and a woolen undershirt.

"Is—is everything all right?" She looked inquiringly toward Derby.

"You go to the telephone," Ryan began.

"There ain't one in this building. Did you shoot—"

"You with the pants on," said Ryan. "You get over to Second Avenue to that all-night hamburger joint and call Spring seven three one hundred. Got that number?"

"Listen, mister, I gotta get some sleep."

Jablonski was trying to get up.

"What's the matter with your friend?" said Mrs. Daniels.

Ryan turned enough so they both could see the revolver in his hand.

"You call that number," he said. "Right *now!*" He spoke doggedly. "Spring seven three one hundred. Tell them an officer is in trouble here. Get going."

The stringy man hitched up a gallus. "Okay," he said. "Okay," and left.

"You shoot your friend?" asked Mrs. Daniels.

"Get him some of your whisky," said Ryan.

She went downstairs without a word.

Jablonski was rubbing his abdomen, methodically and painfully. "Wipe off the beer can," he said, "and get rid of that paper." His voice was a croak.

You nervy old son of a bitch, thought Ryan, as he pocketed the brown paper. Your guts must hurt like hell, but you still remember that Derby mustn't have a chance to prove what we've done.

"Right, Jabby." It was the first time he had ever felt genuine respect for Jablonski.

"Hey, Derby," Jablonski croaked. "Listen. My belly hurts. See? But it'll stop after a while. And just think, Derby. Some night soon, you'll burn. Think of that. And you know what? That night it'll be me who's home drinkin' beer. And waitin' for that flash on the radio. What do you think of that, Derby?"

It was a very silent room when he stopped.

"You can be thinking of me when you get that jolt, Derby. 'Cause I'll be thinking of you." His jaws moved unnaturally, and he retched.

From outside and below came the onrushing sound of an automobile moving fast. Ryan heard the clump of heavy feet on the stairs and then there were two blue uniforms and silver shields and alert faces in the doorway.

They looked awfully good to Ryan.

CHAPTER 6

Fresh-Made Tracks in the Snow

There was a small knot of men standing in front of the shadow-scrawled old precinct station when the radio car pulled up. Ryan paid no particular attention to them. He wanted only to get Derby inside and booked, and to find out how badly Jablonski was hurt. During their fast trip up the empty, late-looking avenue he had once asked, "How is it, Jabby?" and Jablonski had replied from the front seat, "Oh, it's okay," carelessly, as though he had forgotten the whole thing. But his voice hadn't sounded right.

Jablonski got out of the car painfully, and was walking half-bent-over toward the stone steps when a flash of blue-white brilliance engulfed them. Another flash came. Ryan, walking with his hand on Derby's arm, felt him stiffen in terror. Ryan hadn't expected the news photographers to get there so fast; then he remembered that one of the prowl car crew had called the news in on the car radio.

Derby held his handcuffed hands to his face. It made a fine, cringing picture. The flashes burst over them like waves again and again as they went up the time-scalloped steps of the precinct station. Ryan was not only blinded by them but oddly unnerved. He could almost feel the flashes against him, like wind blasts.

Lieutenant Paul Bauer stood outside the desk area at the foot of the stairs, his dark eyes watchful and jaw unyielding under grayed brows and bristle of pompadour. But Ryan sensed Bauer's held-in elation. And in the other men, the uniformed sergeant behind the high dark oak desk, the patrolman with him, and the detective coming down the old stairs, you didn't have to sense it at all. They looked at the tall shambling figure being led in and grinned jubilantly. This was one the department had won, and the whole precinct was filled with the clubhouse spirit of a winning ball team.

"Why's at guy bent over?" a photographer asked his reporter, and the reporter said, "What's the matter, Jabby? You hurt?"

Bauer shouldered into the little group of journalists that clotted around them. "Take Derby upstairs," he told the prowl car crew. "Chief inspector's on his way."

"Yes, sir." Derby's chin was touching his breastbone as they pushed him forward.

"You hurt, Jabby?"

Jablonski did a good job of straightening up. "No, sir. He—he kicked me in the belly. It—ah, hurt for a while. I'm all right now."

"We'll run you down to the hospital."

"It ain't that bad, Paul. Honest." Not for anything would Jablonski miss all this.

Someone plucked Ryan's sleeve, and a tubby young man with horn-rimmed glasses said, "Holcomb—the *Mirror.* You're Ryan, eh? Congrats—great job! Hey, is it true he's admitted it?"

A twinge of nervousness assailed Ryan. This had to be done carefully. One intimation about that hundred dollar bill—but the best thing always was to tell the truth as nearly as possible. "Well, yes," he said hesitantly. "He even sort of boasted about it."

"Boasted? And him already a three-time loser?" And Ryan knew he should not have said that. Jablonski ought to be here to do the talking.

"How'd you happen to spot him?"

He told the story in three scant sentences. The reporter kept looking at his watch because he had to call the city desk immediately. He said, "And the loot—you got the dough, huh?"

Ryan started to say affirmatively, "Oh, he had—" and stopped barely in time.

But Holcomb caught the meaning.

"He had the dough *on him?* "

Full-blown panic now. His thoughts flew like leaves in a gale.

Another reporter who had been listening repeated the question. "Derby had the C-note on him?"

"He had some of the dough." Ryan said wildly and pushed past them. "I got to get upstairs."

The other reporter said, "But wait—"

"Not now. Later." Ryan took the stairs two at a time. As he did, air fanned coldly against his moist brow.

In the squad room off the head of the stairs, Lieutenant Bauer sat at his scarred desk, Jablonski comfortably alongside him. Somewhere Jablonski had obtained a cigar and its blue fragrance fumed the room. Bauer pushed a rickety chair toward Ryan and continued his conversation. "He admitted it, eh?" he asked Jablonski.

"When we were alone he did," said Jablonski.

"Well, he sure ain't talkin' to McGonigle." The telephone at his elbow jingled. Bauer said, "Seventeenth Squad Lieutenant Bauer" into it in one breath, then, "Yeah, Ed…yeah…yeah… Jabby and Ryan…right, kid," and hung up.

"Furtig," he said. "He's been out with the others making the dock joints."

"He can go to bed now," said Jablonski magnanimously. But Ryan knew how Furtig must be feeling—relieved, but envious.

Apparently Bauer knew too. "Well, you know how it is," he said to Jablonski. For a man of his authority and background Bauer had a very mild voice. "Besides, the papers have been making such a—well, I guess you haven't had a chance to see them. You guys have really done a job in case you didn't know it."

Jablonski complacently licked a cigar leaf back into place. "Listen to this," said Bauer and began reading from a paper he fished from the wastebasket.

"…out and out anarchy… Hoodlums have taken over… While the commissioner has said…responsible citizens will bear in mind…action by the Governor…election next year in which…"

Bauer finished it and laughed. "Well, what else should we do?" he asked briskly. Ryan remembered that Bauer had been on duty for almost twenty-four hours. He said, "Well, there's the delicatessen to check, Lieutenant."

"Huh?"

"We picked him up going into a delicatessen on Third to get some beer. He probably broke one of the tens there. He gave another to the landlady. I've got that."

"Good. Anything else?"

"He said he got the dough from a loan shark but didn't know the guy's name. We better run that down before Farragut gets something arranged for him."

"Right. How much did he have on him?"

"Oh," said Jablonski, and Ryan began, "Well…"

Jablonski said easily, "We didn't have time to give him a complete frisk, Paul. Maybe it's in his shoe."

Bauer said, "Yeah," and scratched his unshaven chin. "McGonigle better know that right away." He got up.

"One other thing, Paul," said Jablonski. "The lab oughtta go over that wool jacket of his very carefully. He hit the old dame with a lamp and it busted over her. That heavy wool would be perfect for picking up little bits of lamp plaster."

"Good deal."

When Bauer had gone Jablonski looked sideways at Ryan and smiled a slow, satisfied smile. But Ryan could not smile back. In the last ten minutes something had changed. He did not feel friendly toward Jablonski, and he did not know why. He just wanted to get this over and get out of here.

There was the sound of many feet on the stairs and Ryan, looking over his shoulder, saw Betty Leonard and Mrs. Lombardi go down the hall with two detectives. "The witnesses," he grunted.

"It's a hundred to one they make him," said Jablonski, and that made Ryan feel better. He took a cigarette from Bauer's pack and was lighting it when Jabby muttered, "Hey!" and got awkwardly to his feet. "Good evening, sir," he said very respectfully.

Ryan turned around. A lean man of medium height with a red, knobby face and angry eyes stood in the doorway. His overcoat's velvet lapels framed a high, starched collar, a tasteless flowered necktie and a huge stickpin. He held his head and shoulders hunched forward aggressively as though he expected to encounter violence and expected to return it.

"You Jablonski?"

"Yes, sir."

"You're Ryan."

"Yes, sir."

Ryan had not shaken hands with the chief inspector of the New York police department since the day four years before when he graduated as a rookie patrolman. Now the chief inspector's hand closed on his roughly, as on a nightstick, but the harsh eyes softened.

"You'll be hearing from the commissioner," said Patrick Pembroke. "But I wanted to tell you to your faces what a fine bit of work you've done tonight, men. A fine bit of work." His voice became music. "I thank you for it, and so does every man in the department."

He looked at both of them approvingly and Ryan, who knew that at the age of sixty-four the chief inspector had gotten out of bed and driven here simply to say those words to them, felt his throat close.

"Thank you, sir," said Jablonski.

"It simply shows that heads-up police work can score every time. Have you got a case?"

"We've got a case, sir," said Jablonski with unexpected mildness. "This is the end of Derby."

"Good. The sooner he burns, the better." The matter-of-fact voice was indescribably cold. "You've seen what the papers have said about us. You've given the commissioner the ammunition to answer them with. He'll make use of it later today, if I'm any judge."

Once again the ancient, bony hand shot forward to each of them. "Thank you, Jablonski. Thank you, Ryan. A good job. Good night, men." He went out with slow, cold dignity.

Golly, what a guy, Ryan thought, and out in the hall the chief inspector turned and came back so quickly that for a second he feared he had uttered the words aloud. He was tired and confused enough to do that.

The old man was looking at him. "Ryan," he said reflectively, and the faintest brogue edged his words. "Someone mentioned your name is O'Neill Ryan."

"Yes, sir."

"I once had a man under me named O'Neill Ryan. This would be years ago. Young sergeant, he was." The chief inspector spoke deliberately now. "It was on the shoo—on the confidential squad. He was a fine man or he'd never got there so young. Later some hoodlums—" the knobby face hardened—"some hoodlums met him one night in Carmine Street. They killed him."

"Yes, sir."

The chief inspector's eyes flickered. Then they measured Ryan. "A relative perhaps?" he said softly.

"My father," said Ryan, and all the events of the long night welled up in his throat and to his eyes.

For a long time the harsh angry gaze engaged Ryan's. "Your father," said Patrick Pembroke. "He was a good man. A good man. Good night, Ryan." He went out.

Ryan fumbled another cigarette out of Bauer's pack and kept his head down.

"Jeez, kid," said Jablonski. "I didn't know your old man was a cop." There was a new respect in his voice.

"Forget it," said Ryan thickly, and had to wait a minute. Then he said, "He's really quite a guy, isn't he?" At that moment Ryan would have gone after a cityful of Derbys for the chief inspector.

They heard Bauer coming down the hall.

"Oh, Paddy's a right gee," said Jablonski carelessly. He breathed out a cloud of strong smoke. Then, "What's he saying, Paul?"

Bauer's face was lined with weariness. "Nothing, as you might expect. But the gun looks good. It's a .38, and it was a .38 slug that killed the victim."

"How about the witnesses?" said Ryan.

"They picked him like a flash."

That made Ryan feel even better.

"The young one asked about you, Ryan," Bauer grinned. "I guess you made an impression."

Ryan grinned back. Bauer said, "He hasn't got the bill on him, incidentally."

Jablonski said very casually, "What's he say about it?"

"Nothing. He never heard of it. He was home taking a nap all afternoon—alone. And he says the loan shark's name is Morgan, or something like that." The lieutenant sighed wearily. "I guess that's it. Oh—don't either of you worry about court tomorrow—today, rather. McGonigle can do that. You men get some sleep." He looked at them both. "I guess I don't need to say—well, you know. You did a great job, and it won't hurt either of you. There's reporters downstairs still. The order is to give them everything they want. We want all the publicity we can get on this one."

At any other time the alacrity with which Jablonski rose, and the bored resignation with which he said, "Well, we may as well get it over with," would have made it funny. But the thought of facing more reporters alarmed Ryan. Going downstairs he said, "Look. You do the talking."

Jablonski was glad to. While the reporters listened, jotted and occasionally broke in with a question he told the story in detail and with such flattering reference to Ryan that it was clear to everyone the veteran was trying to give every possible credit to the rookie, even though he himself had been in full command.

Ryan studied the reporters. All were dissimilar and yet alike: knowing, a little rumpled, of indeterminate age. But one, tall and heavy-eyed as though he had been newly routed from bed, wore a sports jacket of soft, expensive tweed and a gray sports shirt. His feet were unexpectedly clad in felt bedroom slippers. His black hair was thick With gray, but his square-jawed face was youthful and forceful.

"Telephone, Ryan," said the desk sergeant.

When Ryan turned, the desk sergeant winked elaborately to the photographers and his lips formed "The P.C." Ryan said, "Detective Ryan," wearily into the telephone.

"Ryan?" said the telephone voice in his ear. "This is Johnson Drumm. I just wanted to congratulate you and your partner on..."

Ryan's jaw dropped visibly. Johnson Drumm was the police commissioner. A flashbulb flared, and then a couple more before Ryan got his mouth closed. He finally said, "Yes, sir...yes, sir," automatically. Then, "Here, Jabby. Jeez, it's the P.C."

They did not shoot Jablonski's picture; he was too assured, grinning, easy. They asked Ryan a couple of questions and learned with excited interest that this was his first murder case. The photographers packed their bags of equipment and then left. It was that simple.

Then Ryan noticed that the one in the sports jacket was still there, slouched silently against the desk sergeant's throne of dark oak, sleepy looking yet watchful. He shuffled forward in his slippers. "Ryan?" he said. "'M Jack Sandalwood. Like to ask a couple questions."

His manner was lazy, but Ryan's hackles rose. Jack Sandalwood was the best-known reporter in the city, a Pulitzer Prize winner whose specialty for more than ten years had been the exposure of venality and crime in unpredictable places. In a sense his appearance was even more of a compliment than the chief inspector's, but it was infinitely more ominous. Sandalwood could ask questions that would never occur to an ordinary policeman, and he could demand the answers to them.

Once again Ryan looked around for Jablonski. "Probably you should talk to my partner."

But Ed Furtig was coming up the station house steps and Jablonski had bustled out to meet him. And Sandalwood was looking curiously at Ryan.

"But you can answer this," he said. "I understand from the *Mirror* man that you said Derby admitted killing the old lady. You were clever to trap him into admitting, that."

"Well..." Ryan's mouth was dry. "We just questioned him. That's all."

"And right away he admitted the murder—just like that?"

"Well...yes. Pretty much."

"Is that how the...ah...fight started?"

Then Ryan saw what he was driving at. "Hell, no. Don't get that idea! We never laid a hand on him until he jumped Jabby."

"I see. Odd though, eh? I mean, he has everything to lose and nothing to gain by admitting it. Why, that puts him in the chair."

"He's denying it now."

"Yeah, but..." Sandalwood squinted his disbelief through cigarette smoke.

"Sometimes guys just get tired of twisting and dodging," said Ryan.

"Yeah." Sandalwood weighed the idea. "But I must say I've never seen a bird of that type break this easy before. Have you?"

Ryan began to feel it would never end. He looked around at the familiar surroundings, the stairway, the patient heads at the desk lighted by dull lights, the plaques along the wall commemorating officers of the precinct lolled in line of duty. Suddenly it was filled with unforeseeable disaster.

"...eh?" Sandalwood was asking insistently.

"Sorry. I didn't get that."

"As I understand it," Sandalwood patiently repeated, "Derby didn't have much dough on him."

"That's right."

"How much?"

"I've forgotten exactly—Jablonski could tell you. I think he counted it up."

"I see. But he didn't have that big bill on him."

"That's right." This was going a little better.

"What had he done with it?"

"He didn't say."

"You asked him?"

"Naturally."

"You mean after admitting the murder itself he wouldn't tell you what he'd done with the proceeds? That's odd."

Ryan could hear Jablonski's complacent drawl from beyond the doorway. That was all he could think of, Jablonski's absence and Sandalwood's unanswerable questions.

"Didn't you try to get *some* explanation…?"

A telephone rang, a nearby clangor. He heard the timeworn salutation. "Seventeeth Precinct. Sergeant Weiner." Then a listening silence. The whole world was silent, waiting, listening for his answer.

And he had no answer. An eternity passed.

But helplessness was a thing Ryan could not long endure, and his temper came to his rescue. "Look here," he snapped. "When you're pinching a guy like Derby you don't think of all the smart questions some second-guesser can think up later. This guy jumped us. He hurt my partner. We didn't have time to… He's being gone over now by Sergeant McGonigle. Talk to McGonigle if—"

Sandalwood began to break in with "I'm sorry. I'm sorry," before Ryan had finished. When he had, Sandalwood smiled pacifyingly and said with soft innocence, "All I meant was that a hundred bucks is a lot of money to get lost so easy."

Once again the full force of Sandalwood's remark exploded belatedly in Ryan's mind, like a delayed-action bomb, which was just how Sandalwood intended it should. Sandalwood suspected he and Jablonski had taken the C-note for themselves. *That* was why he had been curious about Derby's admission of guilt. *That* was the weakness in their story.

Ryan's thoughts began following the pattern he knew Sandalwood's had taken; it was like following fresh-made tracks in the snow. Sandalwood could have drawn two conclusions from what he knew. One was that Derby had admitted killing Mrs. Connors but had given Ryan and Jablonski the hundred dollar bill in return for some favor. The other was that Derby had denied the murder and they had taken the money because he could not very well claim it. Either way Sandalwood had no inkling of the real truth. But he was suspicious, and therefore he was dangerous.

Ryan thrust his right hand with assumed nonchalance into his suit-coat pocket and it encountered the crumpled brown paper sack that Jablonski had used.

That almost panicked him; he withdrew his hand guiltily.

"We didn't thoroughly search Derby," he said. He spoke steadily. "He may have the dough in his shoe or pinned to his underwear—or he may have stashed it some place. Maybe Sergeant McGonigle will get that out of him. I don't' know." The steadiness he had to assume steadied him; he felt his powers of conviction growing as he spoke. "But in any case neither Jablonski nor I have any idea where the bill is—that's for sure."

He looked angrily at Sandalwood's intent face, and he knew Sandalwood understood he had caught the insinuation and was flinging it back. "Maybe a hundred bucks means more to you than it does to me," he added.

"Oh, now wait a minute," said Sandalwood contritely.

"Hey, what goes on?" Jablonski arrived.

Where were you when I needed you?

"I was just asking Ryan about that hundred buck bill." Sandalwood said. "I guess he misunderstood what I meant."

Jablonski grew attentive. "Yes? What did you want to know?"

God, don't spoil it!

"I was just wondering," said Sandalwood, returning to the scent, "why Derby admitted killing the old lady and yet wouldn't tell what he did with the money."

Jablonski looked quickly from one to the other. "Well now, it wasn't exactly like that," he said. "You see, we grabbed him pretty much by surprise and he said some things when he was excited that he probably won't repeat. Matter of fact, after he got his head again he buttoned up pretty much. That's when I asked him about the dough. Of course, we didn't really try to question him."

It was that easy when you were relaxed and experienced.

"I see," said Sandalwood. "I see," and scribbled a note.

Then he looked up and smiled. "Thanks," he said to both of them. "And congratulations." He nodded to the photographer waiting for him and they went out.

"Any time," Jablonski called.

The last Ryan saw of Sandalwood was a glimpse of that well-tailored back going down the steps.

"Whew!" he said.

"Yeah. They can be nosy. But it's over—all over! Wait here a minute 'til I check with Mac—" Jablonski grinned—"then I'm taking you out for the biggest slug of Canadian Club in New York."

Ryan grinned back. "Sounds good—but where do we go at this time of night?"

Jabby punched his arm. "It ain't this time of night where we're going."

"I need cigarettes. I'll meet you on the corner."

As he strolled indolently down the station house steps, a uniformed man came up to them. Ryan recognized him as a probationary patrolman. The young patrolman's eyes widened at the sight of Ryan and he altered his ascent of the steps to give Ryan plenty of room. "Good morning," he said politely. Ryan responded with a careless hand.

That's how little time it takes, he thought.

He took off the expensive light gray hat he wore and re-crushed it into the original fancy crease that he liked to affect as a civilian. Working, he could not wear anything that would make him distinguishable in a crowd. That nightly gesture was an expression of his individuality, a symbol of release from departmental routine.

Buying cigarettes in the all-night restaurant, Ryan began to feel relaxed and thoroughly happy. Sandalwood and the china chip seeped from his mind, and the tension of the last few hours dissolved in a warm awareness of accomplishment and praise. It was the way you felt trotting off the field after having played a good first half. It was the quiet, deep satisfaction of knowing you had come through a hard test well.

He didn't really want a drink or need one, he thought.

But at that moment Jablonski came hurrying along the sidewalk outside. Seeing a cruising taxi he put two fingers to his mouth and blew a piercing blast. The cab squealed to a stop. Jablonski waved to Ryan, coming out of the restaurant. "Hurry up," he called. "This is on me."

"Hell it is!" Ryan laughed, and got in.

CHAPTER 7

C.C. and Soda

The cab carried them West of Broadway and stopped before another old house. To Ryan the comparison between this approach and the other one they had made earlier was startling, but Jablonski had no thought for subtleties. "My girl's meeting us here," he exulted, and rang and then tapped impatiently on the door's frosted glass.

The announcement of Jablonski's girl surprised Ryan, who knew little about his partner but was aware that he was married. He grinned appreciatively. You had to hand it to this old goat at that.

The door opened stealthily on an almost dark hallway. "Evenin', Fritz," said Jablonski, and pushed Ryan quickly inside.

"Evenin', Sarge," replied the thin, elderly waiter. "Everything okay tonight, Sarge?"

"Everything's copacetic, Fritz. Meet my friend, Neill Ryan. He's okay, Fritz. Treat him right when he comes around."

"You know me, Sarge. My pleasure, Mr. Ryan."

Jablonski had opened a door leading down to the basement. Piano music, smoke and snatches of talk and laughter drifted up the stairway. At the bottom of it Fritz look their hats and coats and led them to a corner table. "Inez ain't here yet," said Jablonski.

Ryan looked around. Once this had been the old house's kitchen and servants' dining room. Now, bathed in blue light, there was a small bar of white patent leather and many bottles, attended by a white-jacketed barman. Near it a middle-aged man with unnaturally black hair and a purple complexion was playing "Mood Indigo" on a tiny piano, holding the chords down long. Two men stood at the bar and three tables were occupied. It all looked and sounded welcome.

"Double C.C. and soda for both of us," Jablonski told Fritz.

"Water for me," Ryan corrected.

"Water," said Fritz, and left. Ryan said. "That guy Sandalwood still worries me."

"Forget it. We answered his questions."

"But he suspects something. Not the right things, but—"

"What the hell! What can he suspect? What can he *prove*? You don't understand the beauty of it, Neill. Derby can't say anything without tightening the case against himself. And who else is there but us who knows?"

"Canadian Club with water," said Fritz. "And soda." He put down two heavy water glasses, half-filled with whisky and ice cubes, a bottle of soda and a glass of water.

Jablonski chuckled. "Two bucks a drink and worth it," he said. "At least tonight. Eh, kid?"

Ryan raised his glass. "Here's to your new joint in Mount Vernon."

"New Rochelle. Thanks." Jablonski took a long pull at the whisky.

Ryan took a shorter one. Even with the liquor fumes in his nose he scented the cloud of perfume that enveloped him. A voice said, "So here you are."

A woman stood over their table. She wore a coat that somewhat resembled mink and her ash-blond head was hatless. The lips and eyebrows in her bright, smiling face were well-marked slashes of red and black respectively. Jablonski and Ryan got to their feet. "Inez!" said Jablonski. He kissed her cheek.

Only then did Ryan notice a girl standing behind the blond woman. Inez was forty-five trying to look thirty. The girl looked a couple of years over twenty and she didn't have to try. The brim of a simple felt hat was pulled low over her violet eyes and her hair was coppery and abundant at a time when it was fashionable for hair to be close-cut. Her coat of woolen-pile, cinched to a tiny waist by a leather belt, was inexpensive but chic. Looking from Jablonski to Inez with a faint smile, the girl seemed not to have noticed Ryan. At least, that is how it seemed to Ryan.

He began-speculating about what was under the coat.

Jablonski introduced them. The girl's name was Gee Gee Hawes. She sat down with demure self-possession, told Fritz, "A chilled sherry, please," in a husky contralto and took out a cigarette. When Ryan held his lighter to it, she smiled at him from under the hat and it was like looking into spotlights. The pianist began "The Beguine."

Jablonski said, "This is an unexpected pleasure, Gee Gee."

She smiled at him, making the corners of her eyes crinkle. "A date stood me up," she said candidly, "and Inez was nice enough to ask me along."

"Thank God for Inez," said Ryan, his spirits already lifted by the whisky, and when she made a moue of appreciation at him he began wishing he had shaved recently and had on a new shirt. He wondered whether she lived alone or shared an apartment. He wanted to make conversation and said, "Do you always drink your sherry chilled, Miss… ah…"

"I'm Gee Gee," she said.

"Hey!" yelled Jablonski. He had picked up the *Daily Mirror* Inez had brought in with her. Its front page, devoid of the usual picture, was given over to big type:

COPS NAB KILLER AFTER GUN FIGHT—HARRY DERBY CAPTURED

Ryan said, "Well, well." He did not want to seem impressed in front of this girl.

Jablonski turned to the story inside the paper. "For gosh sakes! Didn't even use our names." He read: "'Bulletin: Detectives of the East Fifty-first Street Station early today arrested Harry Derby, the hoodlum identified as the killer yesterday of Mrs. Thelma Connors in her East Sixty-first Street apartment. Derby was seized after a gun fight in an East Side rooming house. One officer was reported wounded critically.'"

"All you ever think about is the crime news, Ed," said Inez fondly.

Jablonski gave her an indignant look. "How do you like that?" he demanded of Ryan. "Who do you think they're talking about in that story?"

"You and Mr. Ryan?" Gee Gee asked. "Really? You captured that man who—"

"We got Derby," said Jablonski.

"Really?" When her eyes widened they were not violet but incredibly blue. Inez put both her hands admiringly on Jablonski's arm.

A new tray of drinks arrived. Gee Gee said, "The final *News* will be out soon. That may have more on it."

Jablonski said, "Fritz, run out for the last edition of the *News,* will you? Get several of them."

"Soon's I get this other table, Sarge."

"No one was wounded really, were they, Ed?" asked Inez.

Ryan and Jablonski exchanged looks. "No," said Jablonski. "Not really—except Derby. He got roughed up a little. In fact—" he looked at Ryan and winked—"I would say we didn't do him a bit of good. Eh, Neill? We really *fixed* him."

Jablonski laughed with such obvious double meaning that Ryan wished he would shut up. No one could know what Jablonski meant. But it shouldn't be talked about anywhere, before anyone.

"What do you mean, Ed?" Inez leaned yearningly toward him.

Six ounces of whisky had thickened Jablonski's tongue. "I mean that Neill and I managed to make a case against Derby that no defense lawyer is gonna—"

Ryan grew desperate. "How about dancing?" was all he could think of. "Come on, Jabby—while the music's going."

"Hell with it," said Jablonski. "I'm no dancer. I'm a drinker. Where's that lousy Fritz got to?"

Ryan looked at Gee Gee and she smiled at him.

He got up because he had to now, but he hadn't wanted it this way. He leaned over Jablonski. "Keep your mouth shut," he whispered. Jablonski, slack-mouthed, gave him a wise wink.

Gee Gee drew out of her coat. She was wearing a plain dress of gray wool, and the figure beneath it had not been reconstructed into cones and spheres by the usual undergarments and did not need to be. It made Ryan forget even Jablonski.

The piano rippled into "Just One of Those Things," and Ryan put his arm around her.

"You and Ed work together, I gather," she said after a moment. It was strange to hear Jabby called Ed.

"Yes. We've been partners about a week. And you and Inez?"

"We work together too. Or did until tonight."

"What happened tonight?"

"Well, you'll hear it sooner or later. The club where we work let out Inez. They've hired a new kid—a cool singer."

"I didn't know Inez was a singer."

"That's, right. Blues. And you know what cool jazz has done to that."

"You sing too?"

"No, I dance. As a matter of fact—" again the crinkly-eyed smile— "I'm what they call an exotic dancer. You know—a stripper. Although in New York it's not quite stripping."

This was the first time Ryan had ever met a stripper. He said, "I'll bet you're good at it," and then wondered if that had been tactful.

"I've only been doing it a few months. Before that I was in the chorus. Some people think it's indecent. But if you don't have to do anything dirty and you've got a good body, I can't see any harm in it. And the place we're in gets a nice crowd—as clubs go."

"Why sure." But Ryan was off balance. This girl was not what he had thought when she first sat down at the table, and even the knowledge that she was an "exotic dancer" did not alter this new, growing opinion. She was unselfconscious and wholesome, and when her pliant dancing pressed her close to him and a coppery curl brushed his cheek, Ryan, far from considering certain opening gambits, felt embarrassed and respectful, and he could think of nothing to say.

"Well, anyway—" she looked up at him—"I'm not sorry my date had to work tonight."

"I'm mighty *glad,"* and Ryan grinned at her with happy awkwardness. He whirled her around and she followed dexterously; she was really a marvelous dancer. "What's he do—is he an entertainer too?"

"No, but his working hours are almost as bad. He called me at the club just before closing time to say he was on something really big and would be working the rest of the night. He's a newspaperman."

Even mention of the word was enough to alarm Ryan momentarily. "Oh really?" he said. "What's his name? I know a few." Which was an exaggeration.

"I guess he's working on some kind of big scoop," said Gee Gee. "His name is Sandalwood—Jack Sandalwood."

And for Ryan all pleasure in the evening ended. He looked toward their table. Jabby and Inez were deep in conversation.

Keep your drunken mouth shut!

Fresh drinks awaited them when they stopped dancing. Gee Gee excused herself to go upstairs, and for a second an absurd suspicion crossed Ryan's mind that she might be going to telephone her boy friend with what she might have learned from Jablonski's implications. He sat down at the table and picked up a new drink. But he told himself, *You better watch this stuff.*

Jablonski and Inez did not notice his presence. Inez was looking down at her glass; Jablonski, his face heavy with liquor and fatigue and white stubble, spun the rim of his glass with thick fingers.

"Well, that's how it is," said Jablonski. "Sure, we've had fun together. But you always knew I'd retire sooner or later. And Sarah and I figure…"

Ryan realized what he had walked in on. He wanted to leave, but he did not know what Jablonski might have told her while he and Gee Gee were dancing. And now Jablonski was ditching her.

"Sarah and I figure we'll try and make a go of it again. With this deal in New Rochelle…"

Inez looked up suddenly. Her eyes were swimming and her face was a ghastly smile. "I know, I know," she said. "You never made any promises, Ed. And neither did I. But more than once, when you'd been drinking a little, maybe, you told me how one of these days you and Sarah would break permanent. And then you and I…"

She broke off; she seemed about to begin to weep openly. Instead she gained strength from some inner source. She straightened up and her face grew hard and cynical, and even as a tear spilled over one eyelid and down a pale cheek she said, "Hell with it," down in her throat and raised her glass and drained it and put it down with finality. She studied it and her low-held head was no longer ash-blond, but silver-threaded and old.

Gee Gee came back, sat down and, looking at Inez, misinterpreted what she saw.

"Aw, don't feel so bad about it, honey." She patted Inez's purple-taloned hand. "There's plenty of better places you can work. Your agent—"

Inez smiled glassily at her. "This is just my night," she said. "Ed just told me he's retiring and moving out. That's nice too, eh, kid?"

"Well, what else happened tonight?" demanded Jablonski aggressively.

"They fired me," said Inez. "Ol' Max fired me. After all these years. The joint's getting itself a new shouter."

Ryan picked his drink up again and, although he knew he shouldn't, he drank it down.

* * * *

After a time Fritz came in with a bundle of *Daily News*. The dawn cold had touched his pallid cheeks with scarlet. "Hey," he called from the stairs. "You guys are famous."

He distributed tabloids like a newsboy. They were cold and damp and on the front page, almost life size, there was a picture of a man with his hat pushed back over curly hair, holding a telephone to his ear, shrewd young eyes round and the mouth open with awe. It was Ryan, talking a few hours before to the commissioner.

"Holy God," said Ryan.

"Let's see," said Gee Gee. "Oh, look. That's cute. See, Inez?" She looked back to Ryan. "But I don't think it does you justice."

"Hey!" cried Jabby. "Listen!" He had opened his paper and read, "Two fast-thinking detectives of the Seventeenth Squad—one a veteran on the eve of retirement and the other a rookie on his first murder case—fought and shot it out early today with Harry Derby, the dock hoodlum wanted for the murder of a grandmother, and they brought him in.

"'Derby allegedly confessed the brutal slaying yesterday afternoon of Mrs. Thelma Connors, 63, in her apartment at 585 East Sixty-first Street.

"'The two detectives, whose nervy work brought them the immediate commendation of Police Commissioner Drumm, are Detective Third Class Edmund A. Jablonski, 53, who retires from the force next week, and Probationary Detective O'Neill Ryan, 28, promoted from patrolman only four days ago. The two cops spotted Derby, a three-time loser for whom a 13-state alarm was out…'"

As Jablonski read other customers gathered around their table, and when he had finished they broke into applause. Then there was much backslapping and many congratulations, which made Ryan feel a little ridiculous but also very happy that Gee Gee was there for it. Even Inez dabbed powder around her eyes, smiled and congratulated them both.

There were drinks bought for them, and Ryan decided the best way to silence Jablonski's babbling tongue was to let him get as drunk as possible.

After a time he looked inquiringly at Gee Gee, wordlessly suggesting another dance. She nodded almost imperceptibly at Inez. Ryan understood and felt proud of his perception and at Gee Gee's asking a favor of him. With the elaborate gallantry of the half-drunk he asked Inez to dance. She looked pleased, and as they rose Gee Gee smiled warm appreciation.

But later, when the pianist began "I Concentrate on You," which had always been a favorite of his, Ryan asked Gee Gee to dance again. This time he held her closer, and the fragrance of her hair and that lissome body all seemed to make her the most tender and desirable and beautiful thing in the world. Before the dance was over Ryan noticed an unnatural radiance around the window's heavy drape and after a time he realized that it was the light of morning. He didn't care.

* * * *

When they left he had to help Jablonski get to the cab, and early office-goers who passed them turned curious, sleep-wrapped faces to give them a second glance. Ryan took Gee Gee to her door (how incongruous that this ravishing girl should live in a slattern apartment building beyond Eighth Avenue), and at the door he tried suddenly and drunkenly to kiss her. She somehow turned away, it seemed by accident, but she did present a cheek…

Ryan went back to the cab in a daze.

After they had ridden in silence for a few blocks he said, "What the hell did you tell that dame about Derby?" But Jablonski was asleep.

The cab let Ryan off at his home first, for Jablonski lived in Queens. Ryan gave the cab driver instructions.

The first-floor apartment where Ryan lived appeared empty. Then he gratefully remembered this was Friday; his sister worked and his mother would be at the Altar Society coffee to plan the Sunday altar flowers. That was a relief; he did not like coming home like this, and he did not want her to see him. Ryan had grown up in a neighborhood where drunkenness was common enough to be neither smart nor funny but a disgrace.

But as he took off hat and coat his mother came out of the kitchen. "Why, where have you been, boy?" she said anxiously.

He kissed her on the cheek. "We had a heavy night, ma. You'll see about it in the papers." He did not want to tell it now.

"It's always a heavy night," she complained. Complaint did not become her; she was a tiny, merry woman. Ryan held her coat for her, bending over to get the sleeve holes right for her short arms. "I really began to worry," she said.

"You ought to know better," he chided. "You've lived with cops long enough."

She said nothing, but the words twisted a knife blade in her heart. The nights she had waited for his father. And there had been the night... "I'm going to the Altar meeting. There's coffee simmering on the stove."

"Thanks, ma." He took a cup into his bedroom, pulled down the blind and undressed, swaying, while he sipped coffee. He switched on the bedside radio and then lay down, feeling the press of cool pajamas against his liquor-heated body.

The ceiling spun slightly. Ryan, sobering, felt depressed. The radio came on with a little roar.

"...teen minutes to nine, girls," a man's voice drawled.

"All I can say is," and Ryan recognized the familiar voice of Dorothy Kilgallen, "that in spite of my years as a reporter in this town I never cease to marvel at the job New York's cops do."

"Honey, I agree with that completely. And I know what you mean."

"It's that story in the *News*. Just suppose it had been you or me who spotted that—that tough man. Would *you* have liked to follow him into a dark street and into some old rooming house? And just walk in on him?"

"Dear, I'm afraid not. I think that New York's finest are—well, the greatest, that's all. And as you say, these two detectives—what were their names?"

"Jablonski. Edmund Jablonski. And O'Neill Ryan. Isn't that a wonderful name?"

"Oh, for God's sake," Ryan muttered.

"...ought to take up a collection for them," the man's voice said.

"They couldn't accept it, honey. The department doesn't permit that."

"Just keep Sandalwood off my neck," growled Ryan and switched off the radio.

He fell back on the pillow. The ceiling spun again. He closed his eyes... That Gee Gee... He slept.

PART TWO: THE BIG NEWS

PART TWO: THE BRAIN

CHAPTER 8

The White Sheep

A plea of not guilty was entered for Derby when he was arraigned, and since the murder had created so much public indignation his examination was scheduled for three days later. He was bound over to the grand jury and it held him for trial without bail. This was all predictable.

When Ryan returned to work, it was as a hero. His routine and Jablonski's were disturbed for several days by newspaper reporters, Sunday feature writers, magazine researchers, photographers and true crime story authors. At first their questions alarmed him. But when he came to realize that these interrogations were directed less toward discovering anything than to proving an already-established point of view, he began to relax. Circumstances had conspired to make him a temporary public figure; Ryan accepted it and after the initial reluctance even entered in with quiet-mannered willingness. His mother and sister complained about the constant telephone calls at home, but he noticed that his mother was never too busy in the kitchen to dry her hands and come to the telephone, and that when a photographer was coming, Eleanor usually had on a new dress and fresh makeup.

Meanwhile, the department had engaged in the usual tedious and vital routine. The bullet taken from the dead woman's head was found to have been shot from the revolver found in Derby's room. The money that Derby had spent at the delicatessen was recovered and as far as could be told might have been one of the tens that Mrs. Connors had obtained from the bank. The partial fingerprints found in the apartment did not check out; they were the dead woman's. But there were two loan sharks named Morgan who worked the docks; one hung around Pier Ninety in Manhattan, the other in Brooklyn. The first did not know Derby and was eager to testify that he had never loaned him money. The second did know Derby and had occasionally done business with him. But when two detectives found him he had been smoking opium in a Williamsburg flophouse for forty-eight hours, and was white and sweating. He was glad to admit that he had not loaned Harry Derby any money recently.

Far more important, McGinnis and Minor went out to Derby's house and talked to his sister, a thin, blond-haired girl with the calm detachment of resignation. She worked as librarian for a midtown athletic club, and when they asked if she had seen her brother Harry on the afternoon of the Connors murder she said she had not because she developed a sick headache that day and had gone home early in the afternoon.

McGinnis asked whom she had seen there, and she said the house had been empty. Other careful questions elicited that she had arrived home before two p.m., and that she had been alone in the Derby apartment on East Seventy-third Street from that time until sometime between six-thirty and seven, when her younger brother had come home from work. That shattered Derby's alibi that he had been enjoying a nap there that afternoon.

A child found a small black change purse a block from the Connors' apartment; it bore a faint smear of blood which the lab proved was Mrs. Connors'. A police scientist in the lab spent most of one day extracting tiny particles of plaster dust from the hairy wool of Derby's jacket. The spectroscope proved beyond doubt that the particles came from the lamp used to bludgeon Mrs. Connors.

Shortly before Jablonski retired he and Ryan went downtown to the district attorney's office and spent forty minutes with Assistant District Attorney Gil Tilbury. He proved to be an excessively thin young man in an expensively tailored suit, buttoned-collar shirt and casually correct striped tie. He laughed often and confidently, and lolled back in his chair until it creaked to show how supremely at ease he was. He told Ryan and Jablonski that he couldn't wait to try this case and that Derby was as good as in the death house. He twiddled a Phi Beta Kappa key.

That evening Ryan sat at home watching a fight on television before leaving for work; he was now on the late tour, midnight to eight a.m. His mother had gone to a card party and his sister was in her bedroom doing something intricate and time-consuming to her hair.

Ryan in sweatshirt and slippers felt lazy and relaxed after sleeping all day. It was a nice way to feel, lying on the couch watching two other guys over at St. Nick's Arena do the heavy work for a while. Occasionally the camera swept the ringsiders, and one of them was a girl who looked like Gee Gee. Probably he ought to call her again. But he'd called twice and missed her each time, and he didn't want to appear anxious. Maybe tomorrow it would be all right. The doorbell rang.

Ryan lifted himself off the couch and groped his way from the darkened living room to the hall. When he reached the front door he saw through its window that the caller standing outside on the porch was a man and that he was tall and lean.

Then the man moved his head and Ryan caught his profile.

It was Derby.

Even while Ryan watched incredulous, Derby turned and gave the bell an irritable double ring.

Ryan began taking long tiptoe strides back the way he came through the living room and into his own bedroom. He removed the pistol from the holster on the bureau. He cocked it and picked up a flashlight, then returned quietly to the hall. He could feel the beat of his heart.

He moved quickly through the short hall, holding light and gun behind him, shifting the light at the last moment to the crook of his right arm as he reached the door, then pressing the latch with a quick left-hand to throw the door open and bring the gun up as he grabbed the flashlight under his arm.

Derby was wearing a neat bow tie of blue checks, a white shirt and a dark suit. A slouch hat of thin felt was pulled low over his right eye; he carried a trenchcoat and he looked young. He winked rapidly in the flashlight beam.

"What is this?" he demanded in an unexpected voice. "I want to see Mr. Ryan—Detective Ryan, I mean. Isn't this where he lives?"

Ryan kept light and gun on him. Derby could not see beyond the light. He blinked uncertainly.

"All right," said Ryan.

"Oh. My name's Derby, Mr. Ryan. Ken Derby. I'm Harry Derby's brother."

Then Ryan understood—and suddenly felt ashamed of the .38 and thrust it into his slacks. He said, "What's on your mind?"

"I just want to talk to you. Sort of off the record, as they say."

"You're talking to me." It annoyed Ryan to have been frightened.

"It would be better inside." Derby's brother raised his face to the light. "This will take a little while."

"Come on in," said Ryan. He did not know exactly how to deal with this, and that annoyed him too. He followed the younger Derby into the living room, switched off the television in mid-commercial, said, "Sit down," waved to the sofa and sank into the deep, worn, leather chair that had been his father's. When he raised his hands negligently behind his head the pocketed .38 made a hard knot against his thigh.

"I'm Ken Derby," said his visitor again. "Harry's my—my older brother."

"Quite a brother."

"Maybe. Anyway, that's why I'm here."

"Why?" said Ryan.

Ken Derby looked uneasy. "I want to find out what's happened to Harry," he said with an air of dogged determination. "I've been talking to his lawyer. I just don't get it."

"Don't get what?"

"Look. You're a cop. I suppose that you figure anyone connected with Harry is a—crook, or a heel."

Meeting only with affirmative silence, he continued, "We know what Harry's record is. My sister and me, I mean. Harry's like my father was. On the docks and—well, a bum. Let's face it. But the rest of the family isn't like that. My sister isn't, and my mother wasn't. And I'm not."

Ryan kept staring at him.

"The hell with that. Here's what I came to say. And understand, I'm on the level. You can ask about me down at Triple-A. I drive a truck for them—Triple-A Delivery on Varick Street. You ask if Kenny Derby's okay. And my sister. She—"

"You went into that." Ryan said it knowing it must anger Derby into saying more than he had come to say.

And Derby took it that way. He got to his feet threateningly—virtually as tall as his brother although not as muscular. Still, Ryan liked the feel of the .38 against his thigh.

"Okay," said Derby. "Then I'll go into this."

"Before you do," said Ryan, interrupting in a way that he knew would not soothe Derby, "just bear in mind that I'm a police witness against your brother. I can't discuss details of a case that is going to trial."

"You don't have to discuss anything," said Derby grittily. "You've just got to answer one thing. Maybe you don't want to answer it. But I came here to ask it to your face, and I want to see your face when you answer."

Ryan looked up curiously.

"You got a case against my brother," said Derby. "I know that. And he's got a bad record. But almost everything you've got against Harry could be coincidence. The witnesses, the ten dollar bills, all that. The one thing you've really got against him is that there's some kind of dust on his jacket that is supposed to prove he was in that old lady's apartment."

Ryan said, "What gives you that idea?"

"It was mentioned at the examination."

"So you've been talking to Harry's lawyer."

Derby looked alarmed. "Suppose I have? Is that against the rules?"

"No. But do you want to argue with the scientists? They say that dust—"

"I don't want to argue with anyone," said Derby doggedly. "If my brother is really guilty."

Ryan did not feel like answering that.

A door opened behind him and he heard Eleanor say, "Oh, I didn't know—" and concluded she had come out of her room without her dress on. He said evenly, "You said your brother is guilty. Do you have any doubts?"

"No," said Derby. "I don't have any doubts. I don't have any doubts at all." Ryan caught a subtle meaning in that and tried to ignore it.

"Then I don't get you," he said. But a premonition had flared in his mind, swift and ominous as the darkening of an ocean sky before a storm. "If you've talked to Farragut, you know that the scientific evidence—that the dust the lab men found on your brother's jacket—is unmistakable proof."

"That's just what I'm getting at," said Derby.

"What, for God's sake?"

"Mr. Ryan, how did that dust get on my brother's jacket?"

Derby's thin, light-eyed face burned across the lamplit room into Ryan's mind, and time became endless. Ryan's body flickered with impulses—to leap up, or kick over a chair or yell. Instead he must sit quietly and prepare to speak quietly.

"It got there," he said, "when your brother smashed the lamp across that old woman's head."

"No," said Derby. "It didn't."

"Then how?"

"I don't know," said Derby meekly. "If I knew, I could save Harry."

Ryan snorted. "That's only one part of the evidence against Harry. There were plenty of witnesses. There's a bank clerk—"

Derby stood up, his lean frame drooping wearily.

"No." His voice was weary too. "You don't understand, Mr. Ryan. And I know you can't discuss this and I didn't come here to—to—well, try to fix anything. But it's like I said. You have a case against Harry but a lot of it could be coincidence or mistaken identity or something. The one thing that's impossible to figure is that dust. I was hoping maybe you'd be—be honest enough to tell me about that. But maybe you really *don't* know about it."

Ryan could stand this no longer. He too got to his feet. "Why?" he shouted. "What the hell do you want explained to you? Your lousy hoodlum brother killed an old woman. He's guilty of murder. He deserves the chair and he'll get it."

Eleanor's door opened again. Ryan heard her say, "Neill? Is there anything wrong?"

"Maybe he'll get the chair," said Derby steadily. "But he doesn't deserve it. Because he's not guilty of murder, Mr. Ryan... Harry did not kill that old woman. I know."

"Neill?" called Eleanor anxiously.

Ryan could see only Ken Derby's pale, taut face. He was conscious of the rise and fall of his own chest. *"How* do you know?"

"Because Harry was with me that afternoon," said Derby; "No one will ever believe it because nobody knows it but me and Harry. He went around on my truck route. I was supposed to have a helper that afternoon and the helper, he didn't show up—he's a fellow that plays the horses and, well, you know. I had two big pieces to deliver way uptown that afternoon and I stopped off at the house and picked up Harry to help me. That's against the rules, but I didn't want to get Dom, that's the helper, in trouble. And I knew Harry could use the dough. He's been broke for quite a while."

"But—" Ryan could not get his thoughts together. He was afraid to say anything or do anything that would make it any worse than it already was. An inspiration came from somewhere. "If he helped you make deliveries, then someone must have seen him."

"I doubt it. You're bonded on this job. If the company discovered I'd used an unbonded helper, let alone a guy with Harry's record, I'd get fired so fast it'd make your head spin. Harry stayed out of sight, mostly. Oh, he ran a few light pieces in on the way uptown. But I really needed him only for the heavy work. One heavy piece was a refrigerator to an apartment up in Harlem and no one saw us take that in at all. The other was way up in the Bronx and we just dropped this stove on the porch of a new house. There were some carpenters working there inside, but—well, you know how much people notice something like that."

There was silence. "That's why I wonder about that dust, Mr. Ryan."

"If he had an alibi," said Ryan harshly, "why didn't he say so?"

"I don't think he really believes he needs one. And he knows it would get me in trouble if it came out he'd been riding with me—him especially with his criminal record. Harry's funny. He's sort of proud that I—well, I've got a job and always gone straight. And he still thinks that he can't be convicted." He added irrelevantly, "He wants to fight it through himself. He'd kill me if he knew I'd come here."

The full meaning of it began to sink to the bottom of Ryan's understanding. As it did he felt cold and shaky, and he knew Ken Derby was watching him.

Ignored, Eleanor firmly closed her bedroom door.

Derby turned and picked his hat off the sofa. Ryan's gaze remained fixed on the emptiness where Derby had been.

"I hope," said Derby, "that if you hear anything about that dust business, you'll be honest."

Ryan followed him to the door, said, "Good night," and closed the door after him, and wasn't aware of any of it.

He went back to the living room, lit a cigarette and inhaled it deeply. He snuffed it out, and then wished he had not snuffed it out and started to light another and then stopped. He had to pull himself together. He had to-think this straight through. He picked up a fresh cigarette and lit it.

Christ!

The clock tolled ten-thirty. It was time to start getting ready for work.

He was in great shape for it.

CHAPTER 9

Dom the Tailor

A hunchback named Frank Yett ran an untidy candy store just off First Avenue in the fifties. He dealt in pop, comic books, ice cream and novelties, and he took horse race bets on the side. Since this was the kind of neighborhood in which the police liked to keep track of neighborhood gossip, they let Yett make book as long as he took bets from adults only and passed on to them whatever he learned of police interest. Recently he had reported that a teen-age gang war was about to break out.

There was also a man who dealt in used cardboard cartons, lived in East Sixty-third Street and had been missing for two days. His car had been identified as one that ran down a pedestrian and then sped on along Bruckner Boulevard. On this night Jablonski and Ryan had been told to cruise the area where the teen-age war might break out and also to drive past the carton-dealer's apartment occasionally.

It was not cold for November. But it was so foggily humid that the black asphalt was streaked with damp sheen under the street lights and the motor of the well-traveled police sedan responded under Ryan's foot with unwonted power and quiet. They had had a couple of minor runs, but by three-thirty they sensed this would be a quiet night and so they might as well eat leisurely. There was a place on Third near Fifty-eighth Street that served hot sandwiches made with Italian sausage fried in onions and peppers.

At a quarter of four Ryan emerged from it carrying three sandwiches and two cartons of coffee. They pulled into a side street, switched off the lights and with even the radio quiet ate in aromatic silence for a few minutes, sharing the third sandwich.

Jablonski sighed contentedly. Tomorrow night would be his last tour of duty. He did not feel any sentimental twinges. All he could think of was taking it easy for a couple weeks. But something Ryan had mentioned earlier still bothered him. He sloshed his coffee around in the cardboard cup to stir up the sugar in it, drank, made a switching sound with his tongue against a bad tooth and drew a cellophane-sheathed cigar from his vest pocket.

"Well, did this guy offer any *proof* his brother was riding around in that truck?" he asked as though they had been talking about it for the last half hour.

But each knew what had been in the other's mind.

"No. He just said—"

"He didn't say why Harry'd do a thing like that?"

"Well, he needed help with these two heavy pieces like I said, and Harry needed the dough. He got the helper's check, I guess."

"But he didn't say that anyone saw Harry in the truck—anyone but himself, I mean?"

"That's right."

Jablonski crumpled the cellophane and threw it contemptuously to the floor mat. "He's not even a good liar."

"Why do you say that?"

"He's just trying to help Harry, that's all." He lighted the cigar and growled through jets of smoke. "Maybe that damned lawyer... I wouldn't put anything past Farragut."

"But why does this Ken Derby know so much about the dust on the jacket? If Harry didn't tell him—well, why does Ken say if he knew how it got on the jacket he could prove Harry innocent? I don't get it, Jabby. He—he sounded so damned *sure.*" Ryan knew he was sounding like a rookie, but he couldn't help it.

Jablonski laughed a short, bitter laugh. "I'll tell you why. Because he's trying to shake your testimony, that's why. Farragut put him up to that, I'll bet you anything. He's trying to make you less certain. Yup, the more I think of it..."

"Yes, but..."

"The Regal's closing."

Ryan started the car and drove it slowly, lights out, to the cross street and parked. The Regal, a bar and grill across the wide avenue, closed at four a.m. The proprietor usually locked up and left by himself with the night's receipts. Ryan and Jablonski could watch his block-long walk to the subway entrance from here.

The sedan filled with cigar smoke. Ryan twisted his window down a little.

"Don't forget these guys are brothers, Neill."

"Oh sure, I realize that."

"Probably Harry does ride with him occasionally in that truck," Jablonski mused. "Probably cases joints that way."

"I don't know about that. I think Ken's honest. He wouldn't let—"

"You *think*, huh? Personally I wouldn't trust any Derby."

"The younger one hasn't any record," said Ryan. "I checked."

"There he goes."

The interior of the Regal had gone dark. Now its big sign blinked out. A man came away from the doorway's shadow and walked hurriedly down the street. They waited until he disappeared down a subway kiosk.

But Ryan did not start the motor. He had been steeling himself. Now with his hand on the switch, looking straight ahead, he said, "Jabby, do you think there's a chance he's innocent?"

Jablonski removed the wet cigar from his mouth and turned his head to look at Ryan. Ryan uneasily stepped on the starter and slipped the transmission into first.

"Wasn't it you that took the C-note out of his wallet?" asked Jablonski at length. "Innocent, for God's sake!"

"I know, but—" Ryan was doggedly determined to get it all out. "Like his goddamned brother said. That dust is the one thing that convicts him for sure. And we know how that got there."

"God awmighty, Neill. You're getting nuts. If you're serious—I can't believe it, but if you are, check on that alibi and see for yourself. Why, that's the most—and don't forget Derby himself told us he was home sleeping. He didn't say nothing about a truck ride. If I ain't right, you can come out to my new place and—and eat all you want on the house for a month."

Ryan grinned. For the moment at least, Jablonski's hearty disbelief reassured him. "I'm glad the deal went through, Jabby. The Green Lantern Inn, eh?"

"That's it, and you're welcome any time."

The radio said it was four ten a.m. Ryan wondered if he might catch Gee Gee if he called the club, but he did not like Jablonski to know he was calling her. Jablonski said. "Coast back to Sixty-third Street again and see if the guy's come home."

Ryan complied. He felt better for having talked about it. But he still felt a little wordless uneasiness that was like the gnawing of a grave worm.

* * * *

The office of the Triple-A Delivery Corporation was a glassed-in room in the corner of a grimy garage that by mid-morning contained only a few immaculate black vans. An old-fashioned iron stove kept the office overheated and the sagging chair in which the proprietor, a heavy man named Nichols, sat sprawled, scented the hot air with the stink of rotting leather. The wall behind Nichols was papered with calendars old and new, all depicting long-legged girls in advanced stages of undress. Ryan flipped the badge on his wallet toward Nichols.

"It's a routine matter," he said, "so for the present we'd prefer that no one knows anything about it. Especially the people involved." He looked down at Nichols. "That's important," he said.

Nichols' thyroid-bulged eyes, big as olives, looked up under thick lids. "I understand."

"You have a driver named Kenneth Derby. On November seventh he's supposed to have had a run that required a helper."

"Could be."

"Do you keep any records that'd prove whether he did or not—and would they show who the helper was?"

"November seventh?" Reaching behind him, Nichols took one of half a dozen clipboards hanging from worn brass hooks and began riffling the long yellow sheets on it with a wetted thumb.

Ryan looked up at the girls. One had flowing coppery hair. Nuts to that! She'd never pose that way.

"Derby," said Nichols. "November seven. Sure. Here it is. Yeah, he had a helper. Dom. Dom the Tailor."

"Who?"

Nichols grinned a fat-lipped grin.

"Dominic D'Tela, his real name is," he said. "Dom the Tailor, they call him. He's a little dago who part-times for me."

"You sure that's who it was? Is it possible someone else might have substituted for this Dom? Say Derby's brother Harry, who's a—well, a sort of—"

"I know Harry." The heavy lids narrowed calculatingly. "But Dom's the man I paid. I remember now—and I remember Harry was around that night, too. They left together. Maybe he was waiting for Ken to come in. Anyway, I can tell from this, that Dom went out in the morning with Henderson—he's my downtown man. And with Derby in the afternoon."

But Ryan's heart had suffered a sinking spell. Harry had been around that night, all right. Nichols remembered it.

Nichols was saying, "Derby is usually my uptown east guy. And according to this, he drew a full day's check, fourteen fifty."

"Can you tell me where Dom lives?"

"Sure. It's just off Houston Street." Like all downtowners Nichols pronounced it Howse-ton.

"Think he'd be home now?"

"That's hard to say. He jobs around. He's a good strong man."

"Big? Tall?"

"Oh, no. He's a little fellow. Big shoulders, though. Good-natured. And very reliable."

"Yeah. Thanks, Mr. Nichols."

Once again outside in the bright cold street he paused. He was tired. But he was also tired of uncertainty.

Better finish it up. Then he'd know.

* * * *

Dominic D'Tela's midday meal, lasagna, bread and coffee, lay spread before him on an oil-clothed table in the tenement parlor.

"Have some coffee?" he asked cordially.

"No, thanks." But the cheese-laden steam from the lasagna made Ryan hungry.

D'Tela turned a strong face to him and said, "What's on your mind?" then returned to his food.

"Do you remember last November seventh? It was a Friday."

"I'll say it was a Friday."

"You remember it?"

"I'll say I remember it. That's the day Cannon Cracker came in at Jamaica and paid twenty-eight bucks—twenty-eight eighty, to be exact."

"And you were on him?"

"Was I on him!" The memory made D'Tela stop eating. "Ten bucks on the nose. I come home with over a hundred and fifty bucks that night. I worked that day too."

"What was the job?"

The thick cup came down, revealing a suspicious frown. "You checking on me or something?"

"Not on you. On someone else. And it doesn't have anything to do with horse bets. All I want to know is what you did on the job that day."

"Well, let's see." He reverted to the lasagna and chewed thoughtfully. "I was working for old man Nichols that day. Yeah, I remember. In the morning I went out with Henderson and in the afternoon with Derby. Kenny Derby."

"You were with Derby all afternoon?"

"Sure."

"Doing what?"

"Well, let's see. Yeah, that was an easy afternoon—lucky day all round." He grinned. "There were only two big pieces he needed help with. Of course I jumped off with lots of the little ones, too, when we got to a neighborhood where there were quite a few deliveries. I always do my share on a job. Besides, Derby was feeling a little tough."

"What was his trouble?"

"You know how it is. He said something about needing some dough for a friend of his, and he'd had a few drinks at lunch—tell you the truth, I figured he had a broad in trouble. Of course, now I figure he wanted the dough for his brother. But it's odd, sort of."

"How do you mean?"

"Well, he needed money and I told him about this horse I was going to bet, see? He was interested, too. But when I called in to get down on the horse just before post time—around five, if was—he said the hell with it. I just wonder what it might have done for him if he'd given me a ten to bet for him. Maybe his brother wouldn't have bumped the old lady, huh?"

"By that time she was dead," said Ryan shortly. "Let's get back to what you did that day. You said there were two big pieces. Where'd you deliver them?"

"Well, the reefer went to an address in Harlem. The gas range went to a new house up in the Bronx."

"Who'd you see at the new house?"

"No one, especially. There were some painters or carpenters working inside. We just set the range down on the porch and left."

"I see. Now look. This is the important part—this is why I'm here. Was there anyone else along on this trip? In other words was there another man on the truck that afternoon besides you and Derby?"

"Of course not." D'Tela looked surprised.

"At no time did another man ride with you?"

"That's right."

"And you were with the truck all the time?"

"Sure—except when I left it to run packages in. Oh, yes, and...uh... we made a stop so I could pick up that dough I won." He looked uneasily at Ryan.

But Ryan was not interested in handbooks at the moment. He said, "Then you didn't see anything of Derby's brother Harry that day? On the truck or anywhere?"

Surprise opened D'Tela's eyes. "Sure I did. Now that you mention it. He was around the office when we got back, after six. Surly and tough-looking as usual, too. Waiting for Ken. I guess."

"But at no time was he on the truck. You'd swear to that?"

"Sure, for God's sake."

Ryan got up. He knew the truth when he heard it. "Thanks, Mr. D'Tela. You'll probably never hear any more of this, and I'd appreciate it—if you don't mention what you told me to anyone. Especially anyone around the Triple-A Delivery Company."

"Sure. Sure thing, you bet," said D'Tela good-humoredly.

The flights of tenement stairs were dark and noisome, but as Ryan went down them they looked as good as a red-carpeted movie set. That lousy lying Ken Derby! Jabby had been right, all right. They had just been trying to shake his nerve and his testimony. They knew what he and Jabby had done with the dust, of course, and they hoped to make a scared and uncertain witness out of him—the rookie! And they had almost succeeded.

When he thought of what a fool he had made of himself talking to Jablonski in the car Ryan felt his cheeks redden. But it was all right now. He could go home and sleep, and forget the whole thing. Tonight was the party. Everything was okay.

CHAPTER 10

The Y-Shape

Mickey McGonigle was a slim, wiry man who at the age of fifty-four had somehow shrunk an inch under the five feet eight prescribed by the City of New York for its policemen. He had very curly red hair parted on one side over a hatchet face corded with belligerent muscularity. He also had an intuitive, wonderfully penetrative sense for truth, which was infinitely more effective than the popular conception of the "third degree" in questioning suspects or witnesses. Leaning against Manny's bar now, he said, "A beefsteak! A beefsteak for that squarehead Jablonski. I gotta have a drink on that."

He pushed his glass across the broad mahogany. "What are you having, Ryan?"

Ryan was not sure. He did not know what you did on an occasion like this, surrounded by superiors and having to work in a few hours. He said, "A beer."

McGonigle said, "Give him the Würzburger, Charlie." Then he looked down the bar to make sure the subject was out of earshot and said, "You were sure luck for Jablonski."

"Why? He was just as much luck for me."

The thin, conflicting planes of McGonigle's face wrinkled skeptically. "The way I got it, you spotted him, walked him into the house and, when Jablonski let Derby jump him, you pulled him off him."

"That's not exactly right."

"It's not exactly wrong," said McGonigle.

Ryan raised his seidel. "In a pinch like that how do you decide who's responsible for what?" He added quickly, "This is good beer."

Lieutenant Bauer came in, dark-hatted, dark-coated, quick-eyed. "Hi, Mick. Hi, Neill. A Manhattan, Charlie."

Bauer took off his coat, leaned cold hands across the bar, rubbed them and said, "Neill, do me a favor."

"Sure," said Ryan. He knew Bauer too well to call him lieutenant, but not well enough to call him Paul.

"The Fifteenth Squad is getting some enlargements of a print the picture bureau got in a drugstore job a couple weeks back. I have a hunch it may be one of that Little Turk gang we had in. Will you and Lambert pick them up during the night and leave them for me?"

"Sure thing."

"Thanks." Bauer picked the cherry out of his drink and nibbled it by the stem. "How're things going? I haven't seen much of you."

"Just fine, thanks."

"Lambert's a good operator. Quiet but smart. Smarter than Jabby."

Ryan had already discovered that about his new partner, but he was surprised and flattered by Bauer's candor. "Could be," he said. McGonigle was talking Dodger talk with two others who had come in.

Bauer said, "From what I hear they're going to push that Derby case into court as soon as possible. So if you have any special preparations to make or need extra time or anything, just let me know."

"Thanks. I don't think there's anything special, but I appreciate the offer."

Bauer waved that off and sipped his drink. "By the way," he said, and Ryan recognized that the rest had been preliminary and that this was what Bauer really wanted to say.

"Jack Sandalwood called me today," said Bauer, and Ryan's nerves began to jangle.

He said, "I see." Then, "What'd he want?" He took a deep draught of beer.

"Oh, he asked if we'd found that hundred dollar bill in the Derby case," said Bauer very unconcernedly, "and he said something about having talked to Farragut. He—he talked kind of odd." He looked idly down the bar. "I don't know what he was driving at exactly," he finally went on. "He was sort of vague, and that's not like Sandalwood. You have any ideas?"

"No." And then, on a sudden gambler's impulse, he said, "Of course, that night we brought in Derby he was asking a lot of questions, too. He was mainly interested in the C-note then. I think he figured Jabby and I had latched on to it."

Bauer sniffed skeptically and finished his drink. "I don't think so," he said. "I can't believe Jack'd bother with something like that. I think he's after something bigger. But I'm damned if I know what."

"Another, Lieutenant?" asked the bartender.

"No, thanks, Charlie. Well, whatever it is I suppose we'll see it on the front page of his newspaper one of these days. Wonder how the beefsteaks are coming?"

"I think they're about ready, Lieutenant," said Charlie.

* * * *

They ate thick, juice-streaming slices of steak laid on juice-pink bread, and afterward deep-dish apple pie and coffee, and talked shop and kidded Jablonski about his bar and grill. Jablonski sat at the head of the table, wonderfully crisp in a starched white shirt and fresh haircut and shave, flushed with whisky and happiness at being the center of importance. Paul Bauer sat at the other end of the table, and when they had pushed the coffee cups aside and lighted tobacco he said a few words about how swell it had been working with Ed Jablonski and what a good cop he was and how he would be missed. Then he gave Jablonski a big package containing a bar apron as a joke, and a smaller package containing a toilet kit including a gold-plated razor; and everyone clapped and Ed Furtig yelled, "Speech!"

No one expected Jablonski to make a speech. But after accepting with unusual solemnity the toilet kit that was passed down the table to him he rose and stood looking at it for a moment. Then he said, "Well, fellas, all I can say is..." and stopped, and for the first time really, they understood that Jablonski was leaving and how it must feel to be going away from something you've lived with for twenty-eight years, and each of them got a quick, clairvoyant glimpse of what was coming to him some day.

Suddenly Jablonski sat down, his eyes watery, his speech unsaid, but everyone at the table applauded, with a curious sense that he had said it anyway.

Those who were not working that night had a farewell drink with him at the bar and Ryan, going out, punched his arm as he passed. But Jablonski was busy trying to buy that round of drinks and he did not feel it.

It was only ten-thirty. Ryan stopped in a lunch counter restaurant where he knew there was a phone booth, ordered coffee and dialed the number of the club where Gee Gee worked. He had called it only twice before but he did not have to look up the number. The phone was answered with a blast of music and he said to please tell Miss Hawes that Mr. Ryan was calling.

There was an interval during which the music stopped, and then a low, warm voice said, "Hello, Mr. Ryan," and he heard the rush of her breath into the phone, soft and intimate as she held her mouth close to it, and he remembered the scent of her hair and how it had been dancing with her. For a second he did not have any words.

He said, "My name's Neill," and grinned awkwardly in the phone booth's dimness. He heard her chuckle. "I start a forty-eight tomorrow morning," he said, "and I was thinking maybe we could work out a date."

"I think that would be lovely. What's a forty-eight?"

"We work six tours—six days, then get forty-eight hours off. It's really fifty-six hours, but anyway. I thought if you—if the club was closed tomorrow, being Sunday, or on Monday, maybe we could get together in the evening or something."

"Monday evenings I'm free."

"Dinner maybe?"

"I'd love it."

Ryan left the phone booth in a happy glow. He threw a quarter on the counter but left the coffee untouched. He did not want to spoil the way he felt with that coffee.

Lambert had not yet reported when Ryan got to the squad room; so he belatedly crushed his hat into its conventional version, lit a cigarette, propped his feet up on a desk and thought about Gee Gee and where they would go for dinner. Some theatrical sort of place probably. Lindy's or Dinty Moore's.

After a time, mindful of what Bauer had said, he got out the file on Derby that Jablonski had left and began leafing through its slender contents. Notebook pages of names and dates, a couple of typed sheets, a photostat of Derby's police record, a copy of his fingerprints… Ryan stared at them for a long time out of sheer lassitude and a feeling of well-being. Then Lambert arrived.

They had a busy night. Saturday nights usually were busy, but in addition there were two fires, within blocks and minutes of each other, that the fire marshal concluded had been set by an arsonist. Ryan and Lambert spent most of the night on foot patrol, and it was not until after six a.m. that they could drive down to the Fifteenth Squad on East Thirty-fifth Street and pick up the envelope Bauer had asked for. They stopped for breakfast on the way back, each sitting in the car and listening to the radio while the other ate. Ryan idly examined the contents of the envelope over his sandwich. It consisted of big enlargements of some fingerprints and blurred carbon copy of a theft report.

Ryan read it. Several weeks before a man had walked into a small neighborhood drugstore just off First Avenue, handed the proprietor a bottle and asked that it be filled with castor oil. That took the proprietor to the prescription counter at the rear and while he was out of sight the customer dodged around a showcase to the cash register, grabbed its contents and ran out. The proprietor, who was seventy years old, had not noticed the thief especially, except that he wore a dark suit and had no overcoat, although the day was brisk. But the bottle had been oily when he brought it in and so the fingerprint men had found prints of a right thumb and forefinger perfectly delineated on the rim of the cash register drawer.

Things like that were rare, despite what the public, educated by seeing and reading a hundred fictional criminal investigations, was led to believe. Still, they happened, and this was one. Ryan studied the fingerprint photographs while he sipped coffee. He saw something odd in the thumb print—a little Y-shaped scar on the print's right perimeter. That was odd because he had recently seen the same thing somewhere else.

And he knew where. There had been a scar like that in Derby's prints, which he had studied earlier waiting for Lambert. A thumb? What of it? It was coincidence, of course. But it *was* odd. Could Derby have done this one too? He looked again at the date on the smudged report.

And when he did, Ryan felt a crushing weight sag his shoulders and a pervading chill enter his heart. The drugstore robbery had occurred on November 7, at 3:25 p.m., twenty blocks south of the apartment where at the very same time Thelma Connors was being murdered, presumably by Harry Derby.

But the thumb print of the drugstore thief remarkably resembled Derby's.

It must be coincidence. When he got back to the precinct he could compare them.

But the overpowering sureness, the growing conviction that is born of subconscious observation, began invading his mind. Ryan had a precognitive sense of what he would find when he got back to the precinct. The prints were going to be the same.

He knew it because of the way everything—all the incongruous little things that had struck him as odd from the beginning—fell into place with dreadful logic.

Derby had been engaged in a comparatively harmless bit of sneak thievery at the very time Mrs. Connors was being mortally assaulted. That is why he had not told the truth about where he really was at the time. Derby was a three-time loser whom even the drugstore theft would send up for life—but insofar as the murder was concerned he was innocent. He had the strongest possible sort of alibi, proved unwittingly by a police investigation, and now safeguarded unknowingly in the records of the department.

But no one knew about it except Ryan. No one could. For no one would ever think of comparing an odd thumb and forefinger print from a cheap smash-and-grab with the known prints of a tough, big time stevedore-hoodlum like Harry Derby. Not even in the Known Criminal File.

* * * *

Ryan was very quiet during the rest of the tour, but Lambert did not comment on it for he himself was a self-contained man. After they checked in at the precinct Ryan took both prints into the lavatory where he could be undisturbed and compared them, using a flashlight and a magnifying glass in the toilet's dimness.

After that there was no doubt. Derby was innocent. He had an unassailable alibi.

Ryan put Derby's records back in his own desk drawer and the new print from the Fifteenth Squad on Bauer's desk.

Then he went home and tried to get to sleep.

CHAPTER 11

A Million Things Can Happen

Sunday afternoon was desolate. He wanted yearningly to talk to someone; the subject was forever at his tongue's tip, and instead, eating a late brunch, he had to listen to his mother's chatter about the church decorations and Eleanor's talk of the drama appreciation class she was taking one evening a week at Columbia. Eleanor had gone to Katherine Gibbs' and become a secretary after graduating from high school instead of going to college. Now she was working with dilettante interest toward an A.B. degree. She asked Ryan to pick up some volumes of Ibsen she needed the next time he was near the Columbia University library. Twice that day he had to ask her to repeat the name of the dramatist although it was not unfamiliar to him; the second time he wrote it down.

* * * *

Around four he went for a walk, stopping at the first drugstore to call Jablonski. Someone he took to be the bartender at the Green Lantern said Mr. Jablonski had gone to Jersey for the day with his wife to visit her folks. He'd be around tomorrow, the bartender said. Ryan left his name and said he was coming out tomorrow.

He walked thoughtfully toward Fifth Avenue. It was a sunny late afternoon; there were still many leisurely strollers. In Central Park he bought peanuts and fed ragged squirrels and watched a few hardy kids sail boats in the boat basin. The last dull orange gleams of the sun were dying in a striped violet sky and the lights had come on, circling the park, when he turned homeward. The onset of night's gloom depressed him, renewing the anxiety he had partly shaken off.

Tomorrow would be better. Jablonski would have advice to offer, and ideas—just talking to him about it would help. And then tomorrow night, a bare twenty-four hours from now, after they had settled on something, there'd be Gee Gee to see.

Ryan began walking faster. It wasn't just the cold. He wanted to get everything over with as soon as possible—supper and sleep and the trip to New Rochelle.

* * * *

It originally had been a store building, and the first floor front still consisted chiefly of a kind of bayed-out show window that contained a big glass vessel filled with green liquid, the kind that old-fashioned druggists used to display. But across the window glass *Green Lantern Inn* was printed in gold letters and in one corner there appeared "Walter Nowak." Under it in bright, newly applied gold leaf was "Edmund A. Jablonski." That was Jablonski all right—*he* wouldn't waste any time getting his name up!

But when Ryan pushed the door open and walked in there was no Jablonski. A portly bartender, bland-faced and immaculate in a fresh apron, was behind the bar, and from the end of the room an Oriental face under a chef's tall cap looked expectantly up over a gleaming grill. There were tables, neat with green checkered tablecloths and shiny bottles of catsup.

"Mr. Jablonski around?"

"He's not in right now. He should be back about six. Any message?"

"My name's Ryan. I'd phoned him that—"

"Oh sure, Mr. Ryan. He said to tell you to come on out to the house."

"The house?"

"They're renting a house over on Devens Place and I guess the missus has got him doing some work." The bartender, distinguished-looking, smiled a bland, man-to-man smile. "You know how it is."

"Oh, sure. How do I get out there?"

"It isn't far. You take your first right up at the corner…"

He found Jablonski in the unfurnished living room of an old-fashioned double house. He was on his knees in a corner touching up the varnish with a brush and a can of lacquer. From some unseen kitchen came clinking sounds and the rush of water as Mrs. Jablonski washed the glass globes from the lighting fixtures. Jablonski got up painfully but gratefully. "Jeez, I'm glad you're here. My knees couldn't take much more. How you been?"

"Good. And you?"

"Great. Except we're moving in Friday and Sarah figures I can completely redecorate the joint before then. Say, I hear the brass still hasn't gotten over our collaring Derby. You're hotter'n a two dollar pistol, Neill. That's great." Jablonski sounded a little envious.

"You're pretty hot yourself with that bar and grill. That's a nice lay-out, Jabby. I'll bet you do a heck of a business."

"We're doin' all right. We'll drop by and have a drink there after a bit. Mind if I go on working while you tell me what you wanted to talk about?"

"Go right ahead."

Jablonski picked up the brush, sank to his knees, groaned and went on dabbing.

"It's about Derby."

"Oh?"

"Yah. To give it to you straight…in a few words…he's innocent." Only the brush's steady pat-pat against the floor made any sound. Its rhythm did not vary.

"Yeah?" Jablonski sounded surprised but nothing else. He went on brushing.

"You get what I said. The guy's innocent."

Jablonski said, "Why do you say that?"

"Because I know—I know what his alibi is."

"Neill, you're nuts. You must be. Why, he even admitted killing her himself, after he burned the bill. You know that."

"He was boasting," said Ryan patiently. "He was just trying to make us feel worse. You ought to know he'd do that."

"Oh, for God's sake—"

"You can't talk this down, Jabby. I know what I'm saying."

The brush's lacquer-slaps had finally stopped. "I don't believe it." Then, "How sure are you?"

"Dead sure. He didn't kill the old lady. He couldn't have. He was doing a smash-and-run on a drugstore at the time, and he left a clear print there. It's only by a crazy coincidence that I happened to see it and recognize what it was. No one in the department knows, or can know. There's nothing to classify."

"Uh huh." Jablonski, supported by knees and one hand, was bent away from Ryan. He resumed stroking.

Ryan said, "Well, what do you think?"

Jablonski finished touching up the spot he was working on with great care. Then he turned over, to sit and look up at Ryan inquisitively. "What am I supposed to think?"

"Well, you know how you—how we planted that dust on his jacket."

"I know Derby's a hood and a killer."

"Maybe. But now you also know he didn't kill the old lady."

"No, I don't. All I know, and all you know, is that a fingerprint looked just like another fingerprint—to you. You're no fingerprint man. And someone says the time was the same. Maybe yes. Maybe no. I haven't seen any proof."

"As far as the time is concerned, I checked that myself this morning. A radio car got there less than two minutes after the drugstore was hit. And there's a million neighbors who heard the old man yell when he ran out into the street. That job was done just when the report said it was done. As for the prints, okay, I'm no fingerprint man. But I've looked at a few and so have you. Want to argue with these?" The envelope he tossed struck Jablonski's shiny-serge knee.

But Jablonski did not pick it up. He was looking up at Ryan. Ryan had noticed before that his face was fresher looking and less lined. But now it became dark and vigorous with thought.

"The department," Ryan explained patiently; he did not like this or Jablonski's expression—"the department actually has Derby's alibi on record and doesn't know it. Nobody knows about it except me—and now you."

Jablonski said coldly, "Okay. So what?"

Ryan knew what that meant. He had known it by Jablonski's face before Jablonski said it. But he had to go on, to carry the argument through until it arrived at whatever deadlock it would reach.

"So Derby's going to the chair," he said. "And we're sending him there. And he's innocent."

Jablonski, throwing back his head, croaked brief laughter. "For Christ's sake!"

Ryan felt like an undressed child. It made him mad.

"Well, damn it, even a lousy hood is entitled to a square shake!"

Jablonski put a finger to his lips. "Not so loud. Sarah."

"To hell with Sarah!"

"Look, Neill. You're young and you're inexperienced in the department, even though you've done great recently. And I don't want to see you hurt yourself now."

"Hurt *who?*" Ryan had lived with it too long to be patient any longer. The time had come for anger and indignation and he unleashed them, unconsciously seeking to force the decision that would end it one way or another.

But Jablonski had spent his life handling anger and indignation. "Neill, now listen a minute—just a minute. Harry Derby's a hoodlum. He's crooked; it's what's inside him. You ought to know what I mean— you were on the street long enough. He ain't like normal people, that believe in square shakes and giving other guys breaks and so on. He's got a record that—well, he's done almost everything to anyone you can think of. And you know as well as I do that for every time he was arrested doing it, he had done the same thing twenty times more when he wasn't caught. He's an animal, Neill—do you want to turn that loose?"

"No, for God's sake." Ryan responded to emotion with emotion. "For heisting the drugstore he should go up for life."

"He had that choice, Neill. He has it now. As you say, he has a perfect, tailor-made alibi. All he's gotta do any time he wants is to say that he was in the drugstore then. Right away he is out of the chair. Well, he made the choice. He's sayin' nothing about the drugstore. And why?"

"'Cause he figures to beat the murder rap."

"Sure. He ain't crazy."

"But—"

"But nothing! Look, Neill. What do you really think you're going to do about it? Let down all our witnesses? Ruin the case against a guy that should have gone up years ago? Give the newspapers another shot at making the department look silly? And what will something like this do to your career?"

"I'm not thinking about my career," snapped Ryan. "And God knows I'm no friend of Derby's or the newspapers. But I can't stand around and see a guy burn, no matter how much of a heel he is, when he doesn't have it coming to him."

"Well, what do you think it'll do to *my* career?" Jablonski asked quietly. "I'm on pension, Neill, and I need every nickel right now to swing that grill. That's why we're takin' this old house. But what's going to happen if the department finds out about our case against Derby? What happens to my pension, and my reputation and business? I'm in this as much as you. You ought to remember that. And I'm not as young as you."

Ryan lit a cigarette. He hadn't thought of it quite that way. But he said, "Sure you're not as young. That's why I thought you might have the answer. You always said you'd been around a long time."

"Gimme one of them things—my cigars are in my coat. Sure I got the answer. If you'll take it."

"So? What do we do?"

"Nothing."

"But I tell you—"

"Nothing," Jablonski repeated firmly, and put the cigarette to his lips. "Until after the trial. Neill, you're forgetting he isn't convicted yet. And he's going to be defended by one of the best criminal lawyers in the business. If he gets off—and he's got a fair chance of that; they always have, what with hung juries and so on—if he gets off, we can forget the whole thing, and nobody's hurt."

"Yeah, but…"

"Look, kid. You got excited about this before—remember? When that wild-haired brother of his came to see you? Then you found out for yourself what I told you all along—that he was lying. Take my advice again, won't you? For my sake as well as your own? Wait and see, Neill. You won't gain anything by rushing this thing. And you may lose—we both can lose—a great deal."

Jablonski's tone was low and confidential, and it was convincing because Ryan half-wanted to believe it. He had outlined a solution that Ryan had hardly given a thought to.

"Well…yeah." Ryan knocked cigarette ashes into his trouser cuff. "But supposing he's convicted?"

"We cross that bridge when we come to it. Jeez, Neill, a million things can happen. You know that." Jablonski got to his feet. "There's nothing you can do now that you can't do later. Hell with this floor. I want you to meet my wife. Let's drive down to the joint and have a beer."

The three of them drove to the Green Lantern in the bartender's car, which Jabby had borrowed. Sarah Jablonski, tall and black-haired, was a surprisingly youthful-looking woman with fierce bright eyes and quick good humor that made Ryan wonder why Jabby had ever bothered with Inez. He also wondered how much Sarah knew about Inez. Probably everything, he decided.

Once back at the restaurant he protested that he had to get back to Manhattan right away, insisted on walking to the station, and caught an express soon after.

He sat in the smoker and smoked all the way back to Grand Central. He felt relieved of most of the weight of responsibility that he had carried out to New Rochelle; the decision and the need to act had been postponed for a time at least by Jablonski's eloquence.

But not merely by his eloquence, Ryan told himself. After all, he *did* owe Jablonski something—certainly he owed him the chance to let things straighten themselves out, without his own intervention. Jabby's twenty-eight years of plodding still deserved consideration; it was typical of himself to react hotheadedly to any injustice and try to right it. That was what he had done now. But actually that was often the way greater injustices were compounded.

It was a comforting thought and Ryan extinguished the last flickering anxiety by turning his thoughts deliberately to Gee Gee and the next six hours. What would she be like this time, alone with him? And what would he be like?

Ryan had always found girls fairly easy to get along with, except for those he fell in love with. Of those in his twenty-eight years of life there had not been too many, because he did not easily form attachments, although once they were formed they lasted. But Ryan had been almost old enough to vote before he came to realize that while there were some girls you wanted very much to sleep with and others that you fell respectfully in love with, the two were not incompatible but were indeed closely and rightfully associated. Even so, when he met a girl whom he really liked, tensions developed and he felt himself grow shy and awkward. When it was a girl he didn't deeply like, then things went very easily and surely. He felt he was going to be awkward with Gee Gee.

For not since he was sixteen had he met one like this, a girl whose name even was a honeyed fragrance in his mind. He must be crazy, he thought. He'd only met her once—but she had sounded glad he called, hadn't she? And even dames like that don't want to kick around in nightclubs forever. If they have any sense at all, they want to settle down like everyone else, and have a little apartment and kids after a while…and she had sense all right. That was what he liked about her. Pretty girls were a dime a dozen in this town. But the kind that were also levelheaded and could see farther than a mink coat and that somehow you knew were square shooters…

Ryan gazed out the window, looking into the tenements mounting above the train as it rushed down to the level of Park Avenue and the tunnel entrance. But those tenements and the dark, dangerously underprivileged hearts that lived there in the Twenty-fifth Precinct, one of the city's toughest, brought back Derby.

And that brought back something that had occurred to him before but only tangentially, without real meaning. Now, as the train burst into the tunnel with a gasping roar, he thought of what he should have thought of in arguing with Jablonski. If Derby had committed the drugstore theft, then certainly he deserved to go up for life. But Derby was at least in custody and therefore still at the disposal of the law.

But the real Connors' murderer was at large and was not even being sought. He had gotten away with it.

Everything in Ryan's policeman's soul shuddered at that. But what was he, the only working cop who knew this, doing about it?

CHAPTER 12

The Puerto Rican

Ryan chose critically from the shirts his mother had ironed that day, and knotted his tie with precision. It was good to concentrate on unimportant things, and to have a reason for concentrating on them. Putting on his suit he tried not to disturb the creases pressed into it. Then, having arranged a breast-pocket handkerchief, he went into Eleanor's room (after first making sure she and his mother were in the kitchen) to survey the total effect in her long vanity mirror. Ryan decided he looked as good as he could and reminded himself that it was not the world's record.

He left the house giving his hat the fancy crush and resolving to put Derby out of his mind.

Walking to the I.R.T. station took him past the church and the parish priest's house. Only a single dull light burning behind the Venetian blinds hinted at life inside. Ryan striding the frosty sidewalk passed within a yard of that uninviting window. An adviser on Derby, perhaps? A sanctuary to keep in mind, and rely on if need be? Ryan's mouth made a tight smile. No. Not likely.

He remembered the time that he and his mother had come here and were closeted with the priest behind that very window. Ryan hadn't been going to church and that troubled his mother. He had agreed to the interview and he still remembered the platitudes and tired admonitions, the meaningless, emotionless words that should have had meaning and emotion. Now he had not gone to church in a long time, and that had become accepted at home. But he and his problem wouldn't be welcome behind that reclusive window.

At the subway entrance he bought a tabloid and lost himself in the latest doings of café society.

The name Hawes did not appear on any of the mailboxes in the hallway of Gee Gee's building. But *Haas* did. Ryan wisely pushed that button and was gruffly admitted to a second-floor front apartment by an elderly man who had removed the detachable collar from his shirt and the shoes from woolen-socked feet. He said Georgine should be ready in a minute, went back to his chair and continued to stare at a large television set which was portraying the adventures of Sid Caesar.

Ignored, Ryan held his hat and pondered the ways of a world that changes Georgine Haas into Gee Gee Hawes. He did not particularly like Georgine as a name, just as he did not like the heavy scent of cooking in here, or the large oval family portraits that had been hung in Old World style high up near the ceiling, or this grizzled walrus who presumably was her father and didn't even have the courtesy—

Then she was standing there, in the same coat and carrying with her the same faint scent, a perfume of aromatic dryness, and pressing new gloves on over her fingers, smiling "Sorry to keep you waiting," her eyes as deep and large and somehow inviting as he had remembered they were. He got up and dropped his hat and said, "Hi."

She gestured to her father, "Guess you've met—'bye, Pops," and went to the door. Ryan followed, muttering, "Good night." Only Sid Caesar answered him.

In the hall the cooking smell was strong. Gee Gee wrinkled her nose. "I'd never have let you pick me up here if I didn't think you were a nice, sane guy," she said.

"What do you mean?"

A shinily gloved forefinger made a disdainful arc around the stairwell. "Usually I meet dates somewhere else. There are a lot of people I don't want to have know that my old man's a night watchman, and that I support the family—as much as I can."

"I don't think that's anything to bother about one way or the other."

"Neither do I. But some people do, especially in show business. You're supposed to live at the Waldorf and eat at Twenty One."

They had reached the street. "Speaking of which," he said.

"Speaking of which." She laughed and took his arm with the ease of one accustomed to taking arms. "I'm starved. You'll learn not to ask me out to dinner, Neill."

Ryan laughed too, and was emboldened. "That'll take a long time. Where would you like to go? Pick one you really like." His wallet contained almost eighty dollars; he had counted it just before dressing.

"How about Chinese food?"

Ryan did not especially like Chinese food. He said, "Well, if that's what you'd like," without enthusiasm. It did not occur to him that she could have said that because she knew Chinese restaurants were inexpensive.

"I really don't care. Maybe chow mein isn't the thing at that. You name one."

They had reached the corner. Ryan named several, all of them expensive. That was how he felt.

Gee Gee looked her surprise. "You must have got a bonus for catching that Derby," she said lightly.

He'd got a bonus all right.

She saw in his face that it had been the wrong thing to say. "How do you like the Blue Ribbon?" she asked quickly. "I think their food is awfully good."

This time Ryan grinned, shrugged off his irritation and waved an approaching cab to the curb.

They ate oysters and roast duck and got to know each other better. Gee Gee paid an escort the compliment of being neither coy nor arch with him, nor yet determinedly the professional dancer. Instead she was forthright and relaxingly unassuming, as though she felt Ryan was the same sort of person. The effect on Ryan was overwhelming and happily narcotic.

He insisted she select something from the huge, tempting pastry tray over her protests about her figure and her job, and he told her she had nothing to worry about with such obvious sincerity that Gee Gee, who was used to compliments, was stirred. They got on well, and when she remarked idly that after such a meal there was nothing like an *espresso* Ryan instantly suggested taking a taxi down to one of the little Italian coffee shops in the Village. It was an extravagant gesture and Gee Gee, embarrassed because she had never intended to suggest that, protested again. But Ryan looked so disappointed that she gave in.

In the cab they sat quite close together and Gee Gee asked questions about his job, and Ryan answered them, meanwhile dismissing a temptation to try putting his arm even ever so lightly around her shoulders.

"What's it really like?" she asked. "Being a detective, I mean. I know it's not like in the movies and so on. You don't get cases like that Derby one often, do you?"

"Not often," said Ryan, and knew he had let irony edge his voice. "Most of the time it's routine, little things you run down day after day. A lot of it is taking over after a uniform man has made an arrest and developing information, motives and such to use in court. You don't run around with a magnifying glass making deductions." It made him a little bitter.

But she was genuinely interested. "Then what *do* you use? Handcuffs and a gun?"

"Mostly your feet," Ryan grinned. "And sometimes your head. Handcuffs, sure, when you're making a collar—arresting someone. Never your gun if you can avoid it. That's the last resort."

She said, "Uh huh," understandingly in the cab's warm darkness but he knew she did not understand what that meant at all. How many civilians did? She went on, "I guess it's like show business. Everybody who's not in it thinks it's glamorous and exciting every night. But it's routine, too. Except for the opening nights—I guess they are like the nights when you arrest someone like Derby."

"Yes." He could never get completely away from it. So why try? "Derby's something special, all right."

"Derby *is? Was,* I'd say." She sensed this was dangerous ground from his voice, but she had the feminine impudence born of knowing she was liked. Anyway, what was eating him? "Derby's all taken care of—remember?" she said.

But Ryan could not respond to her lightness.

She had not expected him to keep looking like that. She said contritely, "I just remembered Ed emphasizing that night how you two had taken care of Derby."

Ryan recognized the need for getting away from this. "Sure," he said. "That's right. Derby's all washed up. And speaking of that let me tell you something that happened one night down on South Street."

But telling the oft-told anecdote, he could not help wondering if she was looking at him a little oddly, and just how friendly she was with Jack Sandalwood, and how often she saw him. And whether she ever had repeated what Jablonski had said that night.

* * * *

In the coffee shop they sipped black, deliciously bitter coffee drawn from a monstrous hissing machine and sprayed with oil from a sliver of lemon zest. Afterward they went out into the cold black night and walked through Washington Square, past a few hardy oldsters still playing chess by lantern light, and other, darker benches with occupants silent or murmurous. They did not say much, but she took his arm and they walked through the shadowy park content with each other's company and with the awareness that the other was content too.

They walked a long time, past show windows filled with impossible lamps, best-sellers or copies of last month's Paris originals. Once she murmured, "You know, Neill, you're an awfully restful guy to spend an evening with," and looking quickly, Ryan saw her eyes were closed even while walking and yet she was smiling.

Jeez, thought Ryan. He wasn't thinking of Derby now.

They walked a long time like that.

* * * *

He knew the Village pretty well, but after an hour he found they were on one of those little side streets that angled-off another street, and he knew he had taken a wrong turn. It was dark and empty and Gee Gee said, "Golly, where are we?" Ryan said he had pulled a boner, but that at the next corner they should be able to see where...

She pressed a little closer to him in this dark uncertainty, and Ryan put his arm around her waist—how slender, even encased in that thick coat!—and doing that was not surprising to him at all, or remarkable, but natural, and he pulled her closer to him and she raised her face. He started to find her lips...

He saw the movement only as a flash of furtive white, a something on the left that instinctively pulled him from her, and then the man was there, crouched, menacing, barefoot, although not registering immediately in Ryan's consciousness despite the white shirt and snarling brown face, his left hand holding high a clean knife.

It was impossible.

But the little man, legs braced wide, knife high, screamed, "Hello, whore man!" and rushed at them, head down, knife reversed for an upward belly thrust.

Ryan pushed her behind him as the man leaped forward, head low like a tackier in football, knife wavering up. Ryan kicked hurriedly and his overcoat spoiled his aim. His toe grazed the other's thigh, and turned him but did not stop him.

Ryan grabbed for the knife as he came in, missed, grabbed wildly again, caught the man's wrist and twisted it. A knee pumped up and caught him, but his right arm lay across the man's upturned face and he pushed it down, bending the man's head back. Then he lost his balance and felt himself falling. He scraped desperately for footing and went over the curb, stumbled into the street and went down on a knee and saw something leaping. Gee Gee screamed; he did not hear her.

He rolled and made the knife-man almost miss with his leap. Ryan found his pistol even with the man partly on top of him. He pulled it out and shoved it into the brown, intent face and the knife-man incredibly opened a snarling mouth and bit down on the pistol's short barrel, yanking with his teeth. *He's crazy,* Ryan realized. *You don't use your gun on a mental case.*

Light came from somewhere although Ryan would remember sensing that only later. Gee Gee screamed again. Ryan wondered if he would ultimately have to shoot, and if so how he might make sure of hitting the right shoulder.

He saw the knife flash suddenly and he gathered strength from somewhere (a taxi horn honked) to push up with arm and body and knees.

The little man toppled sideways and for the first time Ryan managed a punch. It was only with his left hand, and it hit the man's face, still holding the gun in his mouth, but did not dislodge him. The knife started flashing again and he had to let go the gun to grab that arm. He didn't stop it entirely because he felt something graze his chin even though he was holding the man's arms while he wrestled like a maddened monkey, sitting on Ryan, holding the gun in his crazed mouth.

A shape stood over them. "Take the gun," Ryan gasped and she bent over and wrested the pistol from the man's jaws. Ryan arched his back and moved him a little, then in desperation let go one writhing wrist to swing at the vague face. The punch landed and the man went sideways and Ryan rolled over and kicked him and then, on his knees, punched him again. Someone said, "Hey, for God's sake!" and there was more light and the knife's blade glittered on the black asphalt. Ryan grabbed for it.

So did the little brown-faced man and she entreated, "Here, here," and handed him his pistol. He put it on the man who still lunged forward on his knees, fingers clawing for the knife, and Ryan got up and kicked again and this time he caught the knife-man in the stomach which was what he had intended the first time and the man flew back.

A voice said, "Listen, Buster, that ain't no way to fight."

For the first time he looked beyond the range of his assailant. Two taxicabs had stopped in the street, their headlights illuminating the scene. A big, fat driver whose belly had burst his pants was looking outrage at Ryan.

Ryan pulled out his badge. "Under arrest," he said with thick meaninglessness and went to the brown-faced man. He searched the man and found he was naked under his pants and bloodied shirt.

"You," said Ryan to the cab driver. "There's a call box up on the corner. Tell them to send a radio car here right away."

Gee Gee looked at him, her face white and her eyes haunted. "Jesus," she said. "Your chin."

It was bleeding.

Only after the first radio car got there and dozens of neighbors had come down into the street did someone go up to the knife-man's apartment in the house opposite. They discovered his wife and two babies were dead, their throats slashed as they slept. He was a Puerto Rican busboy in an uptown hotel, the neighbors said, who had lost his job three days before.

Several of them had seen the fight, or the latter part of it, from their windows, and had seen Gee Gee wrest the gun from the madman's jaws. When the reporters came they were eager to talk. When Ryan and Gee

Gee, after his scratched chin had been treated in a nearby admitting room, appeared at the local precinct station, they were photographed together. Finally he took her home, apologizing for the melodrama, embarrassed by the evening's ending and still seeing the knife flashing down. He didn't try to kiss her.

But next day New York read the news, straight from the dark, greasy pavement of Barrow Street:

HERO COP NABS BABY SLASHER

And under its headline one paper added:

DANCER HELPS MAKE ARREST

CHAPTER 13

The Empty Passage

The capture of Derby had made Ryan a one-day hero, but when he returned to work now it was as a celebrity. To the newspapers the combination of show girl, young cop and maniacal killer was a perfect one, and they made the most of it. At a time when the department was under general opprobrium Ryan seemed to be proving singlehandedly that a policeman could be as capable, alert and humane as the most indignant Constant Reader could wish, and the very newspapers that had devoted lead editorials to the rising crime rate now spent flattering front-page space on the work of an unknown rookie. One editorial compared him to the almost legendary Johnny Broderick, and Winchell's Girl Friday column asked, "Why don't they call rookie detective Ryan *Rockie* instead?"

Ryan felt the difference among his associates. Technically, he was still a beginner, but only technically. Now in some subtle yet palpable way he had acquired importance and weight. Even the older men in the station house treated him with the grudging respect of envied prestige. That was pleasant, but to Ryan it sometimes seemed his progress had been too rapid to be healthy, a suspicion heightened by the haunting awareness of what would happen if the truth about Derby got out.

As the opening of Derby's trial drew near, Ryan found himself waking up nights in unrecallable fear, and his daytime thoughts turned often to his father.

What would *he* have thought?

* * * *

Late one wintry afternoon Ryan found himself in Carmine Street.

He did not try to analyze what had led him there after a routine day's work; he simply knew he wanted to be there.

But after he turned into the thoroughfare his mind flooded with the remembered scent of carnations and roses that had filled their home then. And with the huge black case in the living room, his father motionless in it, and the ride to the church, his mother in unfamiliar black; a neighbor had kept Eleanor. And all the policemen who had been there that day in uniform.

"Do you remember him, Neill?" his mother sometimes asked. "Really remember him, I mean?"

A man so enormously tall that the silver shield on the heavy blue uniform was always out of your reach, even on tiptoe. A good-humored man who liked to play and swing you around and carried a rosary in his hip pocket. No, he couldn't really see him. The living memory of his father had been distorted by the photographs kept in honored places in the living room and on his mother's bureau. Yet he *did* remember him, and vividly. Not as a physical being but as a kindly benevolence, a refuge of understanding and admiration, who had been something to him that no one else could ever be.

"Of course," he would say. "Of course I remember him."

He had come here before when he was sixteen. Rummaging through his mother's bureau for a handkerchief one day, he had come upon the envelope of old, crisp news clippings, and had read with sickening shock that pressed tight tears to his eyes what had happened to his father.

Sergeant O'Neill Ryan had been investigating collusion between a lieutenant in a downtown precinct and a gang of young burglars, and he had caused the arrest of three of them as well as suspension of the lieutenant. Some days later he had been lured—how was never learned—into a dark passage between buildings on Carmine Street at night, and two groups of hoodlums had started down it from either end.

As he lay dying on an operating table, drooling blood, one eye sightless, he had described or named five of the seven attackers. It had taken the department years to hunt them down. Two had died in the electric chair, two were in Dannemora and one was dead, shot in a holdup after serving his time. The other two were wanted to this day, and the revolver that Sergeant O'Neill Ryan had carried and fired three shots from that night was still preserved for ballistics tests in the police headquarters annex, in case one of the slugs ever turned up in a prisoner or in a corpse. The case would never be closed as long as there was a chance of one of them being alive.

It had been a warm, pale spring day when he was last here, a solemn boy of sixteen. Yet even with only the matter-of-fact words of the news clippings for clues, he had heard the foot scuffles of desperate defense, the thud of blows, the groans of the fallen man, the kicks and gouges and then the dying echo of coward feet. For months after he had daydreamed of meeting them, all of them, and beating them into bloody slime.

Now the after-knowledge of twelve more mature years, four of them spent in police work, peopled that short passage with a more authentic cast. He knew how the snarls of vicious laughter had sounded to his father, and the eager curses; he felt the overwhelming strength of cowardice and sadism. That was the voice and posture of the other side, the gaudy, boastful, frightened army that every cop faced and fought not because a cop was innately heroic, but because he was instinctively the kind of person who likes order and fairness, and fights for them.

Now he again found the old, thin wood door to the passage and swung it open. He stood a long time looking at where his father had been assaulted and at the new cement that paved the place. Formerly there had been bricks.

He could feel nothing, and the remembered twinges of old anguish were like the pinks of toy arrows. That disconcerted him. He did not know what he should feel or wanted to feel.

But certainly not this empty melancholy, this lack of meaning. What, he asked as he surveyed the scene, had his father's death accomplished— for anyone, his father, the city, even the hoodlums who had caused it? He let the door swing to with a quiet hush. What had his father's death *ever* meant?

As he walked up Bleecker Street the storefronts and grocery trays were as unfamiliar as the slopes of another planet, cold, lifeless, dead, to which he had somehow been transported, a solitary inhabitant.

CHAPTER 14

Farragut

A railing separated the spectators from the official part of the court-room where the judge's bench, the clerks, press, bailiffs and counsel tables were, and just within the compound thus created a row of chairs ran from one side of the room to the other. Ryan sat in one of them, staring down at well-polished black shoes, aware of the blue-centered detective's shield he wore on his lapel as required, trying to forget the impatience that gnawed at him. The jury had been selected on Friday; yesterday had been devoted to motions and the opening statements of the assistant district attorney and defense counsel. None of these held anything unusual, although when the judge asked whether either side wanted the witnesses excluded from the courtroom, pending their turn on the stand, Assistant District Attorney Gil Tilbury said he didn't care and Farragut had said, "No, your honor," rather emphatically. But no one paid particular attention to it at the time.

But that was why on Tuesday, the day on which Ryan had been told to be on hand, he and Jablonski could sit together in the courtroom, in-stead of lounging in the judge's chamber or a witness room. They were both to testify mainly about Derby's arrest and what he had said at the time and how they had found the murder gun. Ryan was desperately anxious to get it over with.

But Farragut was cross-examining with great leisureliness a medical witness who had testified about Mrs. Connors' injuries. Apparently he was trying to prove that the blow across her face could have been deliv-ered by a woman as well as a man, and by either a right-or left-handed person. The courtroom was silent and bored as Farragut pursued his questions steadily, mechanically. He was dawdling, for a sound purpose perhaps, but still wasting time and Ryan hated him. He looked backward over his shoulder at the spectators.

Vacant stretches gaped among the long benches. Not much excite-ment was offered by the certain conviction of an habitual criminal. There was the usual assortment of housewives, some wearing glistening

Christmas ornaments like corsages on cheap cloth coats, and shabby old men to whom the trial meant warmth and possibly entertainment, and a few teen-agers. These were The People on whose unknowing behalf the county in which they lived was moving with lethal intent against Harry Derby.

In the corridors outside The People lounged and talked, cursed and smoked, spat and hoped. But within this high, paneled, punctilious chamber that was the size of a gymnasium, their ordinary conduct wavered and died. Rules were observed and conventions honored in ignorant abstraction. A uniformed officer came forward occasionally to demand loudly, "Quiet, please," or, "Take off your hat!" and the spectators withdrew into themselves and watched and waited without expression. Derby, in a plain blue suit and white shirt, sprawled leanly at the counsel table, frowned and played endlessly with a yellow pencil. Ryan, wishing it were over, tightened his jaws until little hollows appeared under his cheekbones. Jablonski came back from coffee, grinning, and sank beside Ryan with a sigh. Then Ryan's ranging, anxious gaze saw a newcomer settle himself at the little table that accommodated the reporters. He had a young face topped by short-cropped, prematurely gray hair. This time he wore a tie and brightly shined black loafers with tassels instead of bedroom slippers.

Sandalwood had arrived. Sandalwood was covering the trial.

The little hollows under his cheekbones made Ryan momentarily gaunt. Why was *he* here?

The scientist from the police laboratory who had performed the spectroscopic analysis of the dust on Derby's jacket was now on the stand, replying to Tilbury's direct examination with hands-in-lap composure. Farragut, frowning, lay in wait at the table. Derby balanced the yellow pencil on his finger. Sandalwood borrowed a few sheets of copy paper from another reporter, yawned and took out a ball-point pen. Ryan forced himself to think of Gee Gee and how she had looked last night.

He had dropped unannounced into the night club. Three girls' names were billed outside; hers was not one of them. He had stood at the bar, hoping to watch the show from there, but almost immediately someone he took to be the manager deferentially asked him to sit at a table and while he was refusing the cigarette girl came up and said Miss Hawes wanted to see him in the dressing room. There had been four girls there, one a dancer he had just watched finish her act. She was toweling sweat-caked powder from an almost bare body. The other three girls wore short smocks carelessly; one was Gee Gee, who put down a *Mirror,* opened to Winchell's column, rose, clutched her smock and said, "Hi, Neill," with friendly cordiality. The smock showed Gee Gee's fine long legs; that, and the wise inquiring eyes of the other girl, black-edged with mascara, made Ryan self-conscious. He had seen his share of undressed girls but there was an impudent flaunting in this... He said something about going out between shows, and he was a little relieved when she said she could not leave the club and so gave him an excuse for an early departure.

A ballistics man stepped down from the stand after testifying that his examination proved the bullet that had killed Mrs. Connors came from Derby's gun.

"Edmund Jablonski," a clerk bawled, and Ryan came back to reality. Jablonski got up, nudging him confidently.

He was on the stand only fifteen minutes. He told the story of how they had spotted Derby, tailed and arrested him, and identified the revolver and checked jacket. He testified that when they first seized him Derby had said something about "killing the old dame" or words like that, but had later turned sullen and finally attacked him. He gave copious credit to Ryan for coming to his rescue and said nothing about a hundred dollar bill. Then Tilbury said, "Cross-examine," and looked at Farragut. But Farragut waved a thick hand carelessly.

"No questions," said Farragut, and Tilbury looked a little surprised.

To Ryan things looked brighter. Jablonski had told the main part of the story. His role obviously would be that of corroborating witness. When the clerk called "Officer Ryan" he stepped to the stand and placidly raised his right hand, confident he could forget about Sandalwood.

With careless ease Tilbury ran him through many of the same questions Jablonski had already answered and Ryan replied to them readily, keeping eyes and ears trained on the tall, elegant assistant district attorney. Tilbury concluded quickly. Then Farragut lumbered forward for cross-examination, and Ryan got his first close look at Derby's famous lawyer.

Absalom Farragut had a wide, graceless body which he draped in baggy, unassuming suits, high old-fashioned collars and string ties, especially designed according to courtroom legend to impress juries with his genial commonality. His face was a granite slab that could relax into a wide, homely smile or become a black pattern of outrage as Farragut chose, and the shock of hair above it was still more brown than gray at the age of sixty-two. Now he pulled back his coat to thrust a big thumb in the belt of his trousers and began addressing Ryan with the good nature of an old man dealing with a brash neophyte.

"You've been a detective less than a year, I believe, Mr. Ryan?"

'That is right."

"Less than six months perhaps?"

"Yes, sir."

"Less even than three months?"

"Yes, sir."

Farragut smiled benignly for the jury. "You are in fact a rookie—eh, Mr. Ryan?"

Ryan felt rather than heard the courtroom's amusement. He flushed. "Yes, sir." He looked around. At the press table Sandalwood was bent over a doodle.

"So when you and your partner, Mr. Jablonski, arrested Harry Derby it was Jablonski who was in charge of the…ah…detective team do you call it?"

Ryan knew that Farragut was well aware of what they called it. He said, "That is correct."

"And so during that operation you naturally did everything that Jablonski told you to do?"

Out of the corner of his mind Ryan barely sensed Tilbury springing volubly to his feet. He mumbled, "No, not…" but no one heard that, not even himself. A dreadful chasm had opened up before him. Farragut knew everything and was laying for him. That was why he had not wanted the witnesses excluded! He had *wanted* Ryan to see what an easy time Jablonski would have of it, and thus be lulled into a false security. But he was not going to have an easy time of it! He was the carefully-selected victim. Farragut was standing on the opposite side of the chasm that had suddenly opened up and was beckoning him on irresistibly.

There was a wrangle over Tilbury's objection while Ryan felt his neck grow damply cold within his shirt collar. Then Farragut pressed in again from a different angle, and Ryan began answering questions that brought out the physical layout of the room in which they had arrested Derby, and narrated how they had done it.

"Then you searched him?"

"That is right."

"What did you find?"

Ryan enumerated the list of belongings as he remembered it.

"How much money was that again, Mr. Ryan?" A thick tongue circled Farragut's thick lips anticipatorily.

"He had around ten dollars in small bills and change in his pocket."

"And in his wallet? Did you examine his wallet?"

Now he was getting it. "I did."

"And how much money did you find in it?"

Until this instant Ryan had never, finally, decided what he was going to say if that question were asked him under oath. Now he answered it without deciding. "It did not contain any money."

For the first time Sandalwood's head raised.

"You knew the loot in the robbery was one hundred and twenty dollars, did you not?"

"I did."

"And you wanted to find that money?"

"Naturally."

"Answer yes or no, please," ordered Farragut.

The judge interjected, "And louder, witness. Raise your voice."

Ryan took a breath. "Yes. I wanted to find the money."

Sandalwood's expression was quizzical.

"Did you ask the defendant what he had done with it?" Farragut went on.

Here it was again. "Yes."

"What did he say?"

"Objection." Tilbury rose again. "I submit, your honor, that all this is irrelevant and immaterial. The people readily admit that the hundred dollar bill has not been found. The...ah...purpose of these questions—"

"Your honor," Farragut broke in ponderously, "I should like to enlighten young Mister Tilbury if I may. These questions have a definite purpose. Because they help to lay the foundation of the defense's contention that the defendant, Harry Derby, was framed."

Ryan looked down. His palms were wet. His lungs could not get enough air. The chasm had become a bottomless pit, and he, teetering on the edge of it, was losing his balance.

Tilbury chuckled superciliously. The judge told Farragut to proceed.

"Mr. Ryan, what did my client say when you asked him about the hundred dollars?"

"He didn't say anything."

"He didn't answer your question?"

"That is right."

What *could* he say?

"Louder, witness!"—from above.

Ryan was near panic.

"Both you and your partner," said Farragut, his voice rising to thunder, "have testified that Harry Derby admitted he had killed Mrs. Connors—'killed the old lady' or 'old dame' or some such phrase. Now do you say that he refused to tell you what he did with the proceeds of that robbery?"

"Yes, sir."

But the words came out better than he could have hoped, and somewhere in his subconscious there sounded a welcome echo of another conversation about this. "I think you should realize," Said Ryan, looking up, and for a moment his eyes met Sandalwood's, "that we were arresting an armed criminal who in a minute or two jumped—attacked my partner. We—we didn't have time to—well, stage a debate with him. Our main idea was to get him into the station."

Even before he finished speaking he felt he was saving himself, that his words had the simple ring of truth.

The veteran Farragut recognized it too. He waved the answer aside carelessly as though it were of no importance. But in a courtroom everything Farragut said or did was of importance.

"You referred to Derby just now as an *armed* criminal. Was he armed, Mr. Ryan?"

"His gun was hanging on a nail near the door. That's the gun that ballistics—"

"Never mind, Mr. Ryan. Just answer the questions I ask, please. Derby did not have a revolver or any other weapon on his person when you broke into his room."

"We didn't *break* in."

Farragut gave the jury his cracked-granite smile. "He certainly didn't *invite* you in." Again he waved the subject into inconsequence. "In any case, Derby—so you say—attacked your partner."

"That is right."

"Why, Mr. Ryan? *Why?* Why did an unarmed man charge into two men he knew were armed? Were you taunting him?"

"No."

"Were you giving him the so-called third degree?"

"No!"

"By that, of course, I mean torturing him, to make him—"

Tilbury cried, "Objection!" and Ryan said, "You know that's not so."

Farragut did not even wait for the judge to uphold the objection.

"Then I can only conclude," he said smoothly, "that the reason my client allegedly attacked Jablonski is because Jablonski got too close to him, and in some way or other goaded Harry Derby unbearably to attack him. Right?"

"There was no goading, aside from the kind of talk that goes on when you arrest a hoodlum," said Ryan. "Perhaps Jablonski got close— but remember your client, as you call him, knew that this arrest meant the electric chair."

"Never mind that, witness," said Farragut sharply. "In any case when Derby leaped for Jablonski they closed with each other and wrestled. Right?"

"If you call kicking a man in the stomach wrestling. That's what your client did to Jablonski."

"But you had a gun, eh? Yet you didn't fire?"

"That's right."

"Why?"

"Because for a second they were too close together."

"They were too close together." Farragut relished the words and looked down the jury's rows. "Too close together. They were in fact locked in a hand-to-hand struggle, were they not, Mr. Ryan?"

"Well, for a second or so."

"So. For a second or so, you say. Very good. Now then, Mr. Ryan." Farragut spoke rapidly, like a man in a state of unnatural excitement, and Ryan recognized that he was approaching some goal. "Both you and Jablonski were on hand at the scene of the murder earlier. And of course you handled the smashed lamp."

"Of course we did not."

"You did *not* handle pieces of the lamp?"

"No, sir."

"Nor Jablonski?"

"Objection—" from Tilbury. "Mr. Jablonski is on hand to testify for himself."

"Sustained."

"But *you* did not handle the lamp, Ryan?" No polite "mister" now; Farragut's quick, low voice was beginning to cut and tear.

"Objection, please the court. The witness has answered the question once. Besides, Mr. Farragut's questions have no real bearing—"

"Mr. Farragut's questions," Farragut thundered impressively, "are going to show that the dust from the lamp which was presumably found on my client's work-jacket could actually have been placed there artificially."

He was addressing the court. But for a fleet second he fastened triumphant, squinting green eyes on Ryan.

Ryan's face went hot.

This was how it really was. Farragut knew everything, and had purposely passed up Jablonski as too experienced, gambling on Ryan, the rookie, to be more easily tripped. Farragut was betting his client's life that he could make Ryan stumble into the chasm.

"What does counsel mean by 'artificially'?" asked the judge with interest.

"Well, since both these officers were at the scene, and might be presumed to have handled the physical evidence there even if they do not recall having done so, it is the contention of the defense, your honor, that their clothing might have received some of the dust in question—become impregnated, so to speak. And if so, it is not impossible that during a hand-to-hand struggle such as has been described between Harry Derby and Detective Jablonski it is also possible that minute quantities of dust might have been transferred from Jablonski's clothing to my client's. I should like to remind your honor that the spectroscope is an extraordinarily sensitive instrument—"

"Counsel will confine himself to proper cross-examination."

"I'm sorry, your honor," said Farragut contritely, but he was a cat with cream on its face. The idea had been implanted in the jury's minds.

"I asked a moment ago, Mr. Ryan, if you had handled the lamp or any pieces of it," he went on. "Of course, I realize that in the excitement and tension of a murder investigation—your first, I believe—I realize it is possible you might do something and forget having done so later. Consequently, I am going to ask you whether it is not possible that you might have, say, picked up a fragment or two of the broken lamp and forgotten it afterwards?"

He looked brightly at Ryan, smiling a pursed-lip knowing smile.

Ryan had to look away. In the rush of fear that engulfed him like turbulent surf he could not think consecutively. He felt physically off balance as though he might pitch out of the witness chair, and he sensed Sandalwood's gaze on him like a hot, probing lance. He groped wildly for escape.

"Will you search your memory, please?" Farragut went on with smooth rapidity. "Don't you feel it is possible that you might have—"

Ryan shook his head. He looked toward Tilbury for help, as a boxer looks to his corner. But Tilbury was not looking at him. In the front row of spectators there was a patrician blond girl in a lavish mink coat, smiling brightly and making little finger motions at Tilbury, and he, lounging back in his chair, was nodding understanding at her. His socks and tie were both of the same blue and white checks.

"Why are you sure neither you nor Jablonski handled any piece of the lamp? How can you—"

It was almost impossible to pull himself back to Farragut's truculent face, the eyes pinched 'round with tight wrinkles of flesh.

Why didn't Tilbury...?

"No," he said lowly.

"What did you say, Ryan?"

"Louder, witness."

Again he ranged the courtroom. Sandalwood was frowning intently at him. Jablonski's face was a black-and-white scrawl of fear, a caricature of terror.

"No!"

Farragut leaped in with tiger quickness. "Supposing I were to tell you that a beer can was found in the room which also had traces of dust—dust from the lamp. Would you say—"

Ryan did not hear the rest of it.

This was the end. Farragut had him.

He looked beseechingly toward Tilbury. The court was also looking at Tilbury, expecting an objection.

"Answer, witness," cried Farragut, and Ryan brought his white face up to confront the green-eyed sneer. Tilbury turned suddenly, uncomprehendingly, back to the cross-examination.

A low whistle sounded in the courtroom. Ryan knew what it meant. He was dead; there were other sounds, a rising murmur like a boxing audience makes when one of the fighters begins to lurch into unconsciousness.

There came another whistle. The judge's gavel banged; he *had* to answer. Ryan's wet hands twisted. He looked up; the murmur was louder. And then, dumbfounded, he finally realized that no one in the courtroom was looking at him except Farragut. And Sandalwood.

For a tall, marvelously shapely girl with a wealth of auburn hair under a chic low-brimmed hat was coming down the center aisle, followed by a short, slick-haired man in a bright blue suit who carried a polo coat and seemed trying not to smile. The girl's expression was grave until she saw Ryan; then she smiled and waved at him. Her lips were masterpieces of curved lipstick and when she loosened her tightly cinched coat, before seating herself on a front bench, it was with an intimate, revealing air that drew another wolf whistle. The gavel banged ineffectually, two reporters hurried out the side door to telephone the city desk for photographers, and half the courtroom immediately recognized Gee Gee Hawes. Sandalwood smiled indolently at her across the intervening space.

It had taken less than twenty seconds for her to enter and be seated with the nightclub manager who accompanied her. But that was enough to save Ryan and to ruin Farragut.

"I had asked you," said Farragut loudly, trying to recapture the spell he had woven, "if you were aware—" But the court interrupted. "I must remind you, Mr. Farragut, that your question is completely unsupported by any testimony and therefore improper. I will ask the witness and especially the jury to disregard it and its implications."

Ryan was a drowning man finding dry earth under his feet.

Gee Gee smiled at him. The nightclub manager, whose idea this visit had been, tried to appear nonchalant when a reporter asked them to hang around after for an interview. Presently they went out to be photographed, while Farragut returned to the attack with all the irritation of one who knows his chance has slipped. He had led carefully and dramatically up to that last question, hoping it would force a confused, damaging admission. Gee Gee's entrance had wrecked his effect. Now Ryan answered his questions cagily and steadily.

After a dozen more Farragut gave up.

Tilbury quickly paraded the three women witnesses to the stand and all three, with just enough uncertainty to make their testimony convincing, identified Derby. Court adjourned.

The girl in mink rose at once, beaming, and flung herself at Tilbury. "Oh, darling, you were wonderful."

He petted her affectionately. "Wonderful, nothing," he said. "If they were all as easy as this I'd be ashamed to accept my salary."

* * * *

Flashbulbs were still firing in the corridor when Ryan and Jablonski reached it and people were looking at Gee Gee and asking "Who's that? Who is she?" as she stood amid the reporters. Her eyes were bright and she was smiling.

Sandalwood was at one side talking to the nightclub manager. As he and Jablonski passed Ryan heard Sandalwood joking, "Max, you really ought to be ashamed of yourself. Anything for publicity, eh?" Ryan did not look at Sandalwood.

Then Gee Gee caught sight of him and waved and blew Ryan a kiss, and a photographer asked her to do that again. Ryan waved back and pointed to his wrist watch, meaning he had to go; he did not want to get mixed up in that, or have to answer Sandalwood's questions. "I'll call you," he yelled, and she nodded and blew the kiss the photographer asked for. She did it several times.

"Boy, what a dame," said Jablonski as they went down the stairs. "You know what I think? I think you're darned lucky, Neill."

"I'll tell you what I think," said Ryan bitterly. "I think this guy's going to be convicted."

"Wait and see, Neill, wait and see," said Jablonski. "That's all I ask."

* * * *

But when court resumed next day it was not Farragut but his bespectacled young assistant, McCormick, who took over the defense of Harry Derby. Farragut, it was announced, had suffered a heart attack the previous evening and must rest for at least two months. Courtroom veterans smiled. This was Farragut's surrender. It was his boast that no Farragut client had ever been executed in his thirty years of practice, and he knew he could not save Derby. So instead he had had a heart attack, and now it was a McCormick client that would go to the chair.

Three days later after an almost pathetically weak defense the case went to the jury, which deliberated forty-five minutes and then returned a verdict of guilty of murder in the first degree without recommendation of mercy. That made a death sentence mandatory.

CHAPTER 15

The Phone Call

Ryan had the day tour on the day Derby was sentenced so he could not get downtown to hear it, even if he'd wanted to. But he read about it after work, standing at a bar bustling with the hurly-burly of day's end. He had ordered a whisky before he opened the pink sports final, and he drank it straight. The paper did not devote much space to the Derby story, but Ryan was able to reconstruct it in his mind's eye as he sipped the chaser.

There was the loosening of the handcuffs, the leading of the tall, thin man around in front of the judge, the dry recital of the facts and reading of probation reports. "I therefore direct that you, Harry Derby, be transported to the slate prison of New York at Ossining and there be executed in accordance with the laws of the State and at the discretion of the warden some time during the week of February 23. And may God have mercy on your soul." Then he would have been cuffed again and led away, the lean, sinewy back still surly with defiance. But desperately frightened inside.

Ryan ordered and drank another whisky. Then he stuffed the paper into his overcoat, went out and walked down Lexington Avenue.

When he reached Grand Central Station he went in and found a large telephone headquarters containing booths and operators to get long-distance numbers. He called Jablonski at his home. When he answered, Jablonski asked how Ryan was with great heartiness.

"You see tonight's papers yet?"

"No. I been home with a cold all day, Neill. Anything I should have seen?"

Ryan took a breath. "Our boy got the chair."

"You mean Derby?"

"So what do we do now?"

"Well," gently, "what do you think we do, Neill?"

"For Christ's sake!" Desperation tore his throat. "If we don't do something, the guy burns."

From the other end came a long, fully rounded silence. "Well," said Jablonski, "don't you really think he ought to?"

Ryan began to have the helpless, nightmare feeling of being pursued and menaced and not being able to run.

But he said, "God damn it," steadily, "it's not for us to decide that. This is a—" he started to say "human life" and knew how weak that would sound. "This is a guy's life. Even if he is the kind who—"

"Now wait a minute, Neill."

"Wait, hell! We agreed to wait until the trial was over because maybe he'd never be convicted. Okay. We waited. Now he's convicted. And sentenced. And he didn't kill that old woman."

"Where you calling from?" Jablonski's voice had grown cold.

"Grand Central."

"Pay phone?"

"Sure."

But he realized he must be talking loud. The operator outside who had put the call through was looking in at him.

Jablonski said, "Listen, Neill. Take it easy and don't start yelling your head off. You know what I told you when you first got in an uproar about this, and I'm going to tell it to you again for your own good. And mine. You got a great future in the department, kid. You're going to go a long way. I wish I was in your shoes. I mean it."

Ryan knew he did.

"I told you before the trial to keep your mouth shut because I knew this slob might get off and you would only wreck everything if you opened up. And if he didn't get off and got sent up, why that'd be all right too, because it would be too late for anyone to do anything. And Neill, that's just how it is."

"Just *how* is it?"

"Derby's convicted—he's put away. And Farragut's licked—he wouldn't touch the case now for fifty G's. Derby is going to the chair and that's where he belongs. You're sitting pretty. So am I. And why not—? Don't you think cops are entitled to a break occasionally?"

Ryan did not answer.

"So maybe he didn't kill that old lady, like you claim," Jablonski went on. "Although I sure as hell doubt it. But anyway—he was one of the guys in the Moriarity murder in 'fifty-one. You know that."

"I don't know it."

"Maybe it was before your time."

"Was he ever convicted?"

"Of course not. He was brought in but we never had enough to hold him on. Then there was another killing, an old man named Trimble."

"Was he tried for that?"

"No. Derby was never tried for—"

"Was he arrested?"

"No—I'm trying to tell you! We always had a hunch—"

"For God's sake, Jabby, you can't sentence a guy to death just because you suspect something."

"I ain't just suspecting, Neill. I know darned well—"

"You know nothing. And furthermore you lied and stalled before and you're doing it now. What the hell kind of cop *were* you, anyway?"

The other end of the line went silent. The words echoed, and Ryan knew that he had finally hit Jablonski where it hurt.

When he spoke it was with the cold deliberation of mortal anger. "I'll tell you what kind of cop," said Jablonski. "I'm an ex-cop now. But I put in my time, twenty-eight years of it. And I learned a few things in my time. And one was that when you get one of *them*—a guy like Derby—in a spot where you can give it to him, then by God you give it to him. And you sure as hell don't wreck your whole life and your partner's life by trying to give the son of a bitch a break. I'm loyal to the department, that's the kind of cop I am. And I got my own little place out here, and I and Sarah are getting along fine and I want it to go on." There was a pause. "I don't want that changed. You shouldn't either."

Again there was a pause. "But if you try to do anything about it, I'll tell you what I'm going to do. You go ahead and tell your story—and I'll swear to God you are lying. You come in with your fingerprint from the drugstore heist or whatever it was and I'll say that you came to me a while back with a plan to get Derby off, for a payoff. And that you said something about planting or switching a fingerprint. That'll put you and Derby on the same side of the fence, standing against the whole damn department. I wouldn't want that, Neill, and I wouldn't want to do it. But if you force me to I will. You want it?"

Ryan looked out the booth's glass door. The girl was not watching him now. She wrote something on a little pad and then thrust the pencil into her thick coil of dark hair.

"And another thing, Neill. You swore under oath that Derby didn't have the big bill on him. Now if you come in with a different story, who's going to believe you? Once you've admitted you're a liar, you never carry much weight again, you know. It's like an expert witness who gets knocked down in court."

Ryan's hand began moving the telephone instrument from his ear toward the prong that should receive it. He continued looking at that glossy coil of hair. Now she was writing something else.

Somewhere in the telephone booth a tiny metallic voice said, "Well, what do you say? Neill?... *Neill?*"

Ryan kicked at the door. "Go to hell," he said. The telephone girl looked up. He had taken a step out of the booth before he remembered that he was still holding the phone. He latched it into place.

In the wide, murmurous corridor outside he almost ran into a hurrying young couple. The man carried a big valise, the girl a lighter one. "Let me take it, honey," the man said. "Come on. Give it to me."

"You can't carry them *both,*" she protested. But she relinquished the bag.

"Of course I can," he laughed. "They balance." As he took the bag his eye caught Ryan's. Something in Ryan's face made him look again.

"It's all yours," Ryan told him. "All yours. Carry it."

They looked at him, then hurried on. Ryan walked out toward Forty-second Street.

CHAPTER 16

The Long Way Home

He walked fast, through homing commuters and shouting newsboys, slipping past traffic-halted ranks at the curbs to dodge narrowly between taxi bumpers and keep going. At Madison, forgetting he was crossing a two-way street, he would have been run down had a cab driver not seen him walking against the light. The cab squealed to a halt and Ryan looked up; the driver laid his arms over the wheel and rubbed his face in them in an elaborate gesture of patience.

Another time Ryan would have grinned apologetically; now he hurried on, only belatedly aware. He was gripped by a compulsion to get some place in a hurry, to move and keep moving without thinking. He had no real goal. Getting home was as good an excuse as any, so when he came to Fifth Avenue he turned north and walked fast past the glossy, lighted windows of the big stores and the little shops. He wanted to walk, not think.

When he had crossed Fifty-seventh Street and was swinging up the avenue's wide sidewalk, that was almost like broad, scented velvet under the lights of the apartment entrances and canopies, the silent trees and mystery of Central Park on the other side, he did not bear east toward home as he should have done. After a time he remembered Eleanor's request for picking up the Ibsen book at the Columbia library and he seized the excuse to continue walking, fast and anonymous, through the night's cold air, and think only of his errand, knowing his absence would cause no alarm at home, and above all determined not to think about what he could not help thinking about.

He was standing in line in the familiarly stuffy library when something poked his back. A thin, chicken-necked man with the gleam of discovery in his eye was looking at him, tapping finger still extended. "Aren't you O'Neill Ryan?"

"That's right." It sounded surly. Then Ryan recognized the thin man. It was the hair that was deceptive.

"Professor Montagne!" He had not been nearly so bald when he taught Ryan Greek philosophy eight years ago.

When Professor Montagne shook hands his glasses gleamed even more brightly. "I knew it was you," he said. "At first I told myself it was just because I had read about you lately."

"Next," said the woman charging out books. Ryan handed her the book and Eleanor's card, then waited in the corridor for the teacher.

"This is amazing," said Mr. Montagne, and took Ryan's arm. "Do you realize I was going to telephone you within a few days?—here, this way, eh? I know a room."

Ryan permitted himself to be led down a corridor and finally into a small reading room containing a single absorbed girl, student.

Mr. Montagne whispered. "We can talk as long as we keep our voices down." He beamed. "Well, O'Neill, how have you been, as though I needed to ask?"

"Fine, Professor," said Ryan. He still had an undergraduate's respect for a member of the faculty.

"You look well," said Montagne. "And I know you are doing well. You cannot imagine how good it is to learn that a boy from Philosophy 508 is putting into everyday practice some of the Socratic definitions that I—" His laugh deprecated the idea. "But that is not why I intended calling you, O'Neill. Frankly, I have a problem.

"For two years I've been director of the Men Students' Forum. You appreciate what that means—a meeting and a speaker once a month. You are—well, as the students say, let's face it. You are a celebrity. And you certainly must have much to say about the application of your education to the problems of life. If you could come up some Sunday evening and give us a plain, heart-to-heart talk, say thirty to forty minutes, about—"

"Okay," said Ryan. He was suddenly oppressed by time's brevity. He knew what Montagne wanted. But he wanted something, too.

"You'll do it? O'Neill? Really? I can't tell you how happy I—that I—that we ran into each other."

"So am I," said Ryan. He spoke aloud and the girl student looked up.

"Of course," Montagne smiled slyly, "if you were to work in a few references about how Phil 508 helped in your career—in case it did. What I mean is, you are an officer of the law and I hope you remember the time we spent on the Platonic concept of the well-ordered state."

"Yes," said Ryan. "Sure. And that's something I'd like to ask you about. You see, since becoming a cop I've thought about that philosophy course. Occasionally in my work you run into problems that—that make you think about justice and virtue."

"I'm sure you do." Professor Montagne's head bobbed happily.

Dared he? Hell!—why not?

"I guess you've been reading about this guy Derby who was sentenced today."

"I certainly have, O'Neill, and how it was you who arrested him."

"Well, I've been wondering, just as a sort of problem, like one of those abstract problems in ethics you used to give us." He watched anxiously for suspicion in the smiling face. "Supposing I happened to find out now, after helping to convict him, that this guy Derby, this hoodlum, was not guilty of the murder he's charged with?"

It was out. Only in the abstract, of course, but even that had frightened him to say. Yet it obviously had not aroused Professor Montagne. Then he recognized that as a teacher he had dealt for years with the caprices of students. What was one more hypothetical question?

Montagne looked down his nose at Ryan. "Do? There is only one thing you could do. As a virtuous man you know what that is. For a moment I thought you had a poser."

"Well, what? Tell the truth?"

"What else? Can a just man see another punished unjustly—for a crime he never committed—and remain silent?"

"But think of the crimes he *did* commit," Ryan argued, "and never was punished for. Derby himself is certainly no just man."

"That has nothing to do with the case. The just deal justly even with the unjust. It is implicit in the common law—"

"Common law nothing!" said Ryan. "Would you turn loose a known rapist and robber, a no-good—"

The girl student made a meaningful rustle with her book. Montagne bowed apologetically.

"We must be quieter," he said. "Remember, you presented a hypothetical case. I gave you the only possible answer."

"The only *hypothetical* answer."

"Quite. Quite."

"But—if you were a cop as I am, and this was a real problem—" He smiled to show he knew the absurdity of it.

Montagne raised a restraining hand. "My dear O'Neill, I will not let you lure me into arguing theory versus practice—real-life practice—on an empty stomach. I have no doubt that as a policeman I might have to—to compromise. If this fellow is the scoundrel you say, I might not be able to turn him loose quite so readily as I can hypothetically. But I give you the answer of a philosopher. Well! Sorry, I must get on. My wife—"

He rose, still talking. "How about the second Sunday in February? We still meet in the music room. I'll ring you in advance, of course. We could discuss this further then, with the students. Eh?"

"Sure," said Ryan. "We'll do that. In February."

Ryan walked head down, a purposeless night voyager, past murmurous blocks to Central Park and then along a winding park path. When he raised his eyes he saw neat rectangles of lights rimming the park's black quiet; they were not human habitations but remote glitters against eternal darkness.

Why *didn't* he just forget Derby? He did not *have* to be concerned about such animals, did he? Of course he didn't. Then why... For a moment Ryan saw himself objectively, as though he were outside himself, skirting the path he was walking; he saw a tired, anxious, hollow-eyed man of twenty-eight who just wanted this to be over with. Even Professor Montagne had said...

He came to Fifth Avenue. Home was not far away.

No. Not that, now. Keep walking.

At the genteel curbs women in bright evening dress and furs stood with men in sober black, waiting for limousines to take them to theater or opera. Ryan strode on, numbly aware he was walking toward a decision and meanwhile numbly ignoring it.

After a time he found he wanted a drink.

CHAPTER 17

Rosemary

Ryan stopped in a corner bar at Lexington Avenue and drank a whisky, fast and straight. The dinner hour had grown into evening and the men at the bar were beer-drinking philosophers. Ryan walked on to the next bar and again ordered straight rye and put it down fast. He did not consciously desire to get drunk; he had never desired that in his life. Yet as he worked gradually east and south he made repeated stops, to feel raw liquor fire his throat and explode gently in his stomach, barely tasting the water chaser. After a time the alcohol reduced the urgency of his flight and enabled his slowing brain to engage the problem again.

He must not let himself be confused by Jablonski's threats. This was an issue to be decided on its merits. But what were they? By what practical criterion could he justify going to his superiors and revealing that Derby had been framed? What kind of a reception would that get—and what kind *should* it get? The police department's function was safeguarding the city, not debating the subtlest shades of justice.

Yet all the time Ryan knew he was only torturing himself. He could never accept the practical, easy way out. He could never let Derby die, even if Derby himself desired that. *Why* was rooted deeply in him, below the level of understanding. It was not noble; it was automatic and terribly uncomfortable. Right now whisky made it a little easier.

He was standing looking at a drink he had just ordered when he spoke without knowing that he was going to speak. "This is getting deep."

The bartender, arranging glasses in pyramids, looked around. "How's that?"

"I can't touch," said Ryan, trying to explain what he had just heard himself say. "Bottom. Can't touch bottom." He picked up the small heavy glass, spilled a part, and drank the rest.

"You better take it easy, Mac."

Ryan re-buttoned his coat. He did not like criticism at a time like this, but he must not get into arguments at a time like this, either. He went out, and looked up at the corner street sign. He was on First Avenue in the seventies. He had almost walked home.

In the next block was a small pizza restaurant where he ate often when he was late. That was it. One more drink, then a big pie and coffee, because he did not want to arrive home feeling unsteady.

It was a tiny place, with a counter and white tile pizza oven in the back. There were only four booths and a couple of tables in the middle of the floor; one of the booths was occupied by a wrangling couple. The oven man came from behind the counter to serve him with brawny, floured arms.

"Rye," said Ryan.

"No liquor here, mister. Wine and beer."

He'd forgotten. Heck with it. "Gimme a pie. Fish."

The oven man went back behind the counter and began to spin out the cap of dough. When Ryan thought to take off his overcoat, he found Eleanor's book bulging the pocket. He opened it at random, read a few lines, decided it was dull and closed it. He felt the warmth and breathed the fragrance of baking dough. Finally the great, wide pie was slid in front of him, littered with anchovies.

"Coffee?"

"Coffee."

He ate in silence, and the conversational mutter continued from the booth ahead. He could not make out all the words, although the man sounded indignant. Then the woman said with impatient clarity, "Oh, finish your beer and come on home. We can't go back there tonight. It's almost ten."

"Sure, finish your beer and go home." The man welcomed the excuse for new indignation. "Your own brother gets framed by the cops and double-crossed by his own stinking lawyer and on the day he's sentenced all you're supposed to do's drink your beer and go home."

Ryan's sodden mind began pulling itself into awareness.

"Oh, come on," said the woman. She was tired and querulous. "He's out and there's no telling when he'll get back. Detectives don't work regular hours."

Ryan could not believe his ears. Was he right?

"You wanna go home? You go on home."

"Not alone with this pay in my purse. Not in this neighborhood."

"I'll say not in this neighborhood. Cops don't much get around neighborhoods like this, where the ordinary people live. They're too busy."

Where do cops live, buster?

"They're too busy out framing guys. They—" He spilled loud, obscene hatred of cops.

Ryan sipped his coffee and held in his feelings, thinking slowly because of the whisky. This must be Ken Derby and his wife; they had visited his home.

"Come on, Ken," the woman said.

They got up. Ken Derby wore the black whipcord of a deliveryman; he looked thin and fit in it. The woman was a girl of indeterminate age and in a slighter, feminine way she somewhat resembled him. She had dark-blond hair and a slender face with a wide, patient mouth and dark, observant eyes that seemed not to want to see as much as they did. Rising, she dropped a scarf and when she stooped to pick it up and the neckline of her dress opened, Ryan saw small, immature breasts only half-held by a ribbon of bra. Her eyes met his impersonally and she shrugged into her coat without her escort's help.

"How about a beer on the house?" Ken Derby called to the oven man, and turned.

And looked squarely at Ryan.

They looked at each other a long time. "Come on, Ken," the girl said. *"Please."*

Derby exhaled a long breath.

"There he is now," he said, and threw off the visored cap he had just put on.

Ryan pushed the table away and got up. His legs felt shaky. It wasn't fear; he always felt that way when a fight threatened. He was glad the overcoat was off.

The girl, without understanding what was causing this, said, "Oh, for the love of God—" and pressed her angular thinness against Derby restrainingly.

Derby pushed her away and came forward, extending a long right arm, holding his left curled against his chest. That was a disadvantage, for Ryan was accustomed to right-handed fighters.

"Hey, what goes on?" came from the counter.

"Oh, stop it!" the girl cried despairingly and for a perilous second Ryan looked at her, and saw large, fear-widened brown eyes, and a mouth quirked to cry.

Derby feinted twice with the right, not even coming close, and then swung his left with heavy certainty. But Ryan stepped inside it, crouched and dug both fists twice into Derby's thin, muscled belly. Derby grunted and clinched awkwardly, and moved sideways. His thigh lifted the table and Ryan's pizza and coffee cascaded to the floor. Ryan wrestled his way up inside the other man's guard, knowing what he was going to do when the clinch broke.

His head was clear; the whisky's lingering effect only made him confident and strong. Over Derby's shoulder he saw the girl shrink desolately against the booth.

Derby heaved at him to get out of the clinch, and he felt a hand grab him from behind but it did nothing. He took a half step, starting the punch from near his ribs, pivoting his body as he brought it up and it caught Derby's jaw, but on the side instead of the jaw-point. Still, he slumped. Ryan straightened him with a quick left and started another hook, pivoting…

As he did he again saw the hopeless girl against the booth. He pulled the punch just enough so that it thumped harmlessly against Derby's slow left hand. The oven man, who had a toy baseball bat out, grabbed Derby from behind—and found he had to hold him up. The fight was over.

"What the hell?" the oven man demanded.

"Sit him down on the bench," said Ryan. He sucked a knuckle and looked at the girl. She had turned away from them.

"*Sit* him down," said the oven man sarcastically. "For Chrissake, Mac. He won't sit. He's *out.*"

Ryan considered several things, then brought out his badge. "This is a police matter," he told the man with floured arms, and the baseball bat went into a hip pocket.

"Oh. You pinching him?"

The girl turned around. "No," Ryan told the oven man, but he was speaking to the girl. "I'm not pinching him."

"Well, what do we do with him?"

"I said sit him down," said Ryan, and when Derby had been eased into a corner of one of the booths he felt the slackened pulse and lifted an eyelid. "He'll be all right. Give him a few minutes. And bring us some coffee. Or maybe some wine for you, ma'am?"

She shook her head no.

"You look like you could use it."

"No."

"Two coffees."

He sat down at a table, but the girl continued to stand, rebellious and helpless. He said, "I'm sorry about this. Why don't you sit down?"

"You don't have to be sorry. You couldn't help it. He—he gets like that when he's been drinking."

"Sure." He pulled a chair around for her, a tacit invitation, and she finally accepted. She was tired and worn and respectable, cheaply dressed—like a million other women in New York that night. Derby sighed and settled in the booth's corner.

"I gather you're a policeman."

"And you're Mrs. Derby."

"I'm Ken's sister."

That explained the resemblance. "I'm sorry I hit him so hard." Saying that surprised him because he was not accustomed to apologizing under such circumstances.

The oven man brought two cups of coffee, picked up the spilled food and locked the front door. "We close at ten," he said.

Ryan did not like using his authority for personal advantage but there were times when it was justified. The oven man caught his look. "Oh, take all the time you want, loo-tenant," he said hastily.

Ryan said, "That makes you Harry Derby's sister too."

The brown eyes trained a steady sadness on him, and he knew she was refusing to say anything of what she had to say. "I'm Harry Derby's sister."

Ryan burned his mouth with a long sip of coffee. It did not occur to him that there was no necessity for him to make explanations to the sister of Harry Derby. That would occur long after, when he thought about her thin body and patience and gentle eyes. And lack of the obvious prettinesses.

He said, "I'm Neill Ryan, one of the officers who arrested your brother and helped send him up. You were over at my house tonight?"

"Ken wanted to talk to you. We stopped by twice. But—" She looked over her shoulder, and Derby breathed deeply as though in reply to her glance. "But perhaps you can understand how Ken feels."

Ryan said, "Sure."

"Not that we have any illusions about Harry. But Ken—well, don't misjudge him. He doesn't drink often. And he was fond of Harry."

"He sure was." Ryan could not keep the sarcasm out of his voice.

"What do you mean?"

"Your brother came to my home some time back to alibi Harry. He claimed Harry was with him on the day of the Connors murder."

"Ken told you that?"

"He said they delivered some big appliances together that day."

When he saw how it made her look he wished he had not said it.

"He's sort of crazy sometimes," she said slowly, "and impulsive. But he should not have done that. That's—that's obstructing justice or something, isn't it?"

"It doesn't matter. I proved to my own satisfaction that he had lied."

"Yes?" She eyed him oddly and for the first time she sipped her coffee. "Tell me something…ah…look here, Mr. Ryan. Ken was telling me tonight that the word has been out along the docks for quite a while that the cops finally got Harry. Is that true?"

"Got him?"

"You understand me, I think. What Ken meant was that you had not gotten Harry fairly or honestly or on the basis of real evidence. The idea is Harry was framed, that the evidence was manufactured against him. And that the union didn't put up much money and when that lawyer, Farragut, could not immediately disprove the evidence, he simply gave up. Is that true?"

The steadiness of her gaze had attracted him before. Now it disconcerted him. He looked away, feeling again the familiar stab of alarm.

"Wait a minute. I have no idea what they are saying on the docks. But if you think your brother was framed—" to say it was an effort— "you're crazy. Holy God, the evidence against him—"

"I read the papers."

"Then you know—"

"I know Ken was present once when Farragut visited Harry in jail. He says Harry told Farragut that one of the cops blew some dust on his jacket to make the case stronger. I don't understand that, exactly. But did you do it, Mr. Ryan?"

That marshaled Ryan's wits. He looked amused. "Do *you* believe that?"

"I don't know *what* to believe!" she cried. The oven man looked up from the Italian newspaper he was reading.

"Well, it's ridiculous on the face of it," said Ryan. "The evidence against your brother was overwhelming, as you know if you followed the case."

"I know." She sounded uncertain. "And I wouldn't believe it if Harry said it." Her raised voice was near hysteria. "But I believe Ken! And don't think I have many illusions about the police, either. We haven't had a very easy time of it from them—between Harry and my father, when he was alive."

And your brother and father didn't make things very easy for the cops.

Instead, "That's how it goes," he said softly. "Some people go wrong. I saw it happen to kids I grew up with—kids from decent homes and all that. It's nothing for you to be ashamed of."

"I'm not ashamed. I can't help what my father was, or what he helped my older brother to become.

"But I don't know what to think. I don't know what to *believe*. Did you ever hear a bigger cliché?" Her smile was unnaturally bright; her voice cracked. "Listen!" In the intensity of her gesturing she struck her coffee cup and spilled some across the table. "Listen. I lost my job today. I was fired. That's why I've got two weeks' pay in my pocket—from the Fortunatus Club. You know it? It's very exclusive. I was their librarian. When Harry was arrested they found out for the first time who I was. And they were very nice. They said, after all he wasn't guilty until proven—nobody's guilty until proven. You know? AH that. But he was proven. So today Mr. Murchison came around and very nicely told me I would have to leave. He said, 'We feel terrible about this, Rosemary.' And he did. But how many librarian's jobs do you think there are in the city, Mr. Ryan?"

She got to her feet. Her voice was shrill. Ken Derby opened vacant eyes. His sister gestured toward him.

"And you know what, Mr. Ryan? I believe Harry is innocent. By God, I do! I believe what Ken said is the truth and that you framed Harry. You know why I believe it? Because I've talked to you, and seen your face. You're a liar, Mister Ryan. You're a cheap liar—"

Suddenly she began to cry, and she continued talking and crying, disregarding her tears and the saliva that thickened her voice. "That's justice, what *you* are! No truth, or honesty. Justice is what you make people believe. Sure, Harry was no good. But to send him to prison you had to make yourself worse. You had to lie and cheat in the name of decency. That's how the law is upheld! Oh, dear Jesus, I hate—"

She threw herself at him, sobbing, beating down on his chest with her fists, kicking, crying…

"Hey for Pete's sake," said the oven man, alarmed.

Ryan caught her arms. "Call a cab," he said.

The oven man rushed to the front door and unlocked it. The girl was weeping uncontrollably. Ryan waited, holding her thin shoulders and feeling them shake, knowing this would take time.

Ken Derby got up on unsteady legs. "What's now?" he said. "Whatsa matter, Rosie?"

Then brakes squealed outside. Ryan led the girl. "Come on," he flung over his shoulder.

He put them both in the cab, got the address from Derby and repeated it to the driver as he handed him a dollar. "See that your sister gets home all right," he said.

He watched the cab pull away, then went back inside and paid the bill. It was only after he had done that and stood outside again, breathing deeply and seeing the little restaurant's lights blink out, that he really felt what she had said to him.

CHAPTER 18

The Homecoming

As she herself occasionally said, Agnes Ryan had never looked at another man after her husband was killed—and at very few before she met him. She had been a plump little Dresden doll of a girl with the Irish gift of merriment and a fierce streak of possessiveness that was dramatic in one so otherwise kind and docile. When she lost her husband, Mrs. Ryan turned her long-lashed eyes inward on herself and her memories, on her family and her God. She devoted herself to bringing up Eleanor and O'Neill, to working at the church and to making ends meet on a slain policeman's pension and insurance, with occasional help from her brother who had an insurance agency in Worcester. At fifty-five she was a prematurely white-haired little woman with china blue eyes, patience and good cheer. She prayed regularly and lived in the serene faith that her man was watching her from heaven where ultimately they would be reunited forever.

When Ryan let himself in with his key, she was sitting in the living room before a radio turned low, listening to the eleven o'clock news and sewing the hem on a new dress of Eleanor's. After sewing each section she pulled the basting threads out with tiny stubby fingers.

Ryan bent over and kissed her, "Hi, ma," and she caught the reek of whisky and heavy food. It reminded her of his father. Her son reminded her of his father in many ways, although he was shorter and slighter and—it seemed to her these days—quieter and less aggressive. "You're late," she said.

"Yeah. Something came up."

She would not ask what it was although she looked searchingly at his bloodshot eyes and haggard cheeks.

"Some people were here."

"I saw them."

"They came twice."

"They would. It's not important."

"You've eaten?"

"I—I had a bite."

"Let me fix you a sandwich. We had a nice meat loaf."

He really didn't want it but he knew she wanted to fix it. And what difference did it make in a world that had fallen apart?

"Well, maybe a thin one."

While she bustled in the kitchen he leaned back in his father's chair and closed his eyes, and despair flooded in like the sea through a dissolving dike. He did not know where to turn next and he was oppressed with the urgency of doing something *now*—yet what could he do? He thought of the time when he was thirteen and they had hit a baseball through the plate-glass window of Mr. Brodt's butcher shop. Once again he had that hopeless feeling of having done something enormous and frightful, beyond repair or recall. What could he do—what *was* there to do?

Go to Lieutenant Bauer and tell him that the real murderer of Mrs. Connors had been permitted to escape clean and unpursued? Ruin Jablonski's retirement-in-honor—even forgetting Jablonski's threat? Blast his own hopes and chances that were now so bright? And yet...

Everything in Ryan's nature, everything instilled in him as a boy about honor and fair play, his staunch belief in the ultimate supremacy of right, all that he had come to admire and respect as he grew into a man, stood inexorably over and against what he had done. And *he* had done it, he told himself brutally. There was no use blaming Jablonski or Derby or anyone else. They had had a part in it, sure. But he had let himself drift into what was now—as Jablonski had so bluntly told him—an impossible situation. There was nothing he could do. There was no way out. Ryan's closed eyes tightened spasmodically.

"Here, Neill," said a voice and he opened them to see his mother standing over him with a plate and a glass of milk. She was looking at him worriedly. "Is everything all right?"

Ryan munched the sandwich. "It's great."

She picked up the dress and resumed work. After a moment she said, "That's not what I meant. I meant—is everything all right with *you?*"

Ryan knew what she meant. He went on eating the sandwich, looking at his mother's white head bent over the dress, tiny fingers busy with little stitches, and all that he had felt about her as a boy surged into his mind. Suddenly he had to say it.

"Ma."

"Yes?" She went on working, because she knew something was coming.

"Everything's all right—it's fine. I'm just tired. But...something I been thinking of asking you."

"It's about that girl, isn't it? That red-haired dancer?" She forced herself to smile at him. "She looked pretty in the paper, Neill. I'd like to meet her." Her head bent again over her sewing.

"Oh. Gee Gee? No. I wasn't thinking of her. I'd like you to meet her, though. The next Monday night I'm home, I'll ask her up." He put down the empty, milk-clouded glass.

"Good. And so, what then?"

"Oh, nothing much. It's just this—this guy Derby that we sent up. Jablonski and me." He didn't know what he was going to say. He just had to talk to someone—someone he could trust.

"Oh. Well, he surely shouldn't bother you, Neill."

"Well, he does. Suppose—ma, suppose I told you that today I learned something that makes it look as if Derby wasn't guilty after all?"

For the first time she looked fully at him.

"O'Neill Ryan," she said. "Have you lost your mind? Of course he's guilty. By the Holy Mother do you think I didn't read every word of it in the papers, and my own boy in it?"

"Sure. But…"

Carefully she pulled out the basting stitches. "This is the first man you've ever helped send to the electric chair, isn't it, Neill?"

"Yes. That's right."

"I mind the time your father was home on the night a stickup artist was to die in Sing Sing. He'd helped send him there and the man had almost killed the two officers who had arrested him. Yet your father could not stand it, and as it got close to midnight he went out and over to Martin's speakeasy and had some drinks. He told me about it later. And do you know what he did then? The drinks didn't help either, and he left there and began walking and he walked all the way down to St. Pat's and he went in and spent the night on his knees—praying for the man he had helped to electrocute." Her voice suddenly caught and Ryan knew his mother inwardly was crying.

"You're like him, Neill," she went on. "And you worry like him, even over people like this Derby. But you needn't, believe me. For if ever there was justice served to one of them thieving scum—"

"But—" He couldn't let it go on. "But, ma—suppose Derby *wasn't* guilty!"

"*Wasn't* guilty! Wasn't guilty of what, in heaven's name?"

"Well—suppose he didn't kill the old woman?"

She switched off the radio's indistinct murmur. "Well," she said, "*didn't* he kill her?"

Ryan was silent. Could he tell her?

No.

"I didn't say that. I just said, suppose he didn't. And I found it out now. What could I do?"

"O'Neill Ryan, if that's the sort of thing that's bothering you, you had better get to bed and get a good night's rest." Petulantly she resumed her sewing. "You're just the kind to lean over backwards about things like that, you certainly are. But let me tell you this. Even if that Derby had not killed the old woman, he has done so many other evil things, and well you know it, that the electric chair is no more than he deserves. Think of your father, boy, and what they did to him. That man Derby is that kind—if he hasn't killed some decent, brave officer it is only because he hasn't had the sneaking chance to. Why, Neill, of course he's guilty."

It was getting beyond his control. "But, ma," he cried out, "supposing—suppose I have to go to the department and tell them that—that we've got to set Derby free?"

He was on his feet. He had not been aware of getting up.

Wonder filled her face. "Tell them he must be set free," she repeated. "Have you had too many drinks, son? God in heaven, you're—you're having a nervous fit, I think. Neill! How can you say such a thing—how *can* you? A crook like Derby? Think of what you stand for, and what your father stood for." She waved to the large framed photograph on the table and Sergeant O'Neill Ryan in uniform stared at his son with expressionless, retouched eyes. "He felt bad about the man he sent up too, Neill. But it didn't swerve him from his duty. He didn't flinch—he prayed for strength. And he got it. He knew when it was time to force himself to be—to be steel."

"But a man's life—"

"And what was your father's life?" she asked. She was being steel too; the blue eyes were night-dark. "What's the matter with you—you're not that new at the business. Don't you have the courage to put a—something like Derby where he belongs? A decent citizen must be treated with respect until he's proved guilty, anyone knows that. But a crook like Derby—what's come over you?"

The front door opened. Eleanor came in laughing, pink cheeked, followed by her date. "Hi, ma. Hi, Neill. Come on in, Jerry."

Ryan rubbed his hand over his face and nodded to Jerry. "I got your book," he said, and went into his room.

He undressed slowly. *Was* he having some kind of nervous fit? Was he crazy? After all, what was Derby to him—or to the world? Nothing. Less than nothing. As Jablonski had said, Derby himself knew where he had been at the time of the Connors murder. If he didn't want to say, why should O'Neill Ryan interfere?

But it wasn't that, and he knew it wasn't that. Maybe Derby was better off to the world dead than alive. Maybe he deserved extinction, like some deadly reptile. But something else was involved here. It was the basic acceptance of right and order toward which mankind had been moving for aeons, the faith in a well-ordered society that had led Ryan, and his father before him, to make themselves society's instruments for preserving what was good and decent. Ryan could not put it clearly into words, but he felt it.

That was what was being violated. That was what had given Rosemary Derby's face its desolate look. If Harry Derby were executed Ryan knew he could never tolerate himself again, nor pleasurably accept praise or kindness from others, or even accept their company. Then what must he do?

Suddenly he flung himself out of the bed and sliding to his knees beside it tried to pray. But he could not; what was there to say? That he was sorry for having made a mistake? That he would not do it again? That had made it right when he was a child. That had made everything right then.

Suddenly, from deep inside himself he started to cry, silently, face pillowed against the sheeted mattress, his tears wetting it, shoulders twisting and belly wracked spasmodically with sobs. For a long time he wept, not trying to halt it, sensing that this was something that had to be gotten over with.

Then he dried his face with a clean handkerchief and groping for it his hands grazed the pistol and holster on the bureau. That was another easy way out, he told himself contemptuously. But a thought struck like a bullet from the gun. If he were to be killed in the days to come, Harry Derby would go to the chair as surely as if Ryan himself had sentenced him.

There was one thing he could do. In the student's desk he had used as an undergraduate he found paper and pen. He wrote:

> To whom it may concern:
>
> In event of my unexpected death I want it to be known that when Ed Jablonski and I arrested Harry Derby we applied some dust made from a part of the lamp at the Connors murder to his jacket. Subsequently I learned that at the time of the murder Derby was holding up a drugstore on East Thirty-first Street, as a fingerprint obtained there and now in the file on the case will show. I swear before God this is all true.

He signed his name and shield number, put the letter in an envelope and addressed it to the judge who had tried Derby. Then he put the envelope in the little tin box in which he kept his insurance policy and his few other papers of importance.

He lay down again on the bed. He felt cold and exhausted and yet calm. He had the sense of something being about to happen, of his being about to go away, like on his last night at home before going to Uncle Frank's summer camp near Worcester as a kid. He was passing some kind of turning point. A new time was coming in.

He began to breathe normally, and as he did he began to think logically about the real killer of Mrs. Connors. That was still a way out, of sorts: if he could get the real killer then they would have both him and Derby. It had fleetingly crossed his mind before, but he had dismissed it as impractical. Now he faced it squarely and fully.

That would take some of the curse off as far as the department was concerned. And even Jablonski might be saved, he thought in this spell of new clarity, for there was always Farragut's explanation that the telltale dust had been transferred by accident during the fight.

He thought of the truculent, snarling man for whom he was considering undertaking this alone, without the usual help of the department, and he smiled bitterly. Still, it was an honest, satisfying bitterness, born of growing certainty of the direction he would take. Thinking on it, after a time he fell asleep.

He slept well.

PART THREE: THE BLOW-OFF

CHAPTER 19

The Things That Really Happen

He and Lambert had agreed to begin afternoon tours next day to spell another team, one of whose members had a daughter who was getting married. But Ryan dropped into the station house at twelve-thirty when he knew Bauer would be at lunch, telephoned downtown, and without explaining his purpose quietly set in motion the identification machinery that would give him the names and records of all known criminals in the metropolitan area who had two vital characteristics: a physical resemblance to Harry Derby and a working method of robbing women as Mrs. Connors had been robbed.

Then, since it was still early, he walked to the apartment where the murder had occurred. The afternoon was bright and warm; north of the city snow was melting among Westchester's hills, wetting the sunny rocks and making rivulets for children to play in on their way home from school. But amid Manhattan's concrete and steel geometry there was no snow except where a taller building cast, in this brightness, a blue shadow across lower rooftops. Even so, you felt the catch of distant spring in your throat.

Mrs. Lombardi sat on the steps, a heavy shawl over her shoulders, a cigarette between her lips. "How are you?" she said.

Ryan asked about Mrs. Anders and Betty Leonard and learned that Mrs. Anders had since moved to Tulsa. Gloria Connors still had the apartment but was living with friends and was moving out the first of the month—maybe sooner if she could arrange about the furniture. Meanwhile, it was being shown. Ryan asked if he could borrow the key and Mrs. Lombardi said she didn't know why not and took it off a large key ring she fished from her pocket.

"Thanks. Oh, one other thing I wanted to ask you. Remember you identified this guy Derby without any trouble? You picked his picture out right away, and then again that night at the precinct and so on?"

"Sure I did."

"Well, there's one thing I'm curious about. Was there anything about that guy when you saw him, either at the precinct or later in court, that made you think he might not be the right one after all? I mean, maybe just one little point that might have made you wonder?"

A landlady's perpetual suspicion squinted at him through her half-closed eyes.

Ryan smiled easily. "I guess it sounds nuts, now he's convicted and all that. But I'm making a—a sort of study of witnesses' observation, Mrs. Lombardi. I was just wondering how the whole process of identification struck you."

"It struck me," she said, "that you fellows did a pretty good job of locating him fast. When I looked at that picture there wasn't any doubt. And then when I saw him..." Her forefinger skillfully flicked the cigarette butt into the street. "But I'll tell you one thing. Maybe it was having seen the picture that did it. But I sort of got the feeling when I saw him in court that I'd seen him before—I mean some place else. You know what I mean?"

"Did you ever live near the piers? Or have anything to do with stevedores?"

"No. My sister's husband's cousin is a steward on the *Roma,* though. We go down and visit with him when the ship's in sometimes."

Ryan shook his head. "Did you and the other ladies talk about this afterwards—Mrs. Anders and Miss Leonard, I mean?"

"Well, you think something like that happens every day around here?"

"I just meant, did either Mrs. Anders or Miss Leonard say anything that might suggest they weren't as sure about the identification as they might have been? In other words did they notice any single point that didn't quite correspond—that they remembered later, as sort of out of key?"

"Not that I know of."

"Did the man's voice sound the same in the courtroom? Did he wear his clothes the same way? Did the way he walked correspond with what you remembered?"

She shook her head continuously to the questions.

"Or did any of the others say—"

"Listen, why don't you ask them? You're a detective."

"I will," said Ryan. "Thanks, Mrs. Lombardi."

He went into the building. A girl he had never seen before answered the door of Betty Leonard's apartment and explained she was Betty's roommate. Ryan told who he was, and the girl said Betty was working days now and would be for the next couple months. Betty would be very sorry she missed him, the girl added, and Ryan recognized that he had been the subject of sororal discussions. He said he'd be sure to drop back a few evenings from now.

When she had closed the door he let himself in the Connors apartment as quietly as he could, although the front door stuck a little at the bottom. This was the beginning, he told himself.

It hadn't really changed since he was last here. Someone had cleaned up the living room and straightened the chairs, and now it was simply a gloomy, overheated living room, furnished cheaply and in need of airing—hardly the appropriate background for murder.

Ryan sat down in a chair, pushed his hat back on his head and lighted a cigarette. He could not really expect to find anything. The lab boys and the various squads who had been here were good, and at the time they had worked under the stimulating pressure of having to crack the case in a hurry. He could not easily imagine finding anything that had been overlooked, here or elsewhere. Yet he had to.

When he had smoked a few minutes he rose and began examining everything in the room, touching things gingerly. He tried to imagine how it had happened, how the man would have pushed his way in and how the old woman would have backed up, crying anxious, unfinished questions. The invader would have shut the door. And then... He went over every physical action that could have happened in the handful of seconds in which it all did happen.

Then he sat down again and looked around, breathing in smoke from the cigarette hanging between his lips. He thought of Ed Furtig and how Ed had sat here in this same chair, smoking and wondering. Then it had been Ed's to carry.

Ryan got up. This was getting nowhere.

Well, he could always come back. He yanked at the door knob angrily and the door gave and then stuck. He remembered it sticking when he came in and he yanked harder. The door stuck at the bottom near the threshold. Ryan lifted on the knob and it opened. He went into the hall, slamming it behind—Before it could slam he wheeled and held it open. Suddenly things were whirling in his head. There was a closet door at home that stuck often, especially in winter. To open it he always...

Ryan went back in and closed the door firmly, hearing its lower edge grate on the threshold. He was a murderer now and in his imagination in the next few seconds he had killed an old woman. He took a deep breath, then he grabbed the knob fast like a man in a hurry and yanked, and again the door partly opened and stuck at the bottom, an inch of it wedged tight. Ryan's hand went automatically up to the top corner that was free to pull on it as he lifted the knob, just as he did at home when the closet door stuck. Just, he thought, as any man would do naturally and unthinkingly. And especially one set on escape.

He stood looking at the door a long minute. He could not dare to hope that much. Yet thoughts of how doors stuck only at certain seasons and at certain temperatures and humidities thronged his mind; this was a warm day, possibly the warmest since Mrs. Connors died.

Ryan opened the door carefully, got a chair and stood on it to examine the upper corner with his small flashlight. On the inner surface there were only smudged streaks that could have been made by anything. And on the other side there was only dull green paint.

The vital part was the door's top edge. Where a man's fingertips would naturally grab and press. He raised up on his toes and pressed the flashlight's tiny button.

Its beam revealed grimy, worn wood innocent of any mark.

Ryan put the chair away dispiritedly, too let down to care about anything. Somehow he had felt so sure, so intuitively certain...

He pulled his hat down over his eyes and yanked the door doubly hard. He almost ran into a woman standing before him on the threshold.

"Why, what are you doing?" she demanded. Her sallow face went yellow around the cheek bones. She held a key.

Ryan said, "Who are you?"

She turned, frightened, seeking help.

"Wait a minute. Miss. I'm the police department."

She turned back.

"I'm Detective Ryan. I'm—I'm just rechecking some of the evidence."

"But...I thought the man was all sentenced and everything."

"Oh, he is. But there's always a chance of an appeal at the last minute. We want to be ready for it. I got the landlady to let me in."

"I see. Well, you didn't find anything new, did you?"

"That's right. But as long as you're here I'd like to ask a few questions."

She walked rapidly past the spot where her mother had lain and threw up the window as though fresh air would clean the room of its cruel memories. She said, "Know anyone who wants to buy some bedroom furniture?"

"Not at the moment, but I'll keep it in mind, Miss Connors. Tell me something. You saw this Harry Derby in court, eh?"

"Yes."

"Did it occur to you that you had seen him before?"

"No."

"Did he remind you of anyone?"

"No. No, he was a complete stranger."

"There was just you and your mother in the family?"

"And my brother Philip in Chicago."

"Miss Connors, this will strike you as an odd question, but did any of you have any enemies?"

She shook her head mutely.

"Your mother especially—she hadn't had any trouble with anyone shortly before she was attacked? Think back, please."

"Who could have had trouble with my ma?" she asked sadly, and Ryan felt a pang of sorrow for her.

"How long had you lived here?"

"Six years going on seven."

"No one ever broke in before—into your apartment or somebody else's?"

"No."

"After—after the murder, you didn't hear from anyone, or find anything around the house that in any way might have had anything to do with what happened?"

"No."

It was hopeless. At best these were the routine questions you asked as a last resort. Anyway he was simply going over ground that had been covered before when the trail was fresh and memories keener.

"Well…" Ryan twirled his hat in his hand. "Thanks, Miss Connors. If anything does occur to you I wish you would call me. At the Seventeenth Squad. Plaza 3-4483. The name is Ryan."

She got up too, but as Ryan moved toward the door she walked into a bedroom without answering. I suppose she feels pretty bad, he thought.

The door was about to close on him once again and finally, when he heard her say from inside, "Wait a minute, detective. Maybe you can explain—" She was holding something in her hand, something that glittered.

"You may remember that the cops—the officers, who were here at the time, found a cuff link near my—near mother's body."

"I remember. It was one of hers."

"That's right. One of the officers said that the other one might have been carried away by the murderer—that it might have caught in his clothes or something."

"That's possible. But it never turned up, Miss Connors."

"That always puzzled me a little. You see, Phil had given those links to ma with a shirtwaist. It was a birthday present. She had packed the shirtwaist and I always figured she wanted to wear it with the links when we visited him—you know, to show she liked them. I thought she probably had the links in her hand when that Derby came in. And then in the struggle—well, you know."

"That's probably what happened."

"No," she said. "I don't think it is. Look." She held up something for him to see. It was a cuff link. "See this?"

"Sure. That's what was returned to you after the trial, eh?"

"That's right. But look at this."

She spoke tartly, as though she expected him to understand something he clearly did not understand. She held out her other hand, thin and weedy, clenched tight. Then she opened it.

He saw two links in one hand—and one still held in the other. All three were of the same little silver scimitar design.

"I found these two in ma's jewel box a week ago," she said. "Just by accident. What do you think of that, detective?" It was a triumph for a vinegarish woman of lean, dark-browed homeliness, happy to discomfit a member of the sex that had long refused her.

What the hell! Ryan thought. "Miss Connors, are you sure you found those two links where they ought to be?"

"I told you I did. Ma had never gotten them out that day at all."

"But why didn't you ever find them before?"

"I simply never went through her things. I—I didn't want to stay here and a friend of mine in Jersey asked me to stay with her. It was only the other night when I came by to—to sort of get ready to close up the apartment that I found this. But it doesn't make any sense, does it?"

"No."

But Ryan was paying no attention to the explanation. "Look. You're sure this is the cuff link you got back from us? You didn't mix the three of them up?"

"Yes. Of course I'm sure."

She was an insurance clerk, probably good on details. She could be sure of something like that.

"And can you be sure that this set of cuff links didn't contain an extra one—a spare, so to speak?"

"Of course. I remember when she opened the package on her birthday. Anyway, did you ever hear of a spare cuff link?"

Ryan was wordless. He looked at the three links. God! he thought again. Things like this didn't really happen. And yet they did. He knew they did. That is how things *really* happened. The most unlikely, far-fetched, one-in-a-million chance, *that* is what happened, even though you could not believe it when you saw it face-to-face.

"It doesn't make any sense, does it?" she asked again with acid triumph.

"Maybe it does," said Ryan. "May I borrow these, Miss Connors?"

"Are you sure I'll get them back?"

CHAPTER 20

The Scarlatti Sonata

It was still too early to show up for work and Derby's home lay only a dozen blocks north and east. Why not? He had something to do there. He would not try now to determine what the cuff link might mean, although he sensed the possibilities. And Rosemary Derby might be able to help there. Ryan walked uptown, energetic and buoyant.

It was an old, dingy apartment building—but an apartment, not a cold-water flat as he had thought. He rang the bell under a hand-lettered *Derby* and the door buzzed without any challenge from the speaking tube.

She stood at a third-floor door, slim in black slacks and black sweater and some sort of thin-soled slippers that made her seem smaller and more girlish. She did not see him clearly until he came abreast of the door which streamed sunlight into the dark hall. She said, "Oh." Her hair, tied with a wisp of ribbon, looked more tawnily blond than it had last night. Her level-browed face was calm.

"Can I come in a minute?"

"Why not?"

She stood aside and he walked down a short hall into a small living room that seemed to contain a lot of books, on tables and in painted wooden bookcases. On one wall were several reproductions of paintings which he suspected were by Picasso, one of the few names in modern art he knew. An odd pattern of tinkling music that sounded like a guitar came from a table phonograph.

"Sit down," she said noncommittally, and turned the phonograph to a whisper but did not turn it off. Ryan felt like an intruder.

She sat down on a couch and extended slender black legs before her. Ryan took out his cigarette package and offered it and she shook her head.

"Mind if I do?"

"No."

These were the stiff formalities before a duel.

"Ken's not here?"

"He's at work."

"There are a few things I didn't get a chance to say last night."

She waited, not making it easier.

"My sister is a secretary in an ad agency. They always need secretaries. I could talk to her about a job—a job for you. Can you do typing and shorthand?"

"Theoretically. But my shorthand's rusty. Anyway, I'm not interested."

"I thought you needed a job."

"Perhaps you don't understand the difference, Mr. Ryan, betwixt—between library work and stenography." She bit her lip and Ryan could not know it was because his unexpected appearance had trapped her into using an archaic word.

"Maybe I don't. But this job would pay seventy-five bucks a week. Is that so far under a librarian's pay?"

She did not say anything. To Ryan she looked clean and well scrubbed—not pretty in any glamorous sense, but level-headed, willing to accept things on their own terms. It was a quality hard to define, but he liked it in a girl. The music that Scarlatti had written three centuries before stopped momentarily and then started again, an intricate twanging in the mid-afternoon quiet.

"Why this?"

"Why what?"

"Is the police department running an employment agency?"

Ryan pulled slowly on his cigarette and held the smoke in his lungs, extended the cigarette to an ashtray on the little table before him and very carefully dumped the ash, making a gesture of it. He did not want to get mad, or even show irritation. What he was about to say had been on his mind since last night, yet he had never analyzed it or arranged it logically. He just wanted to say it.

He leaned back and exhaled the smoke. When it was gone, "I owe you and your family a debt," he said. "I plan to repay it."

Her calm gaze was a triumphant challenge.

"You were right," said Ryan. "Last night. We framed your brother."

It was out. She was the first person he had ever said it to. He had a wild sense of relief.

"I knew you did." She reached to a box and took out a cigarette. "I could tell it last night." She flicked a lighter at the cigarette.

"Don't misunderstand me," said Ryan. "Your brother's a no-good bastard." He liked using the word to her. "And if he died it wouldn't hurt anyone in the world." He stopped and looked at the smoke spiraling up evenly from his cigarette. That was how it was—justice, evenness, balance. Things had to go straight up and down, and no other way. He went on.

"He's a rat. But that doesn't mean he should suffer for something he didn't do."

She looked at the baseboard across the room. Then she talked through thick smoke.

"And taking care of his sister and getting her another job will fix everything? Make everything even?"

That did something to Ryan and he had to knock the ashes off again, this time impatiently.

"That's not the idea. I said that he shouldn't suffer for something he didn't do. I don't think he should. And he won't."

"What are you going to do about it?"

"I've already done one thing. I've written a letter that will be found immediately in case anything happens to me. It will free Harry."

"And in the meantime?"

"You'll have to leave that to me." He got up. "I'm not going to let him get the chair, I promise you that. I hope to vindicate him. By bringing in the guy who really committed the murder." He laughed, masochistically. "Probably the chances of that are not good. But that's what I'm going to *try* to do. Anyway—" he spun the light fedora in his hand—"there's one thing I can guarantee, Miss Derby. Your brother won't burn. I'll see to that, no matter what else happens. But there are other people involved here, and other people's rights. I'm going to protect those too. So for the present Harry stays in Sing Sing. He belongs there, you know."

She was looking at him steadily and, the sun outside being temporarily darkened by a cloud, her cigarette made a firefly glow in the twilit room.

"In the meantime," Ryan said, "well, you've suffered on account of this, losing your job. There was something I thought I could do that might help and so I mentioned it." He pulled on his hat. "But forget it. If you have something else to do, fine." He had said what he had come to say. The heck with her.

He turned and remembered something. "One other thing. What I've been saying is between ourselves. I really didn't have to say it. I thought you might feel better if you knew. But if you tell anyone else what I said just now, I'll swear you're a liar and I never said it. You couldn't get anyone to believe it anyway. Take it or leave it, Miss Derby. That goes for the job offer, too."

He started down the hall, and she said, "Oh now, please!" but so quietly he could not believe it had reached him. Yet when he opened the door she was beside him. "Please don't go like that." The size of her eyes and the solemnity of her mouth surprised him.

"I've got to get to work."

"But you—please take a moment. I want to ask you—" A shrill whistle came from somewhere. "Oh! I was making tea. Every day at the library we had tea. Please—"

He allowed himself to be led back and when the tea had properly steeped during a few minutes of strained politeness he found himself sitting with a cup and a little cookie, undergoing thoughtful inspection. He sipped and readied himself.

"You're an honest man," she said with crashing frankness, and Ryan flushed.

"An honest cop," she reflected.

That graveled him. But he remembered the principles that the department had ingrained in him: you could not do your job effectively if you treated the public as enemies. You had to make friends of them, even those who regarded you as an enemy. This level-eyed girl was a part of the public.

"I think you're too well educated to believe that policemen are generally dishonest, Miss Derby."

"I don't say that. I'm sure some—most are—are honest. You are, certainly."

But her skepticism was an acid eating into his mind, filling it with cynicism. This was the public for which you worked late hours for small pay, and took chances, this dark-blond, small-breasted dame with the tight lips and critical air. He owed her something of course, but he was paying it off—suddenly it burst out.

"Where the hell do people like you get off? You and your lousy brother? And your old man! You're a great family to be squealing about cops! The Derbys! The lousy, crooked, mugging Derbys!"

He paused, surprised at himself. But he went on in a vibrant tone that was even more emotional.

"Let me tell you something, Miss Derby. One of the greatest things that could be done to make this country more—more law abiding, and a better place for decent people, would be to make a rule that everyone—everyone—at some point in his life should put on a police uniform and walk the streets for eight hours."

"And what would that accomplish, aside from giving him a little taste of power?"

"I'll tell you. It would make people realize what it is to be a cop. Because the instant you step out in that uniform you realize that whatever happens that's rough or unpleasant or dangerous along your beat in the next eight hours, you have to settle it. You're the one everyone will turn to. If some donkey comes home drunk and starts beating up his wife, you're the guy who has to walk up and cool him off. If some hoodlum tries to stick up the corner liquor store, that blue uniform of yours is the first thing he's looking for when he comes running out. If some teen-age kids get goofed on tea and go hunting trouble, you're their best target, because you're a cop. They won't go up against you openly. The first thing you know is a scuffle behind and then a baseball bat across the skull. That's how hoodlums begin. Later of course they graduate to be big shots—like your brother Harry." He looked bold hatred at her.

"Try directing traffic, Miss Derby, and discover how some truck drivers like to see how close they can come to you. Or there's the so-called honest citizen, who parks overtime and flies into a rage if you give him a summons, and threatens to get your job. Cops are human beings, Miss Derby, and sometimes we wish the people we serve would at least give us a minimum of cooperation, instead of thinking we're all bribe-takers or sadists or boneheads."

She had watched him throughout what he said and Ryan stared back, bitter and angry and waiting. He was not prepared for what she did say.

"I guess I had that coming. I'm sorry, Mr... Mr. Ryan. Sometimes when…well, when a girl has two brothers like Harry and Ken…what I want to say is this. If you mean what you said, and I know you did, I'd like to help you. And I know Ken will, when I tell him what you told me. Not all Derbys are—well, antisocial."

"I told you that if you mentioned this—"

"I understand. I completely understand, and you needn't worry. You can trust me, and you can trust Ken. He'll want to help, because he is fond of Harry. Do you know, on the morning of the day Harry was arrested they quarreled? It was about that jacket of Harry's that Ken wanted to borrow because his uniform was at the cleaner's. Harry wouldn't let him. Ken called him cheap or tight—you know. Then, when Harry was arrested and charged with that murder Kenny sat where you are and cried like a baby because of the quarrel. But tell me this. How did you—why did you come to frame Harry?"

How far should he go? How much dare he trust her? But if he did not trust anyone, how would he ever get at what he had to get at?

"It wasn't exactly my idea. Not that I'm not as much to blame as anyone." He looked at his wrist watch. "I'd like to tell you about it, Miss Derby—"

"My name's Rosemary."

"Okay, Rosemary. I'd like to tell you about it." It was true. He suddenly realized how much he wanted to tell every detail of how and why it happened. "But I'm due at work. Maybe I could come back sometime."

"Tomorrow afternoon?"

"I'll try to."

"And—Mr. Ryan?"

"People call me Neill."

She smiled shyly. "Neill. I think it's wonderful, what you're doing. Not because it's my brother. Because you have honesty and decency, and it's nice to know there are people like you around. I'm sorry about what I said about the police."

"Forget it," said Ryan. But he couldn't help adding, "We hear it all the time."

* * * *

When he and Lee Lambert came in that night, a Manila envelope was in his mail slot near the stairs. It contained copies of the police records of four men, all of whom from their description resembled Harry Derby, were at liberty and were known to have robbed women in the past. Two usually operated in and around Brooklyn and one far up in the Bronx. But one, a man named James Mackie and known as "Big Mackie," ran a small Turkish bath and athletic club in the east fifties and lived over it. He was a former prize fighter, he had been arrested a half dozen times in the past decade although not recently and he had twice been convicted of crimes against women.

Ryan studied the photograph. Mackie looked darker than Derby and had bushier eyebrows. But his dimensions were the same, and the address made it look good. If it turned out that Mackie had some connection with Harry Derby that would explain Derby's possession of the bill...

A note had been clipped to the records. It was from the IB man who had compiled the information. It said, "For your information this same description was given one of the boys here for checking a couple days ago by Jack Sandalwood, the reporter."

CHAPTER 21

There's a Story in It

Next morning rain, thick and gray as a twinkling theater curtain, made a steady beat on cars and pavement; it would last all day. Ryan took off his raincoat and sat down to doughnuts and coffee before the restaurant's lighted windows. He unfurled the *Herald Tribune,* turned to Red Smith's column and sipped black, sweetened coffee. It was in between times, late for the crowd that got to work at eight-thirty, but early for the nine o'clockers. You felt those things when you had worked all hours long enough. Ryan bit into crisp doughnuts and savored the wry humor of good sports writing. For a while he forgot where he was and what lay ahead of him, and how little time he had.

But when the coffee was finished and the sports page read, he paid his check, stood at the restaurant door yanking his raincoat tight against the weather and thought of Gee Gee. She'd be in bed at this hour, sound asleep, her body sweetly scenting the warm bedclothes... Ryan went out into the rain. Forget it. There was work to do.

Mrs. Daniels was in a faded housecoat when he knocked at her door. She said, "Oh, it's you?" apprehensively.

"Anyone in that room where we arrested Derby?"

"No. It's empty."

"I'd like to look around it, if you don't mind."

"Help yourself. The door's open." She was waiting for him to say something else.

"And I'll take ten bucks, if it's convenient."

She sighed—of course he wouldn't forget that.

"Can I give you five now and send you the rest on Saturday? Honest, most of my roomers have been slow this week. And I never got the other ten back, you know."

"Sure," said Ryan. It was as good as you could expect. She'd never have sent the money voluntarily, of course.

He mounted the stairs they had crept up so cautiously that night. No need for silence now. Even so he walked quietly. He had a surreptitious feeling about what he was doing. There were a lot of people he would not want to meet here, nor would want to know that he was still concerned with the place where Harry Derby was arrested. Lieutenant Bauer, for example, or anyone from the precinct station.

He pushed the door open, took off his coat, draped it over a chair and sat down. Rain whispered fitfully at the windows; otherwise the old house was gloomily quiet.

Nothing had changed since the last time; he almost expected to see Derby's long back against the wall, arms spread-eagled upward. Ryan tried to remember exactly what Derby had looked like and exactly what he had said. That was the only purpose of this visit, if it had one: to strain for every possible hint he could get. For Derby must have had *some* guilty knowledge of the murder; otherwise how had he come to possess the hundred dollar bill?

He got up and walked around the bare and chilly chamber, remembering where he had stood, and Jablonski's chagrin, and Derby's taunts… He took his place at the wall where Derby had stood, put his hands up against it like a prisoner. Then he turned and moved forward into the room, imagining for a moment he was confronting two cops…

"What the devil are you up to? Re-enacting the crime?"

Even in his first start of guilty fear Ryan recognized the voice.

A man stood in the doorway. Under his open trenchcoat a gray tweed jacket was visible. His confident, good-looking face wore a mocking smile.

It was Sandalwood.

Ryan stared, then tried to pull himself together. Clinch—play for time.

"Where did you come from?" he asked with intentional naïveté.

Sandalwood grinned and came in.

"Supposing I tell you I've been following you for a while?" he said. "What *are* you up to, Ryan? Derby's up the river—you're certainly not still building a case against him. Do you just like this place?"

And when Ryan remained silent, he drawled, "Or are you looking for something—say a hundred dollar bill that got lost one night?"

Ryan cursed him and Sandalwood laughed. He was trying to overpower Ryan with his confidence and his reputation and his tactical position, and he was doing it.

"Yesterday you dropped in on the Derbys. What's the attraction there—the sister?" Sandalwood's eyes bugged out impudently; he was trying to lure Ryan into rage.

"And now you're here. Why don't you get it off your chest? I can give you a break, you know, if you cooperate. Let me tell you something,

Ryan. Give it to me straight and then I'll tell *you* whether you are telling the truth or not. Want to know something? I always figured you guys were up to something that night. So before Derby went up the river I talked to him. And he leveled. I've known Derby a long time. He told me pretty much what it was all about."

Was he lying? Was it a bluff, intended to trap him into admitting something? Or did Sandalwood know? He clearly had been following him.

Ryan had to make a move. He seized on the first inspiration that came.

"Okay," he said steadily. "I'll tell you the truth. Not many people know this. But Harry Derby is the greatest slide trombone player you've ever heard. He really is." Sandalwood's jaw sucked turtle-like into his neck.

"His tone is clear as a bell," Ryan went on. "What Jablonski and I were trying to do that night was to recruit him into a little jazz band we're forming."

Sandalwood's face darkened. Ryan knew he had turned the tables. "You know how it is," he went on. "There's just never enough good trombone players."

Anger was making Sandalwood's eyes kindle.

Ryan grinned. "What's the matter? Aren't I telling you the truth? Suppose you tell *me.*"

Slowly, visibly, Sandalwood swallowed his rage. It took time. But he was too skillful to let himself be twitted into further error. He had attempted a well-timed bluff, but Ryan had called it.

"Okay," he said. "You can't blame me for trying. I played a hunch, that's all. But on the level, Ryan—what the hell *are* you doing?"

"Just call downtown to the deputy commissioner," said Ryan, "and get permission. Then I'll be glad to give you an interview."

Carelessly Sandalwood threw a porkpie rain hat over an unruffled brow. "Okay."

He went to the door. "I was bluffing and you called it. I haven't talked to Derby. But I will now. Know why? Because now I know I'm right. Something went on here that night—I can feel it. Maybe it wasn't a hundred dollar bill. Maybe it was something else. But whatever it was, there's a story in it, and I'm going to get it."

Over his shoulder Sandalwood smiled deliberately. He did not feel like smiling, and he knew that Ryan knew that. Then he paused, going out, and the smile was replaced by calculated malice.

"By the way, seen Gee Gee Hawes lately?"

Ryan could not think of an adequate reply that would not involve the swinging of fists.

When Sandalwood had ambled down the stairs whistling with studied loudness, Ryan lighted a cigarette and noticed his hands were trembly. He inhaled deeply. Sandalwood had been following him! It couldn't have been for long, and it was probably the result of luck more than intent—maybe Sandalwood had happened to see him on the street yesterday and had tagged along hopefully. Ryan was certain he would have sensed it if anyone had been following him for any length of time.

Even so, the thought was alarming, and Sandalwood's threat was more than alarming. He crushed out the cigarette in a rush of desperate helplessness and jogged down the stairs. Twice on the way home he checked to make sure no one was behind him. He had not intended returning home, but in this new uneasiness he wanted to be doubly certain no one could overhear the telephone calls he would make.

The house was still. Ryan heated coffee, poured a cup, lighted another cigarette and then dialed the number of a stool to whom Lee Lambert had introduced him. "He's a barber over on Third," Lambert had explained afterward. "Slip him a fin occasionally but never go in the shop. Though you can call him there." When the barber whose name was Connie answered, Ryan told him what he wanted to know—everything he could get about Big Mackie, and fast.

"It won't be much. That party's out of town."

"What do you mean? When did he go?"

"Oh, some weeks. Quite a few weeks," said the barber in the cryptic locution of one who is being overheard.

"I want to know when he left town," said Ryan. "The exact date. And where he is now. Check it hard."

"Okay. Sure, Mr. Johnson. I'll call you in a few days."

"Call by tonight. I said I needed it fast. Call my home and leave a message—here's the number. Make damned sure I hear from you. This is a big one."

"Well…okay. You gonna drop around for that scalp treatment?"

"Let me hear from you and you'll hear from me."

He gulped coffee and dialed a Brooklyn precinct where a sergeant who had helped break him in as a rookie was still stationed. He was working on a little hunch of his own, he lied glibly, involving a Manhattan job some time back that might have been done by either of two Brooklyn muggers with records. What could Oley tell him of either?

"Ferris you can forget about," Oley said promptly. "He ran into someone a little tougher than he is last summer in a bar and got badly mauled. He lost one eye and the other's just about gone I understand.

Anyway, he was in the hospital all fall, and now he has to be led around. Who's your other guy—the Drummer Boy?"

"Vince Van Loan. Thirty-one. Five feet—"

"Sure. Drummer Boy Van Loan. He's always been nuts about playing snare drums. I think you can write him off too, Neill, though I'll check further if you like."

"How do you mean?"

"My missus was telling me—she went to school with the Van Loan girls—that last summer Vince met some broad who sang with a little band out Nassau County way. Well, this singer gets Vince a job drumming with the band and damned if he's not going straight. He's nuts about drums and he likes the dame, and I guess it's working out. I'll ask Mary about it again tonight, but I think you can forget him. Got any others over our way?"

"That's all, Oley. Thanks a lot."

He hung up the phone thoughtfully. The Bronx guy would have to wait until he could sound out Lambert on their contacts up there. Meanwhile, pending word from Connie what else could he do?

He looked at his watch—twelve-thirty. He was hungry, and he'd be getting to work before long. But something Sandalwood said came back and he dialed another number, and as he did his tight mouth relaxed in a smile for the first time that day.

A sleep-husky voice said, "Hullo?" and Ryan, instantly contrite, said, "If I woke you up, I'll kill myself."

"You didn't wake me up," Gee Gee said. "Hello, Neill. Good morning," and he could tell from the way she sounded that she was smiling at the recognition of his voice. Ryan took a deep breath and forgot Derby.

"I haven't seen you for a long time—six days, to be exact. I was wondering if you'd like to have brunch or something."

"I think that would be lovely. Just give me time for a shower."

"I *did* wake you up."

"Oh, now stop! But wait—is it raining?"

"Cats and dogs. So what?"

"Then why don't you come here for lunch? I blew myself to a coat—a real fur coat. Neill, wait'll you see it! I can't wear that lovely thing out in the rain."

"You could wear your old one."

"With a new one? Never! You come here. I'll make you *plintzen.*"

"What is plintzen?"

"They're a German pancake like crêpes suzette. But simpler."

Waiting on the subway platform Ryan inspected himself in a gum machine's speckled mirror. Under his eyes were blue shadows. He didn't like that. Weariness shamed him. He hoped she wouldn't notice.

* * * *

"I don't know why I'm so good to you," she said as he reached the top of the stairs. "Cooking lunch and everything." She was wearing a small apron over a simple blue skirt and sweater. He had never seen her dressed so plainly.

Ryan took both sweatered arms and kissed her warm, unresisting lips. He had been kissing her since the third date. "Now what have I done?"

"Where have you *been?*" But he knew he was welcome. "I feel neglected—and I have a right to feel neglected." She took his wet hat and raincoat.

"I'm sorry. But you knew I was on the day tour last week. And when I work days and you work nights what can you expect? Besides, something came up."

"What came up?"

"I can't go into it, Gee."

She was tempted to say, "I know what came up—something with baby blue eyes and blond hair," but she gave him a look of quick inspection and was glad she had not. Something was wrong, obviously. Still—he *had* neglected her!

"Oh! You wait a minute."

She ran out of the room. "Close your eyes," she called. He closed them. Something sweet-smelling was cooking in the kitchen. "Now you can open them," she said from close at hand.

She stood before him swathed in a coat of dark, long, glossy fur. The big collar stood luxuriously up around her smiling, sparkling face, and its close-held skirt hugged her thighs. Ryan thought of mink and sable and some of the other furs that wealthy dames were always being robbed of. He was quite sure it was not one of those, but it was pretty close.

"Like it?"

"Sure. It's—it's terrific."

She turned, modeling it. It was hard to tell whether the coat made her look better, or whether she made the coat look as opulent and chic as it did, but whichever it was the effect was overwhelming. She had always looked too pretty or too...too big-time for him, he thought in sudden dispirit. A guy with a lot of flash, like Sandalwood, was more her style. Ryan would have been stunned to learn that Gee Gee felt hurt because he had not called her, and because he now was not being as enthusiastic as she had hoped.

She slipped out of the coat. "That's all of the fashion show," she said lightly; "I just thought you might want to see it. It's—it's the first *good* coat I've ever owned."

"It's great."

At the door she turned, holding the coat, and said. "You don't know what it's like, growing up in neighborhoods like this, wanting a fur coat—and finally getting it."

She went out.

You'll never get a coat like that on a cop's salary, cookie. But why assume she would ever be dependent on a cop's salary? Still, the idea, and the day's rain, and his anxiety and weariness all helped make him bitter and defeated. When Gee Gee reappeared and said, "Oh, it's silly, but you know in show business you have to put up a front, and a coat like that helps," it did not help at all because Ryan innately disliked people who put up fronts.

When she said, "Will you excuse me a minute?" he said, "Sure," and left alone, had a feeling of guilt, of having been mean without knowing precisely how, and certainly not understanding why.

The plintzen were warm, tender egg pancakes with sugar and cinnamon rolled inside them. The coffee was fresh and fragrant. As they ate, she said, "That reminds me. Will you be through at midnight?"

"Far as I know. Why?"

"Because you're invited to a party."

"A party?"

"At the club. This is Max's birthday, and after the last show tonight he's giving a party for the whole staff and their husbands and boyfriends and so on. I thought if you didn't have anything better to do—"

"Sounds wonderful." Then he remembered he'd have to be up early tomorrow morning. There was the guy in the Bronx to work on. And Betty Leonard to see. And the cuff link distributor to locate and question. "Gee whiz. I don't know."

"Don't know what?" Very casually.

"Whether I can make the party. I don't think I can."

"Another girl, Neill?" Quietly.

"Don't be silly. It's—it's business:"

"Police business?"

"Well. In a way. I'm sorry, Gee."

"It's perfectly all right. Don't give it another thought."

"Now don't be like that. I honestly can't help it."

"Of course. I think I can find someone else to invite."

Ryan looked at the table, at its cotton cloth and old-fashioned cruet set, at his plate that was bare except for a few sugar crumbs, and his freshly filled coffee cup. He felt helpless and tortured. He didn't like this; she was getting away from him somehow. Not that she had ever really been his. Yet he was losing her.

"Gee Gee?"

Now it was she who was looking at the cruet set.

"Maybe I better tell you something." But dared he? No. She was a friend of Sandalwood. He said, "I'm in a little jam at the moment. Not too serious. But I've got to work it out. It's—it's about Harry Derby."

"Derby? Why, he's all put away and done with."

Ryan frowned over the cigarette he was lighting. "Well...yes. But still...I can't tell you about it, Gee."

But somehow that relieved her. If it was Derby then it wasn't another girl. Things added up, in a way.

"Neill, I remember that night we met and Ed Jablonski got sort of high and began talking about how you and he had *fixed* Derby. Is it that?"

"I said, I can't tell you about it."

"I remember Ed saying that you two had made a case or something against Derby that no one could break. Is that what's gone wrong?"

"Oh, for God's sake!" The torture suddenly strained his voice. "Listen, forget anything that—that drunken idiot said that night. You hear me? Forget it! And don't repeat it!"

It was the violence more than what he said that hurt her. And his refusal to confide in her. It made her think of overheard parental quarrels. Why did things always have to go like this with someone you really liked?

"So anyway, I can't go to your party," he went on. "You can get somebody else, all right. How about your friend, Sandalwood?"

She was silent.

"Seen him lately?" He spoke mildly, trying to bring the conversation and himself back to normal.

"No." She shook out and lit her own cigarette. "He's been busy, too. He's writing a new series of articles."

"Oh?"

"Something about famous miscarriages of justice."

There it was, once more. He would never escape it.

"Oh, fine." He added, "Maybe I'll get in the papers again," before he thought.

"What?"

He shouldn't have said that. "Do you like him. Gee?"

"Not especially. But he's not too bad. And he's press, you know. That's important in show business."

"Another part of the front to keep up?"

She flushed. "So what? I want to get somewhere in my business, just as you do in yours. Soon as that coat's paid for, I'm starting dramatic lessons with one of the best coaches on Broadway."

But the coat came first, he thought bitterly. He got up, knowing that somehow he had been cutting his own throat, and feeling helpless about how it might have been avoided. "The pancakes were wonderful."

"Glad you liked them." From a cool distance.

"I really would like to be there tonight."

"Well, come if you can make it." The distance did not diminish.

He knew he wouldn't get there, and he knew that a breach of unfriendliness was deepening between them. Walking toward Eighth Avenue he felt the rain's thousand prods on his damp shoulders. They did not make him feel worse.

In the apartment that he had left the telephone rang and Gee Gee, busy clearing the table, stopped to answer it.

"Baby?" said a sleepy voice. "This is Jack. Look. I've been working my head off all week on that lousy series. I feel like coming up for air. How about a long lunch at the Harwyn?"

Well, why not? What did she owe Neill Ryan? And when would she see him again? And when did she want to?

"Sounds lovely," she said into the phone.

Even so, she felt a little guilty about putting the film-like plastic rain cape over her new coat. And going out in it.

* * * *

"On a day like this?" said Sandalwood. "Of course you must have another. I'm going to." He signaled to the waiter standing at alert attention just out of earshot. "Two more Martinis on the rocks. We'll look at a menu after that."

Why not? Gee Gee thought. What was there to do until dinner? And maybe she could learn something for Neill. Instantly she asked herself: why should she bother?

"But you have work to do. My day doesn't begin until evening."

"I beat that typewriter for four hours this morning," said Sandalwood. "That's enough for one day. From here in I coast." He grinned lazily at her.

"How's the series coming?"

"Oh, all right. I could write it in my sleep. They are old cases that everyone should remember but doesn't—I hope. People who were executed and later proven innocent, guys who served twenty years and then someone else confessed to the crime. You know."

The waiter put down two enormous glasses.

"They are all *old* cases? No—no recent ones?" She tried to speak inconsequentially.

Sandalwood, sprawled in his chair, liked this expensive place and the gin's warm comfort, and the looks of the girl across from him. He felt luxurious and relaxed. But for years he had made his living by catching nuances in what people said to him, by daring to guess at what they meant and by probing imaginatively for more. It was a kind of intellectual short-circuiting and was one of the reasons Sandalwood was a great reporter. Now he had caught something.

"Oh, there'll be a few modern ones," he said, although it wasn't true. The Derby case was something apart, a private interest of his own.

He was too old a hand to look up and watch how Gee Gee took that. Instead he studied his new drink and added significantly, "There'll be one or two *quite* recent ones, in fact," and saw her fingers tighten on her glass.

Suddenly she was afraid of him—for Ryan's sake. He was too wise, too able, too knowing.

And Sandalwood had caught her alarm. But what was she scared of, he asked himself. What was on her mind? He rehearsed the calendar of recent crime; there hadn't been anything of importance involving nightclubs or entertainers. But she was a friend of Neill Ryan.

Sandalwood raised his glass to her, said "Here's to us," and looked at her over the rim. "One of the recent cases in the series will be the Harry Derby case," he said, watching.

Gee Gee raised her glass hurriedly. "The Derby case?"

"Sure."

That was it. It was cat-and-mouse now.

"But—Derby was guilty. He's been convicted."

"Oh sure." He smiled superiorly.

"You mean—what do you mean? There's more to it?"

"I'll say there is." And he was sure he was right, although he did not know where this was leading him. But he was on the right track.

"And *you* know all about it?"

Sandalwood gave no sign that he appreciated the emphasis on that "you."

"I'm a reporter, cutie."

"Well, then," she said helplessly, "you know."

What would this do to Neill? For even in her moment of alarm she felt a surge of warmth for him. He *had* had something on his mind, after all. He way in trouble. It hadn't been another girl.

What was he supposed to know, Sandalwood wondered. And, equally important at the moment, where did her sympathies lie? He said, "This could cause a lot of trouble for your friend Ryan."

"Well, whatever it is," she said instantly, "you can be darned sure it wasn't Neill's fault."

"'Whatever it is,'" he repeated. "Don't you know what it is?"

"No, I don't, but I know this. It was all that damned Ed Jablonski. I remember the night they arrested Derby, he was boasting afterward about how they'd fixed Derby good. I know that Neill is not the kind to…"

Sandalwood wasn't listening. *Fix him good.* That didn't sound like taking a little money from a prisoner. But he had never put much stock in that idea, anyway. What was it, then? Some kind of frame?

He remembered Ryan's guilty start when he came on him up in the old brownstone's bedroom.

"…and if anything happens it will be poor Neill who'll suffer," Gee Gee was spying. "It's not fair." She looked meltingly at Sandalwood. "Unless you give him a break in your story. That could help, couldn't it?"

"Sure, it could," he said. He had enough for now. He had a lead. *Don't press, Jackie boy.* And there was no doubt about where she stood. But maybe there was a way to make her open up a little more next time, in case she should learn more from Ryan.

"You seem to think a lot of Ryan," he smiled at her. "It sort of surprises me—the way he's been seeing Harry Derby's sister lately."

"What?" said Gee Gee. "Derby's sister?"

"Care to order now, sir?" the waiter asked.

"Why not?" said Sandalwood.

He felt good, and very wide-awake. And voraciously hungry.

CHAPTER 22

The Girl in the White Jaguar

Someone who knew what a chisel was made for had been prying open automobile windows in the east fifties, mostly near hotels where out-of-town visitors parked on arrival and left their bags. It sounded like a team of three, two to get into the car quickly and a third in another car to pick up the loot. Bauer mentioned it when the afternoon tour gathered in the squad room.

"They haven't hit for five days and they're about due. They may figure the rain'll help them. Lee, you and Neill cruise as far up as Fifty-seventh. Take your meal period after nine, because they haven't been doing anything after nine o'clock. Harry, you and Al do the same about Fifty-seventh until you get a call."

For the next hour Lambert and Ryan shuttled back and forth in a well-worn Plymouth sedan through wet, shiny side streets from Fifth Avenue to Third, saying little, listening whenever the hoarse radio rasped into communication. They had worked together long enough so that they did not have to say much. Lambert was driving, inching and stopping and inching again through the dense traffic of a gloomy, rainy afternoon. They both scanned the parked cars for luggage that would attract thieves.

A frustratingly long line of cars had halted them in Fifty-second Street when Lambert touched Ryan's arm. Twenty-five yards ahead of them two men in dark overcoats were standing, hardly sheltered from the rain, against the wall of a building. In front of the two men a yellow Cadillac convertible was parked. One of them kept looking down the street in the direction from which Ryan and Lambert had come.

Lambert said mildly, "They seem to like it in the rain."

Ryan unlatched his door. "Probably their car's behind us," he said, and slipped out of the Plymouth. He walked back a few car lengths, then reached the sidewalk. From here he could not see the men so well; a restaurant's well-lighted canopy over the street interfered with his vision.

The traffic in the street began to crawl again, taking Lambert with it. Ryan studied the cars coming up behind. Two cabs, then a glossy Buick fresh from a garage, then a small white sports car—it would be none of those.

But behind the white Jaguar were two nondescript sedans. Ryan strolled toward the bright canopy and the two men beyond it. The Jaguar had pulled up before the restaurant canopy and the garage attendant who had delivered it took the parking slip from the doorman on duty. Ryan looked again for the two men; one had walked over near the Cadillac and was still looking west down Fifty-second Street. The first sedan had gone past, but the second one blinked its lights.

This looked good. And by now Lambert must be at the corner.

Ryan moved forward—and collided with the doorman coming out of the restaurant, hurrying with an open umbrella. "Watch it, Mac," said the doorman. Immediately behind him came a copper-haired girl in a new, glossy fur coat with a film-like rain cape over it. She was followed by a hatless man in a gray sport jacket. He was laughing. "Thanks, Joe," he said to the doorman. A dollar bill appeared between their hands.

The doorman opened the Jaguar's door and held the umbrella over it. Ryan forced his mind away from the fact that she was the girl who had just told him she hadn't seen Sandalwood lately. He made himself look ahead. The two men were near the Cadillac.

He hurried across the bright canopy. She was getting into the little car's jewel-like interior. The second sedan that had blinked its lights had stopped alongside the Cadillac. The two men walked around the Cadillac without touching it and started to get into the sedan. Ryan came up behind them.

"Where you been?" said one.

"Ethel made me drive her to the employees' entrance," said the driver. The door closed on them.

Ryan walked up to the corner where Lambert had pulled in near a hydrant.

"False alarm." He got back into the car.

"Next time lucky," said Lambert.

So she couldn't wear that coat out in the rain, huh?

* * * *

Ryan called in at nine to say that everything was quiet and that they were taking their meal period at the Polish sausage restaurant. All evening he had fought the thought of Gee Gee and Sandalwood being together. Sergeant Weiner said, "Wait a minute. Your mother phoned and said to tell you Connie called."

"Who?"

"Connie. She said you had called her earlier."

"I get it."

"Call her at this number."

He kept Lambert waiting while he called the barber. "Connie? This is Ryan."

"Yeah. About that party you were asking about. He left town in November. Quite sudden."

Ryan's worry and weariness left him. "What date was that?"

"I can't get it exactly, not so far. I'll keep tryin'. But it was well before Thanksgiving. Because he paid a—a person I been talkin' to some money he had owed him a long time. This person says it was about two weeks before Thanksgiving. I looked that up on a calendar. Thanksgiving came on a Thursday."

"It usually does."

"Yeah? Well, this one was Thursday the twenty-fifth."

That could figure. If Mackie had done it and had heard of Derby's immediate arrest he would feel relieved. Naturally. But after a few days he would start worrying. He would wonder if the cops weren't putting out a newspaper phony to lull the real killer... Then he might worry himself right out of town.

"How much did he owe this person?"

"Two hundred bucks. He paid him only a hundred, though."

God! This was coming too fast. *Derby* had still had the hundred dollar bill.

"You know this Mackie?"

"A little. I used to box at his place."

"Box?"

"His joint is part Turkish bath and part health club. Or it used to be. A few fighters trained there, prelim boys and like that."

"Remember any of them? Or do you know anyone who might have heard from him recently?"

"I dunno who'd of heard from him. The old man who helps him. Or that screwy kid who gives out the towels, maybe. I dunno who else. I hear when he left, Mackie said he was going to visit his mother in Chicago." Connie sniggered. "I'll bet she lives in a kennel."

"Who else did he know?"

"I'm telling you, boss, I don't know. I ain't seen Mackie in three years myself. Maybe five. Today—hey, I know one. And you do too. That guy who's gonna burn in Sing Sing."

"Who?"

"That guy Derby," said Connie. "What's his name—Harry Derby? The one who killed the old lady. Sure. He wanted to be a fighter. I've gone more than a few rounds with him at Mackie's. Mean, he was. But Mackie always thought he'd make a fighter."

Ryan said, "Can you think of anyone else?" but it was only habit. He didn't listen to the answer.

When he climbed into the car, Lambert said, "They had something for us, huh?" disappointedly. He was hungry.

"No. I had to call home. Sorry."

But when they were both seated in the restaurant, Ryan could not think of food. All he could think of was Sandalwood and Gee Gee, and how little time he must have left, and the facts Connie had given him that twirled and flittered in his mind like a deck of cards in a gale.

"Lee, do me a favor? I'm not hungry. And I've got an errand to run."

"Sure," said Lambert. Ryan had had a phone call. He was a nice-looking kid and unmarried. "Better gimme an address."

Ryan knew what Lambert thought, but it didn't matter. He gave an address twelve numbers away from the Derby apartment. "Blow two long and two short if we get a call." He would be able to hear it from that close.

"I won't unless I have to," Lambert grinned.

* * * *

She said, "What I don't understand is why the fingerprint at the drugstore didn't tell the police right away that Harry committed the—that robbery." She was sprawled back on the day bed in the tight slacks. Her hair was pulled tight in a pony tail. She looked young and thoughtful.

"Everyone thinks fingerprints are a big thing," said Ryan. "Actually they're valuable mostly after you've made the collar. If even a partial print is found at the scene, and then you make an arrest, you can tell fast whether the suspect is your man. But what good is one fingerprint in itself? Individual prints are not classified by themselves. The whole system of fingerprint identification is based on getting a complete set— it's only the habitual criminal or specialist whose individual fingers are classified. Say you go over a safe job and find one left thumbprint. You look at the file of left thumbprints of habitual box men. Then maybe you make it.

"But we can't file and classify all ten prints of every guy who ever hit a drugstore. If Harry had been arrested in the drugstore job, then that print would have helped us make him fast. But no one could go through all the sets of prints on file downtown to find one that matched. It would take forever. Don't put your trust in fingerprints. For one thing we don't often find them, no matter what you see on television."

He sipped the Coke she had insisted he take, and which he had accepted because he knew she wanted to be a thoughtful hostess. Ken would be home soon, she had said. Ryan was glad he wasn't there now.

"What I really wanted to ask you about," he said, "was what you might remember of the day that—that Mrs. Connors was murdered. And also about a guy named Mackie."

"Mackie?"

"Big Mackie, he's usually called. He runs some kind of athletic club near Fifth Avenue. Ever hear Harry mention him?"

"I don't think so. Harry tried boxing once, though, ten years ago or so. Maybe Ken would know. He'll be along any minute."

"I can't stay much longer." He looked at his wrist. "One other thing. I wish you would tell me everything you can remember that happened here the day of the murder."

"Happened? Here?"

"I won't try to explain. Please." He was oppressed by time's swift passing.

"Well." She drew on her cigarette and considered. "Harry was staying with us then."

"Didn't he always?"

"Harry came and went. Sometimes he roomed alone. Sometimes he—he stayed with a friend." Ryan caught the intonation's meaning. "When he was broke he often came here for a few days or a week at a time. He slept on this couch."

Ryan listened to a car braying outside. It wasn't a Plymouth.

"That's how it was that day. I remember Ken woke Harry up when he was getting ready to go to work, and Harry got mad. I remember him swearing he'd find some other place to stay where he could get a night's sleep. But they'd been arguing the night before; this was just a continuation."

"What about?"

"The night before? They'd argued about money. Harry had some sort of chance to buy into a little gum vending machine business. He could have swung it with five hundred dollars. He wanted Ken to lend it to him."

"And Ken wouldn't?"

"Ken didn't have it. He helps keep this place going. And he's got a girl who—who likes to go out and spend money."

How about you? Ryan wondered. Don't *you* ever want to go out and spend money? Or is your whole life just looking clean and working in a library?

She misinterpreted his look. "Really, I know Ken didn't have it," she said emphatically. "If he had, he'd have loaned it to Harry. He was awfully anxious for Harry to go straight. It—they had a strange relationship, Ken and Harry. They liked each other and sometimes I've thought each one took a kind of vicarious pleasure in the other's goodness or badness. Harry was proud of Ken, I know. He used to kid him about looking like a traffic cop in his uniform. And I suppose Ken sometimes admired Harry's wildness."

"Yeah. What else happened that day?"

"Well, I straightened the house and got breakfast—Ken leaves a lot earlier than I do—than I *did*. I didn't get to work until ten. So I made breakfast for Harry and me, and Harry was still here when I left. That's the last I saw of him. You—you arrested him that night."

"Did he get any phone calls that morning? Or the night before?"

"No."

"Or have any visitors?"

"No. He and Ken just argued." She said it matter-of-factly, but in that monotone Ryan heard the shouts and curses that had echoed in these quiet walls.

"That's how they always were. Emotional. Pulling and tearing and yanking at each other. And liking each other underneath. Ken wanted to borrow Harry's jacket that day—his uniform was at the cleaner's. Harry told him to—to go to the dickens." Ryan could imagine what Harry had said.

"The checkered jacket?"

"That's right."

Hell, thought Ryan. What was he getting—a stronger case against Harry? In these few minutes he had confirmation that Harry had needed money that day, was in an ugly mood and had his telltale jacket. "Tell me this. Did you ever see a cuff link like this?" He took it from his wallet.

She looked long and carefully. "No. I never did."

"Harry never had cuff links like that?"

"No. I don't ever remember seeing them."

Outside a Plymouth honked, then honked again. The apartment door opened.

"Ken?"

"Hi, kid. How's tricks. I just got a big—" He caught sight of Ryan. "Well, well." He grinned and held out a hand. "Hi. I'm sorry about the other night. Any hard feelings?"

"No hard feelings."

Ken Derby pulled off the black whipcord jacket, unclipped the shiny leather bow tie from his shirt collar, and unbuttoned the collar. Then he rubbed his jaw. "That's quite a right you got," he said amiably. "Quite a right."

"Thanks. I was lucky, too."

"How about food, Rosie? Listen, I know a good right when I see one. I used to box. I still follow the fights on television."

"Where'd you box?"

"Down at Mackie's. With Harry."

Ryan had a sense of things falling exactly into place.

Rosemary said, "There's liver and bacon."

"Mackie's?"

"That'll be fine." Ken looked at Ryan. "This'd be a long time back."

The Plymouth honked again.

"You familiar with Mackie's?"

"Sure. Why not?"

Something began taking shape in Ryan's mind. "I'm working to try to clear your brother."

"So Rosie told me. If I can help…"

"Can you keep your mouth shut?"

"If it'll help Harry," said Ken doggedly, "I can keep my mouth so damned shut—"

"Good. Because there's a chance—just a bare chance, according to some information I have—that this guy Mackie killed the old lady Harry got sent up for."

Ken's expression was eloquent. "Listen. If that's so and I can help prove it—"

"It's a long shot, and besides I've still got a lot of things to check." He waited for another bleat from the car below. "I understand Mackie has living quarters above his joint, right?"

"He used to have an apartment on the third floor."

"Could you draw me a plan? And show me how to get into the living quarters?"

Ken Derby put hands on knees and leaned forward earnestly. "Listen. I know the joint and I'll draw all the plans you want. If you're trying to spring Harry, there's nothing you can't ask me."

Finally it came, a loud impatient entreaty.

Ryan jumped guiltily. "I've got to go. Listen, draw that plan. Although I can't get back for it until after midnight."

"You come any time you want," said Derby. He held out a hand. "It'll be ready and so will I. If getting into Mackie's joint will help, you're as good as in."

"Okay," said Ryan. "I just want to frisk it. Okay. But keep your mouth shut."

When he reached the street a tawny Plymouth convertible was panting at the curb across the way. The boy in it leaned impatiently on the horn. Lambert was nowhere in sight. Ryan grinned. This half hour had been better than food.

CHAPTER 23

Liniment Scent

They were drinking coffee around a dining-room table, late. Ken Derby gestured toward the sheets of paper before him, each bearing a neatly drawn diagram. "I haven't been there for quite a few years, you understand," he said. "But that's how it was when I hung there."

Ryan sipped the coffee Rosemary had made. It was one-thirty. She had talked a few minutes and then gone to bed because she had a job interview coming up in the morning. Ryan said, "But you don't know anything about the top floor?"

"The building was originally a laundry. That was on the street floor, of course. The top floor ought to be basically like the second. We can find our way."

"We?"

Determination made Ken Derby's face almost as thinly mean as his brother's. "I want to go," he said. "If I can't help, at least I can't do any harm. I know the place, and you're going to be operating alone. And I'll tell you this." He looked up suddenly, levelly, at Ryan, and Ryan heard the emotion in Derby's throat. "If there's anything I can do to save my brother, I want to do it. Believe me."

"The chances," said Ryan, "of Mackie being our guy are probably one in a hundred thousand. All I know at the moment is that he looks something like Harry, and—but there's another guy in the Bronx—"

Ken Derby's face narrowed with earnestness.

"Wait a minute. Maybe the odds aren't quite one in a hundred thousand."

"What do you mean?"

"This Mackie could look like Harry. Sure. But what I was thinking was, he's a tough guy, in a queer way."

"A fag?"

"No. Well, I dunno, now that you ask. He hates women, that's for sure."

"He's got a record along that line."

"I guess he has been pinched for mugging women at that. But what I mean is, Mackie's always been against dames. He used to tell jokes about dames, jokes where they got beat up, or something. Tell you something else. Nobody ever saw Mackie with a broad."

"But right now he's out of town."

"He is?"

"He left soon after Mrs. Connors was killed."

Ken Derby whistled softly. "Hey, if you could extra—What is it? Extradite him? Get him back here. And—"

"From where?"

"From *where*, for God's sake! From wherever he is."

"That may be Chicago," said Ryan, "but I doubt it."

"You don't know?"

"That's one reason I want to frisk his joint." He rose. It was almost two a.m. He was dead tired and the days were growing fewer.

Ken Derby got up. "I'll go with you."

"No, you won't," said Ryan. "This is police business."

Derby looked malevolent. "Yeah? Like hell it is. The police department isn't doing anything for Harry. You're swinging it, all alone. Like I said, maybe I can help and maybe I can't. But he's my brother. And you're my friend."

Ryan was ashamed to find he wanted company. "Okay," he said.

The cab dropped them in front of a bar two blocks away from Mackie's place. Derby suggested a quick drink but Ryan curtly told him no. They walked down the shadowy street to a point opposite the narrow, inconspicuous building that housed Mackie's business and home. It was dark and so were the taller buildings on either side.

"Funny," said Derby. "He used to stay open all night."

"Subway rides used to cost a nickel," said Ryan. "I thought you *knew* this place."

"I do. But Mackie or somebody was always here this time of night. Maybe the kid who helps him has been goofing off. Or the old man."

"Maybe." Ryan strained his eyes across the dark street. "An old man?"

"An old white-haired coot." He sounded anxious. "The sign was *always* on nights!"

Nuts with it. Either you hit or you quit.

"You sure about that back door?"

"Dead sure."

"Then stay here. I'll call you."

Ryan walked boldly across the street. There was no one in sight, but he knew well that the chance of his being observed was not a small one. He got to the other sidewalk, found a space between the buildings, moved into it—and saw a light moving up behind him. He wheeled and crouched in the shadow. A white-marked police car rolled by. For the first time in his life he knew how it felt to be on the other side.

The RMP car went on and Ryan looked around. Ken Derby was nowhere in sight. He had ducked fast and expertly. It must run in the family, Ryan thought contemptuously, then remembered Rosemary. That hadn't been fair.

He got around to the back, walking boldly in blackness. There was a cellar door, as Derby had said. He found the old-fashioned knob, then felt the key plate and keyhole. Above them he fingered the cold circle of a barrel lock. Ryan took out a thin-bladed Swiss knife that his father had carried and made sure the old bolt was not in place. Then he took some wrinkled wires from his wallet and worked on the barrel lock. The third wire made a click and the door knob twisted open. Wet, heavy air poured out, hot with steam.

Ryan advanced into it, closed the door and listened. There was a hissing noise and a steady, rhythmic dripping. And the tropic, humid heat of the equator at noon, and the strong scent of liniment and cheap soap. After a few minutes of uncertain silence, he flashed his pencil light around. This was the boiler room; there was a furnace and a boiler with gauges. And this was breaking and entering in the night time, a felony for anyone. A disaster for a cop.

He silently retraced his steps and when he found the sidewalk empty, he whistled softly. Derby ducked swiftly across the street and followed him to the back door.

"We're in. Maybe there's no one here. Maybe not. I want the upper rooms where Mackie lives."

"I can find 'em."

Ryan closed the door silently. Steam and soap-scent warmly enveloped them.

The second floor stank of stale liniment. Ryan's small light showed boxing gloves, tied in pairs on nails along a wall, a sandbag and two punching bags, and an elevated ring with little stools below at one corner. Beyond were doors that would lead to sleeping and dressing rooms and showers.

"How about the third floor?"

"We go back to the stairs," said Derby. "I never been up there."

"Lead the way."

They went up narrow stairs. There was a door at the top of a small landing. It had no barrel lock, and when Ryan used his knife blade for a minute along the frame, it opened. Once inside, he listened carefully, then felt for a light switch and flipped it. They saw a small, dark living room, heavily draped and massively furnished, and illuminated with big lamps whose shades dripped thick gold fringe. In corners large bronze statues gleamed; all portrayed naked athletes.

"Aren't you taking a chance with that light?"

Ryan went to the room's two windows, pulled down the shades and drew the drapes. "I'm taking a chance being here at all," he said.

"Yeah. What should I do?"

"Stand by the door and listen in case someone starts poking around."

Ryan pushed his hat back on his head characteristically. There were two doors at the back. One led into a kitchen, the other into a bathroom. Where did the guy sleep? Then he saw another door.

But he took the kitchen first. The cupboards, half empty, held only a few dishes and the usual staples. The refrigerator contained a half bottle of milk turned to moldy cheese, a can of tomato juice and some eggs. He looked over the stove, into its oven, and pulled it out from the wall.

In the bathroom he examined the contents of the medicine chest and then flashed his light in the toilet tank box. He felt around the back and underneath surfaces of the washbowl and tub for anything stuck or hidden there.

There was a scraping noise from the other room. Ryan froze. He waited to hear from Derby.

He did not hear. He waited.

He did not hear anything.

He went to the door, flicked out the light so as not to be silhouetted, decided against drawing his gun, and peered into the living room. Derby stood still at the door, looking out into the hall.

Was someone holding a gun on him?

Ryan waited another moment. Then he whispered, "Derby!"

Silence.

Ryan took out his gun. He reminded himself that a gun was the worst thing he could use here. He walked into the living room.

Derby wheeled nervously.

Ryan said, "What was that?"

"I thought I heard something." Derby's whisper was husky.

"It came from out there?"

"It came from somewhere!"

Ryan went to the living-room door that was still open, and flashed his light out. There was nothing on the stairs.

"Maybe the bedroom," said Derby. Ryan looked around.

"I heard *something*," Derby insisted.

Ryan had heard it too. He went, gingerly, silently, to the bedroom, gun ready, and switched on the light beside the door. It was a small, pale-blue room with a single bed. Ryan studied it, then searched it. There was a small desk slanted across one corner with a telephone and old magazines on it.

That might be where he'd find what he needed. But first... Derby peered in.

"Watch that door!"

Derby straightened, said "Check," and went back.

Ryan felt behind the pictures on the walls. He got under the bed and explored its springs with his light. He looked at the hair brush and the other toilet articles on the bureau, and shook out the magazines on a small table. He up-ended a floor lamp, looked at its base, then critically examined its shade. Finally he lifted all the drawers out of the bureau carefully, and slowly and inspected their contents: several shirts and socks rolled into balls, a couple big sweaters, a sheaf of physical culture magazines, some blankets.

And, with the blankets, a heavy woolen; black-and-white checked lumberjack shirt.

The checks were not as big as those on Harry Derby's jacket, as he well remembered. And it was a shirt, not a jacket. But witnesses in the excitement of the moment could have made that mistake. Ryan fingered it unbelievingly.

The telephone rang.

Ryan looked to the desk. The phone rang again. He glanced out the door at Derby. Derby was watching him and looked scared. The phone rang again.

Ryan went to the desk and picked it up. "Hello?" He held his voice low and indistinct.

"St. Louis calling—one moment please." Then, "Ready with New York, sir."

"Hello," said Ryan.

A man's voice rasped in the receiver. "Damn it, Bobbie, how many times do I have to tell you how to answer the phone?"

Ryan waited.

"'Mackie's Baths!'" the voice quoted testily. "If I've told you once, I've told you a million times how I want the phone answered."

Ryan took a chance. "Yes, sir."

"How's business?"

"Fine," said Ryan.

"That's good. Bob?"

"Yes?"

"How's everything?" The tone grew guarded.

"Everything's good," said Ryan. He held the mouthpiece away from his face, so he could not be heard well. "Everything's okey doke." He took a chance. "You in St. Louis?"

Derby watched wondering from the door.

"Yeah. But I may fly into town tomorrow."

"Good."

"You sure you don't hear anything?"

"Everything's quiet as all hell," said Ryan. "Come on home."

"I got it all paid off but the one, and that'll be arranged this week. But meanwhile I don't want the big man on my neck."

"Come on home," said Ryan tensely. "You'll be okay. I heard today the big man ain't—ain't mad at nobody." It was taking a chance.

But the other end of the line chuckled with appreciation. "You're a good kid, Bobby. But where were you earlier? There was no answer."

"I went out for a little while. I felt like a beer."

"A *beer!*" said the other incredulously. Ryan knew that had been a mistake.

"When'll you get in?" he asked quickly.

"After dinner tomorrow night," the other replied angrily. "See that you're there! When did you start drinking beer?"

He had to take the real chance. He had to know who he was talking to. "I was kidding, Mister Mackie," he said. "I'll be here."

The telephone chuckled more happily. "Don't hand me any Mister business."

They rang off. Ryan turned from the phone. He could not believe it had happened. Derby was still watching from the door. "Huh?" he said.

"God," said Ryan.

"Who was that?"

"Mackie. He's in St. Louis. But he's flying in tomorrow. Or today. Or whatever the hell time it is."

Derby's wide eyes fixed on Ryan. Then his face lighted up. "Jesus!" he yelled. "We *got* him!"

"Shut up," said Ryan. "That kid may be back any minute."

The bureau drawers were still on the floor. He began to lift them back into the bureau. Habit and training reminded him to run his hands around their bottoms and backs. That's how he felt the little Scotch-taped protuberance on the back of one.

He turned the drawer around. Then from its rear panel he yanked the small object taped to it.

It was a cuff link. Ryan recognized its miniature scimitar pattern instantly. But he looked a long time at it. All he could think of was that this is what comes of living right.

"Let's go," said Derby. "Want some help?"

Ryan did not answer. He re-taped the link into place and restored the drawers after inspecting each one. There was nothing taped to the others.

He went through the desk. It was full of letters tied in ribboned bundles, to Lester Mackie from his mother. And old receipted bills. And boxes of nails, and pins and loops of string. Mackie was a saver.

Thank God for that, he thought, recalling the cuff link.

They went down the narrow, liniment-smelling stairs in silence. As they groped through the boiler room, Derby said, "You think he'll show up?"

"He's got to," said Ryan. And the way things were going, it was true. Maybe things were going *too* good. Still, he was filled with the glow of imminent triumph.

Ryan insisted on walking several blocks south and west before hailing a cab. He dropped Derby at his home, noticed it was almost three-thirty and realized he was famished. After all he'd been moving at high speed for almost twenty-four hours—and getting places! He was entitled to a sandwich and maybe a beer. But where could he go? Then he thought of Gee Gee's party.

It shocked him to realize how long she had been out of his mind, especially considering the circumstances in which he last saw her. He'd told her to get someone else for the party, and he had a pretty good idea who that would be. And this was the girl he had almost told about Derby! What might she have told Sandalwood?

Well, why not go to the party, and find out? It would sure surprise her. Ryan grinned without humor.

"I want to go to a joint between Fifth and Sixth," he told the cab driver. "On Fifty-second."

"One of the strip joints?" said the driver. "We gotta hurry, Jack. It's almost closing time."

CHAPTER 24

The End of That

Ryan was led to a tiny table while a raucous band crashed and tub-thumped its way to the end of a song. He was barely seated when an unseen voice told the customers, in sibilant confidence through a public address system, "And now, friends, the concluding number…the star of our show… Maxie's Rendezvous is proud to present for your enjoyment… that titian-haired temptress of the dance…lovely *Gee Gee Hawes!"*

She appeared from somewhere near the bandstand, looking tall in a gown of long white pleats that was like a negligee. Not only her hair but her eyelids sparkled with sequins and her lips were parted expectantly. She wasn't the lissome, natural girl in the brown coat now, but self-consciously glittery and sure, enameled and eager. Ryan sipped beer as she undulated around the dance floor. He had not expected her to be so professional. She slipped unexpectedly out of part of her dress and her jeweled bra was small and revealing.

A man at the next table said, "Jeez, Lili can take a night off any time she wants." He saw Ryan looking at him. "Lili St. Cyr's sick tonight," he explained. "This dame's a substitute. Not bad, huh?"

"Not bad," said Ryan.

The music increased in volume and tempo, slowly. Gee Gee glided around the floor, gradually freeing or losing garments. The spotlight grew deeper blue, until it was hard to tell whether what was visible was cloth or shadow. Then men at the next table made comments. Ryan tried to disregard them.

Finally, in a flare-up of music she disappeared near the bandstand, and there was a jet roar of applause. She reappeared briefly, the white dress held in front of her. She took several bows. Even the musicians grinned. The show was over.

"Chef's left, Mac," the waiter said to Ryan. "No steak sandwich. I can get you a nice ham on rye."

"I'll take it. And another Prior's dark."

The orchestra played a final number, then went back stage. The lights went up. Ryan looked around. No Sandalwood. Was he back stage? The customers finished drinks and began leaving. The waiter brought the sandwich and Ryan munched hungrily. His eyes were on the door near the bandstand. Other girls came through it dressed for the street, but instead of leaving they sat down at tables. Finally Gee Gee appeared. She walked slowly, the new coat draped with affected casualness over her shoulders. Then she saw Ryan.

"Neill!" She came over quickly, smiling. "You made it! I'm so glad."

Ryan grinned and he didn't want to. But seeing her always made him feel like that. Besides—as his weary brain reminded him—he had to find out what had happened. This wasn't a pleasure trip. She should think it was, though, he told himself cynically. "Sit down and have a drink. You must feel like it after all—after your dance."

She looked at him. "You were here for the show?"

"Your part of it. It was terrific."

"You're sweet. But what did you *really* think?"

"I said. Terrific." He looked around. A few people had straggled in and were hailed by those at tables. No Sandalwood. Yet.

Her cool, long-fingered hand closed over his knuckles. "Okay," she said. "Neill, you've got to remember that in this business you don't always do what you want. Maybe in any business."

A waiter came up and Gee Gee said she would take tomato juice. "I gained a pound and a half this week."

Ryan said his beer would do for a while, then brought up the subject on his mind. But a little regretfully. It would have been nice to just sit and talk. "I thought I'd run into Sandalwood. I figured he'd be the one you'd ask to the party."

"He was," she said right back. She thought of what Sandalwood said about Derby's sister. "He had to go up the river today. Tonight, I mean."

Ryan flinched. Up the river could mean many things. But to a policeman and to a police reporter it meant one thing. Up the Hudson River was Sing Sing.

Gee Gee misunderstood his expression. "Oh, honey, why think of him? I don't feel that way about him at all. And maybe there's something I could get mad about too, if I wanted. But there's something I really must tell you that Jack said."

"What?"

The waiter came with the tomato juice. "Have a drink, Neill. You look like you need it. Bring a big Scotch, eh, Benny?"

"Sure, Miss Hawes. You were terrific tonight, Miss Hawes. You killed 'em. You shoulda heard what they said onna way out."

"Thanks, Benny."

"I mean it. When Lili leaves. Max doesn't give you the spot he's crazy."

"Thanks. Benny. You're sweet." The waiter left. "See? I have a public."

"Everybody's sweet tonight."

"Now, Neill, don't be like that. I don't want to quarrel with anyone. Not tonight. This is a big night. Do you know what happened? Lili St. Cyr is the headliner here now. So tonight her manager phoned in that she was sick and Max had to rebuild the show. And who did he put in the top spot?" She was radiant.

"Congratulations." He appreciated her excitement. But he hadn't liked seeing her dance like that, or the artificial sweetness she seemed to be showing everyone. And she'd been talking to Sandalwood.

"There are girls here who've been in the business over three years," Gee Gee went on. "And I'm just getting started. But Max—well, *Max!*"

A man stood over their table, short and purple-suited and dominant. Ryan recognized him from the day in court.

"You were sensational, doll," he said. "Sensational." Pudgy fingers with big rings squeezed her shoulder. "Some people been saying when Lili leaves Saturday night you oughtta replace her." Gee Gee looked up hopefully. He saw the look. "I'm thinking about it."

"Thanks, Max."

"Have your friend stay for the party." Max walked away.

"Thanks, Max," she called after him.

"You forgot to tell him he is sweet."

"Now, lover, don't act that way. This might be my chance. Max isn't so bad."

"What was it you wanted to tell me?"

But waiters began moving the tables around, including theirs, to make one long table.

Apparently everyone had read about Ryan. When Gee Gee introduced him they were very nice, with that combination of friendliness and respect for even a minor public figure that characterizes the stage. They sat at the long table and drank toasts to Max and ate turkey slices and listened to the music. It wasn't the raucous thumping of before; the pianist's fingers had acquired a melancholy delicacy and the trumpet a beautifully timed sadness. Gee Gee raised her face to the horn's golden bell, listening, chin and neck white in the smoky light, and the trumpet player saw her and played straight to her while her red nails tapped rhythm on the tablecloth. The band rambled slowly through "Confessin'," yearned into' "After I Say I'm Sorry," and mourned with "When Your Lover Has Gone." Ryan found his arm around Gee Gee's shoulders.

After a time she sighed and nestled. "What's with you, baby?"

"I'm fine."

"Sure? Not mad?" She was anxious about it.

"Sure," said Ryan. "Not mad." It was almost true. Then Sandalwood's taunting face, the Harwyn's canopy, the white dress held before her at the end of the dance, swam through his mind, and it was a lie.

Her glass was empty and she sipped contentedly from his, which he had not touched. She had to tell him about what Sandalwood had said, but she didn't want to right now; this night was too perfect to spoil. He had come to the party, after all. Everyone had told her how well her act had gone. And she knew it had; she had felt the crowd's electric reaction.

"Baby." She had never called him that before. "You don't like Harry Derby's sister better'n me, do you?" It was a rhetorical question, asked in drowsy confidence that the answer would be the right one.

Behind them the unmuted trumpet took up "Dream," huskily, sweetly.

But raw gasoline had been poured on smoldering coals.

"What else," Ryan demanded, taking his arm away, "did Sandalwood mention today?"

He had never seen her eyes so round. "Why, Neill. Don't get the idea—"

"I've got the idea. Incidentally, Rosemary Derby is a very decent sort of girl. But what did Sandalwood say about her—or me? Today. At the Harwyn Club."

That hit. "How—how did you know that?"

"I'm a cop, you know," said Ryan bitterly. "Just a cop."

She was silent a second. Then, quietly, "Neill? That night you and Ed Jablonski arrested Derby—what really went on?"

"What do you mean?" Ryan demanded truculently. But it alarmed him.

"Because whatever it was, Jack Sandalwood knows about it. And he's going to publish it in his series. He said so. What happened, Neill? Is Derby's sister in it?"

Ryan made a snorting sound. "What'd he tell you?" he asked thickly.

"He didn't tell me anything—and I didn't tell him anything. Except that I knew, whatever it was, that you were not to blame, and that the night we met that damned Jablonski had boasted of fixing Derby and all that."

Oh, God! He could hear it all, just as though he had been there. He knew how Sandalwood had got it out of her, and what he was figuring on, and why he had gone up the river. It was very, very late and the night had grown old and the fatigue was back. And he was beaten.

After many highballs the man sitting across from them had arranged matches in a geometrical pattern on the tablecloth. Now he lit the first match and waited for the next one to ignite. So did Ryan. And there was Sandalwood, all the time. Always ahead of him.

"What does it mean, Neill?"

"Mean? To whom?"

"To you—and me. To us."

"*Us,*" Ryan repeated. "You're not mixed up in it."

She did not answer. The man across the way got his chain of matches burning. They made successive brown spots on the tablecloth.

Ryan reached some obscure conclusion. She had fixed him up, too. The cute kid in the big fur coat. "The hell with it," he said.

It was hardly lucid but she knew what she meant. And even before he could enlarge on it, she answered understanding.

"Sure. The hell with it. You know what, Neill? The night that we met—well, I've been thinking. That night, I got to looking at Inez when she was crying about that slob of a partner of yours. And I remember later, when you tried to kiss me, I thought, 'What's with hanging in clubs?' I thought to myself, 'You fool around joints like this'"—she waved—"'where do you wind up?' And I believed it. But suppose I go along with you, pal?"

The s's were coming out slurred and the "pal" was too loud. Ryan, who had been studiously refusing drinks, realized that Gee Gee had had several. He had never seen her like that.

"Then where do I wind up?" she asked. "With some guy who's never around when you want him, and gets jammed up in some jerky way and won't talk about it, even when you try to help him and everyone else will be reading about it in the paper in a few days. And two-times you with some gangster's sister, and…"

"Sure," said Ryan. It would still take Sandalwood a few days to get the story together and print it. So if he had any chance left at all, he'd better get going. That meant getting some sleep, not the kind that was a luxury or comfort, but the raw commodity that kept you going and thinking straight, and alive. *Fit for duty* was the departmental expression.

Why had he ever thought she was for him?

"Okay," he said. "I never could have taken you to fancy joints like the Harwyn Club. If we'd hooked up, you'd have wound up in Queens, buying groceries at Bohacks and having a baby. Two or three, after a while. No strips. No daiquiris on the ice, or frozen or whatever you call them. No Max." He looked at her. "No Max. And I'll say this. I don't go for dames that let every slob who hires them get cozy—"

The chain of matches had burned out on the tablecloth. The man who had lit it, finding their conversation more interesting, was listening attentively. The pianist drifted into "Avalon."

"Go to hell," said Gee Gee a little hoarsely. "You heard me, buster. You go to hell. No one talks to me like that. I'll work for Max. I'll go to the Harwyn Club if I please. And I'll tell any spying, sneaky son of a bitch cop who thinks he's going to tell me—" She flung her glass's contents, backhand, in his direction.

Ryan jumped up to avoid its ice cubes.

But being up, there was no reason to sit down. "I was going to take you home," he said. "I guess I needn't have bothered. Max'll be glad to." There was another full glass near Gee Gee.

The man across was listening so intently that when she picked it up and threw it wildly he did not react quickly enough to dodge this second shower of ice cubes.

Ryan got his hat and stalked out. There was a cab stopped at the Sixth Avenue corner and he got in it.

That ended that.

CHAPTER 25

You Get to Waiting for It

There were gaudy placards on the newsstand where he bought his morning paper a few hours later. They announced the beginning of "Prosecution of the Innocents," a new series by Jack Sandalwood. Ryan apprehensively read the first article over toast and coffee in Grand Central waiting for the Ossining train. In it Sandalwood referred to half a dozen historic miscarriages of justice and to several familiar recent ones, and explained his purpose: to reveal how the courts and the law are less than completely omniscient and just. The name of Harry Derby did not appear. But, Sandalwood concluded, the series would also include some new, unsuspected cases of gross injustice that would stun the reader.

Having hardly touched the toast, Ryan left a tip, paid his check and walked toward the train gate. As he did he felt his burden sag his shoulders and bend his head. If he felt that way now, how would it be this afternoon? And tonight? And tomorrow? Tonight and the possibility it offered seemed remote and hopeless. But Sandalwood was near and overpowering and inescapable. Sandalwood knew all, or certainly most of what he needed to know.

Presently the sun glittered like strewn diamonds on the Hudson, and the landscape that rolled past the train window looked newly raked and tidied. But to Ryan the day was at midnight.

Since Ryan was an official visitor ostensibly on police business, he was to see Derby in one of the second floor attorney's rooms in the death house. In the center of the room was a table with a pad of white paper and some chairs. On the sterile walls were framed etchings. Ryan heard a voice say, "In here!" and Derby came in. The guard remained just outside the door.

Derby looked even leaner, and his face and hands were pale. Yet he also looked healthy and well-knit, and the gray denim shirt and pants were almost dapper. He stared at Ryan a moment, then slouched in one of the chairs. He clasped his hands before him. He did not say anything.

Ryan waited. When there was no sound in the room or outside, he spoke very softly. "I'm not here on police business. This is personal. We framed you a while back. Now I'm going to spring you. I thought you ought to know."

Derby watched his own hands twist.

"You heard me?"

The breath went out of Derby's lungs, but Derby did not look up or speak up.

"Ask your sister. Rosemary."

"Why?"

"Because she knows all about it."

"I mean, why are you doing it?"

"Because you're innocent, for God's sake. I won't let an innocent man go to the chair."

Derby looked up, wary but interested. "How do you know I'm innocent?"

"I know where you were at the time of the crime."

"Like hell you do."

"Think I don't?"

"I know you don't."

"All right. I'll tell you. And if I'm right, you'll tell me."

"I'll tell you nothing."

"Your eyes will." He lit a cigarette. "On the day and at the time Mrs. Connors was murdered you were cracking a drugstore down in the Thirties near First Avenue. You needed dough. You had hoped to buy into a gum-machine business; maybe you thought you'd get part of it that way. You went into this joint, sent the old guy who runs it into the back, then you grabbed what was in the cash register. You ran out, and you made it—easy."

Derby's lynx eyes were still trained on his hands. "Where'd you get all this?"

"What's it matter, if it's wrong?"

Derby said nothing.

"But it's not wrong. Because you left a thumb print on the drawer. And of all the people in the department I'm the only one who could recognize that print if he saw it. I saw it."

Derby was silent.

Ryan said, "Look, Derby. I didn't come up here for a joyride. I came to tell you I realize now what happened."

Derby's glance ranged nervously over the floor's waxed linoleum. Ryan knew what he was thinking: this was a trick. Derby could not readily interpret something like this in any other way. He said, "And the other reason I came was to find out if you could give me any leads on someone who might look like you, or wear a checked jacket, or might have been operating in that neighborhood." Ryan took the last drag on his cigarette and snuffed it out against his shoe sole. "I don't have all day. Let's go."

"What the hell *is* this?" said Derby. "First the reporter. And now you."

"What reporter?"

"Some mutt named Sandalwood," said Derby, and Ryan's empty stomach spasmed. "He was up here late yesterday. What goes on?"

How much did he know now? "What did you tell him?"

Derby's lips twisted their habitual contempt. "I didn't tell him nothing. I told him to come back later, I'd think over his proposition."

"What was that?"

Derby looked at Ryan with cold insolence. "I'll tell you one thing, copper," he said. "That guy knows something. How much, I don't know. But he's not shooting in the dark. Somebody filled him in. He talked about getting me out. Everybody's going to get me out. You—him—even the damn union."

"What does the union say?"

"They had some jerk up here last week. And I got a letter. Everyone says, 'Don't worry, Derby—you'll never burn. We're workin' on new evidence.' Not that I believe the slobs." Derby's laugh was unnatural.

Ryan said, "Why do you think I'm here?"

"I don't know."

"I'll tell you. I want to get any lead I can as to who killed the old lady. And one of the suspects is a guy named Big Mackie. You know him—the guy who runs the boxing joint."

Again Derby looked at his hands. Then he looked up. "Let me tell you something. I been living with this a long time. Ever since that verdict come in, sure. But longer than that. You know me, cop, and I know you. Maybe every now and then I've did something could get me in real trouble. Maybe once or twice it did. Maybe sometimes I was lucky." For a second he glanced at the wall's etchings.

"But after a while you get to waiting for it. And when it happens, you're almost—well, relieved or something. You know what I mean? So don't get too friggin' gay. I ain't too unhappy." Derby's voice had raised momentarily to normal volume.

The guard at the door looked in. "Everything okay?"

"Everything's okay," Ryan said. Then, "Tell me something, Harry. Why'd you take the rap? Even though you didn't know about the fingerprint, you knew there was a chance that the old guy who runs the drugstore could identify you."

Derby laughed. "Gimme a cigarette. And next time bring a carton. You crazy or something? Look at my record. I'm three times gone. If I got tagged for that drugstore thing, I go for life. What difference does it make *when* you die, if you're gonna die in prison? You think I want thirty years in this can? Besides, that Farragut is pretty good, you know. They're still workin' on it for me."

They've sold you down the river and you don't know it. You'll still be expecting a miracle when they shave your head. "Yeah. Sure," said Ryan.

"Anyway, I ain't as dumb as I look. You think I believe this hero play you're making?"

"What are you driving at?"

"You think I didn't read the papers? Think I don't know where framing me got you? Why would you kick all that in the face?"

"Look, Derby, before I'll let you go to the chair I'll tell everything that happened the night we pinched you."

The Adam's apple in Derby's throat rolled as he laughed.

"You think they'd believe you? You think they'd let you talk about that? When they got Derby all buttoned up and another murder written off? You *meathead!*"

Hunger and weariness and most of all defeat began again. Why had he bothered? Why had he started it?

The guard put his head in the door. "About finished?" he asked.

"Big Mackie, for the love of God!" said Derby contemptuously. "How's that screwball mixed up in it? He couldn't hurt anyone but dames."

"Dames?"

"He used to collect pictures of broads being whipped."

"Okay," said the guard, coming in.

"Gimme your cigarettes, if you want to really do something," said Derby.

CHAPTER 26

Steam

That night Ryan and Lambert, among others, were loaned to a Bronx precinct that was anticipating a triangular war between three teen-age gangs. Nothing happened and so after driving and walking unfamiliar streets until one a.m. they were able to return to Fifty-first Street and check in. There was a message for Ryan in Sergeant Weiner's legible scrawl: "Ken called and said your boy is back. Ken is at home."

In the cab that he took simply to save energy Ryan tried to relax. He could not. He kept thinking that luck never lasted forever. They'd been lucky taking Derby. He'd had luck with the Puerto Rican.

And now?

When Rosemary let him in she smiled cheerfully, then her face grew anxious again. Ken sat at the dining-room table, a gin rummy game before him. At sight of Ryan, he swept the cards away. "Let's go."

"Not so fast. What do you know for sure?"

"He got back around seven. I saw him drive up in a cab. I was in the beanery across the street, drinking my fourth coffee." He grinned. "I'd been there since I got through work."

"And then?"

"He went out around eight for an hour or so. Then he came back. That's when I called the precinct."

"He's still there?"

"He was there when I checked at eleven-thirty. At least, lights were on in the apartment."

"Good." Yet he could not help hesitating. Might there not be a better way?—this was a long gamble. Either they shocked a confession out of Mackie, or else he himself could be in the worst jam a cop could get in. But time was running out, with the special assistance of Sandalwood. And Ryan was tired of tiredness and anxiety. He wanted something to end. "Let's hit it."

Rosemary was watching him. "I don't think you'd better."

"Why?"

"I don't feel good about it."

"Nuts," said Ryan. He had hesitated too long already. "But I'll do this one alone."

"No, you won't," growled Ken. "We're in it together now."

At the door as they went out Rosemary rose on tiptoes to kiss her brother. He went on into the hall.

And then, quite unexpectedly, she kissed Ryan. Her lips were cool and fragrant. It was nice.

* * * *

The lights were still on, and the red sign over the door brightly announced, *Mackie's Baths.* "We'll go in as customers." Ryan had decided that earlier. "It'll be simpler."

"The old man will remember us later."

"What he remembers later," said Ryan, "either won't matter at all, or it'll be just a drop in the bucket to everything else."

The old man looked up from a racing form, made his appraisal of them, then lowered his feet from the counter and stood up. "You gentlemen will want beds?" He smiled. His lips were purple from the indelible pencil he had been wetting.

"That's right."

He put down paper and pencil and led them upstairs into a side room containing two blanketed cots. "There's plenty of steam up." He gave them bath sheets and brown envelopes for their valuables. "That'll be seven dollars for the night."

"We'll give it to you when we check our valuables," said Ryan. He made a pretense of taking off his suit coat. The old man went out and downstairs.

"We're the only ones in the joint," said Derby.

"Then let's move before someone else comes in, or that kid that Mackie thought he was talking to." Ryan put his coat on again and examined his gun. "You haven't a gun on you?"

"No."

They crept across the gym and up the stairs to the door of Mackie's apartment. Ryan turned the knob stealthily and the door swung open; it had not been locked. They went in and locked it behind them. Ryan waited a moment, then switched on a lamp. "The bedroom," he said.

They entered it quietly. Light from the living room dimly showed the bed and the desk. From the bed came the regular sighs of deep sleep. Ryan moved to it and took out his flashlight. "Now," he said. He shone the light in the sleeper's face.

It showed a narrow-eyed face, harshly lined and topped by white hair. Blinded by light, the eyes opened to panic. "Who's that?"

Ryan's hand swept under the pillow for a weapon. There was none.

"Police," he said. "You're under arrest for murder, Mackie."

Mackie tried to see beyond the glare of light that Ryan kept in his eyes.

"Did Beef send you?" he demanded. "Is that you, Beef? This is a hell of a way to collect."

"This is the law, Mackie. I'm pinching you for killing the old lady last November. Want to tell me about it and make it easy for everyone?"

"What are you talking about? Lemme see you!" He started to throw the covers aside. Ken Derby reached across Ryan to push Mackie back and when he did Ryan felt a gun bulging Derby's hip pocket. "Start talkin', you," growled Derby.

But Mackie had nerve. He found the chain to his bedlight, pulled it and saw them better.

"What the hell *is* this?"

"Why'd you leave town last November?" said Ryan.

"What's it to you?"

"Why'd you do it?"

"Are you really law?"

Ryan showed his badge.

Mackie said, "I drop a little dough on some races about that time." He sat up. The white hair made him look old, but Ryan could tell it was prematurely white. "Some bookmakers were getting tough. I thought it'd be simpler to get out of town until I could get the dough together to pay them off."

"Did you?"

"They're taken care of now, except Beef Wurtz. I sent word to him tonight I'd be square in a week. That's why I thought—"

Derby pushed Mackie's shoulder contemptuously. "Don't try to hand us that. You killed the old lady to help pay your debts."

"Stop that," Ryan told him. "Get out of bed, you."

Mackie complied slowly. Ryan switched on the room's center light and studied Mackie, a tall, thin figure in pale blue pajamas. But a muscular sinuousness belied the white hair; Mackie probably could punch. His appearance bothered Ryan.

"Why'd you dye your hair?"

Mackie looked indignant. He said, "That's a fathead cop question if I ever heard one. My hair changed two years ago. It just happened. Ask anybody who knows me."

"Walk over to the bureau."

"Why?"

"Walk."

"Get going!" Derby shoved him.

"I told you to lay off," said Ryan. "I'm running this."

Mackie stood at the bureau. "Take out the middle drawer," Ryan said.

Mackie looked puzzled, but he yanked at the drawer. It made an odd scraping noise.

"Put it down on the floor. Now reach around behind it and give me what's stuck there."

Kneeling, Mackie felt around the drawer and encountered the taped link. He pulled it off and looked at it curiously. Then he extended it to Ryan. His eyes were blank.

"This what you meant?"

"That's it."

"What is it?" asked Mackie.

"You know damn well what it is," said Ken Derby. "You dropped it the day you killed the old lady on Sixty-first Street."

"Just a minute, sonny," said Mackie. His eyes became gimlets; for the first time Ryan saw the resemblance between him and Harry Derby. "Maybe this guy's a cop"—he gestured toward Ryan—"I don't know. But I know damned well you're not. You're young Derby."

"So what?" Derby moved ominously forward. Ryan moved with him. He had it now. He had it *all.*

Mackie crouched, his hands moving to a boxer's defense. Derby's left hand went for his gun.

"Put that away, Derby!" Ryan started for his own gun.

"You're not going to frame *me* to save your brother," said Mackie.

Derby's gun came up and Ryan hit his arm; the gun exploded and its slug tore the ceiling. Derby swung the gun around. To Ryan the barrel's opening looked like a tunnel entrance.

"Put it away."

Derby's jaw was set. "I'm going to get a confession out of this guy, whether you like it or not."

"No, you're not. Because he's innocent. All you had to do was to see his face when he found the cuff link. And there's his hair. In the police records, that are four or five years old at least, his description might sound like Harry's. But not since his hair has turned white. No witness would mistake one for the other. And anyway, it sounds like he can prove an alibi for having left town."

Just out of Derby's range of vision Mackie was edging toward the door. Ryan kept talking loudly.

"Last night when I was searching the bathroom. I heard a scraping noise. By the time I looked out, you were over by the door. You said you heard the noise too. But as a matter of fact, maybe you made that noise. Eh, Derby? The same noise that Mackie made when he yanked the drawer out just now? He's right. You were framing him."

Mackie was out the door and forgotten by Derby. Ryan said. "Just one question. Where'd you get the cuff link?"

Derby took a breath. "I found it in the truck," he said.

"A *pair* of them?" asked Ryan. And answered his own question. "Of course, a pair of them. You dropped the other one in the Connors' apartment."

Realization of what Ryan had said swept Derby. He turned and discovered Mackie gone. He moved to the door, turned again and Ryan saw in his face that he knew. So now he would start shooting.

As Ryan simultaneously jumped and crouched to one side, he thought incongruously that he had been right. The luck had run out. He hurled himself forward in a flying tackle and felt a hot sear along his neck even as fire flashed in his face. Then darkness.

Had he been blinded?

On the floor he pulled out his gun, then there was light—a little—from the doorway, and he saw Derby plunge through it.

Ryan jumped up, ran to the door and leveled his gun. But not in time. Derby was making a clatter down the stairs.

Ryan went more quietly after him, his mind working as fast as his body. He had fallen, so Derby might think he was dead or at least unconscious. Now Derby was going for Mackie. If Derby got them both, it would be perfect—for Derby. He could tell the entire story as they had reconstructed it. Mackie, the supposed murderer, would be dead; so would Ryan. Harry could be freed and Ken unsuspected.

That was the one thing he must not let happen.

He leaped down the last few steps. The second floor was empty. From below he heard Derby bellow, "Get away from that phone," and then a shot. He hoped he had won Mackie enough time to get the call through. But he hadn't.

There came the unnatural, animal scream of a man in agony.

Ryan went on. The first floor was hot with vapor. He heard the hiss of steam.

The old man who had admitted them sat on the floor near the telephone, looking puzzled. Blood spilled over the fingers he held to his throat. The telephone instrument dangled from its pay box, and the door beyond, leading into the steam baths, showed no light. But white vapor floated out through it. The hissing became a high keening.

Getting through the door was the critical thing. The light would be behind him. Ryan gathered himself and burst into steaming darkness. He heard the hiss come toward him like a snake and ducked; a searing stream passed above his head. One of them was playing the live steam hose around the room. A second later there came another scream, close. Its horror penetrated his nerve fibers. A gun fired repeatedly and the blasts made a steady, echoing roar in that confined, heavy-aired space. Ryan moved toward the leaping flashes but did not dare shoot. Mackie was nearby, too.

Someone fell to the wet floor heavily, and the hissing became erratic. Whoever had been holding the hose had been hit and now it was free to writhe.

Blinding pain sprayed his ankles; he jumped in agony and cried out.

He bumped a body. A pistol barrel dug his side—and fired. The sound came to him muffled by his own clothing.

Something he had never felt before attacked Ryan's belly; it was nauseated and prickly hot, and cold, all at once.

Deliberately he reached out and felt the jacket Derby was wearing, brought his own gun up, pushed it into Derby's side and pulled the trigger. This was all that he had to do now and he wanted to do it well. He felt himself falling, and as he fired again he aimed upward, to allow for that. He heard Derby's knees hit the floor. He did not hear himself go down. He aimed lower and fired again.

He knew he was dying. He heard a sound and he aimed his pistol in darkness toward the sound and fired its last shots.

Having done all he could, he sank into unconsciousness.

CHAPTER 27

A Word With The Chief Inspector

For an endless time there were white shapes and indistinct voices, and blurs of sound and feeling, and medicated smells. When he became conscious it was so slow and weak a process that he was not conscious of consciousness, or that there had been a change. During the period of a long morning he became gradually aware of a bed and sheets and of a ceiling, of nurses who came frequently and a male voice that called him "old kid" with accented heartiness. Then time separated itself into periods and brought awareness, and Ryan knew he was in a hospital, and that his chest hurt, and sometimes his mother was there, and Eleanor. There seemed to be a great deal of concern about his temperature.

Once he caught the flick of a brown coat out in the hall, and he hoped with sudden illogicality that it was Gee Gee; she must have missed the number on the door and would come back. But she did not, and even while he waited for her to, he realized how ridiculous it was. That was over.

Then one day the doorway darkened and a man in a blue overcoat said, "Neill? Can I come in?" and it was Lieutenant Bauer.

Bauer shook hands and took off his coat, and said in his soft way, "The doctor said we could talk a little. But if you're not up to it, just say so."

"I'm fine."

Bauer sat down. "It's about Derby. Both Derbys."

"Both?"

"Well, mainly Ken. The district attorney's office is anxious that nothing goes wrong with the case. Harry's out on bail."

"On *bail?*"

"Well, Farragut put in quite a plea, and I guess after he spent time in the death house, the court figured maybe he was entitled to a little freedom. You know judges. But he's going up eventually, no doubt about it."

"Paul, tell me something. How'd I get here?"

Bauer looked stunned. "Hasn't anyone told you?"

"This is the first chance I've had to think about it. Yesterday I was kind of groggy."

"*Yesterday?* You've been here nine days, Neill. This is just the first day you've been thinking straight."

Ryan said, "I have?" Then, "I guess Mackie got the call through to the department, eh?"

"No. Mackie never called us. It was an RMP that hauled you out. The boys were cruising the street when they heard the shooting. When they got inside—well, I guess you know better than anyone what they found."

Ryan felt the hot steam on his ankles.

"It's funny you don't remember," said Bauer. "Because after they got you out, you were lucid as anything. You explained the whole case against Ken Derby to one of the uniformed men. Then you conked out."

He shot a quick look at Ryan. "They found the three of you in the steam room with the hose jumping around. Apparently that daffy Mackie had got it out. The old man on the desk was dying of a bullet through the Adam's apple. Mackie was wounded, but not seriously—there were two slugs in him, both from Derby's gun. Your gun was empty. You'd hit Derby twice. Once right through the mouth, and once near the heart. It's a wonder he's alive. Could you see in there, Neill?"

"No."

"You shoot real good by ear."

"An RMP crew?"

"Sure. Derby fired at them, then gave up. They shut off the steam and carried you out."

Ryan felt a wave of gratitude. It had been a department operation after all. He had tried to carry it by himself, but in the end it had taken the department, the alert, ever-present department, that was always ready for trouble and knew how to meet it. Ryan's eyes stung, and he knew from that how weak he was. He hoped Bauer did not notice.

If Bauer noticed he was tactful.

"Under Derby's bed—Ken Derby, that is—we found his bag packed and a ticket to Montreal, and a letter that he was going to mail if the frame against Mackie didn't work."

"He wasn't going to let Harry burn then."

"No. The letter admitted everything. He really liked Harry."

"Sure he did," said Ryan. "You know he came to my house after we pinched Harry and tried to tell me Harry was making deliveries with him on the day of the murder? What a bluff!"

Bauer smiled crookedly. "I don't know. By alibiing Harry he alibied himself, and if the lie was detected, it would always be explained on the grounds of brother loyalty."

A nurse came in and made Ryan drink something cloudy and bitter through a tube. "Only a few minutes more," she warned.

"I better get down to business," said Bauer. "What have you got on it—what first tipped you off?"

Weak as he was, Ryan grinned faintly at how ridiculous it was. "The scraping sound that a drawer made," he said. "That's what did it. All the other indications had been there all the time; I suppose I'd noticed them subconsciously. But it was when I heard the scraping sound again that I realized Ken might have made it scrape the first night we were in Mackie's. And if he had, then he had framed Mackie. Why? To help his brother, of course. And then—it was like a spark jumping a spark gap—why couldn't he have done it *to help himself?* Why couldn't he be the killer?

"He'd been in the neighborhood that day, as D'Tela had made clear. He looked a lot like Harry and could be mistaken for him. He wanted money—for Harry perhaps, but also perhaps for an expensive girl friend his sister mentioned. He was left-handed, a characteristic of the killer, if you'll remember how all Mrs. Connors' injuries were on the right side of her head. Harry was right-handed of course as I know. I saw them both fight. And he certainly might have Harry's jacket and his gun available to him."

Bauer nodded. "His sister threw some light on that."

"You questioned Rosemary?"

"She came to us. She said she had misled you, unknowingly."

"Yes, although it was an honest mistake. The two brothers had argued about the jacket that morning and Harry had refused to loan it to Ken. So she assumed Ken had not taken it. But, as she said, she left the apartment before Harry did, and so before he might discover it was missing. Later, when he robbed the drugstore, Harry was described by the druggist as wearing dark clothes. If he'd seen it, the druggist couldn't have missed noticing that jacket. If Harry didn't have it, where was it? And once you conceive of the possibility of Ken having the jacket, like any brother who dresses first in the morning, and presumably finding the gun in it, you don't have to go much further. D'Tela had supplied the motive: Ken needed dough and D'Tela had talked of a tip he had on a horse that was running that day and would pay long odds. If Ken could pick up a little quick money, bet it and win, he'd wind up with big quick money."

"Yes. We'd figured it as a chancy, spur-of-the-moment job from the start."

"Sure. Who cases an old lady in advance? And it was even chancier than you think. He took the jacket, found the weapon and had the motive. He had a few drinks at lunch, D'Tela said, and I can testify he gets out of hand when he's had a few drinks. Everything combined.

"I figure he went into the bank to get change like a deliveryman often has to do. He saw the old lady and the hundred buck bill. Perhaps it was only chance he spotted her again, going into the apartment. In any case he saw his opportunity to follow her in, put the gun on her—and escape out the back through the building behind. Remember, he worked that part of town regularly, as his boss told me, and could know these buildings pretty well. And D'Tela was busy running bundles, too. Derby had only to circle around and get back on the truck, which was the perfect escape vehicle. Who'd suspect a delivery man of an armed heist? Of course, after what happened he was afraid to flash that C-note on D'Tela."

"Was D'Tela in on it?"

"No. Why need he have been? He was on and off the truck a lot that day. Ken would not have told him anything. Another thing: look how Harry's peculiar behavior confirms it. He'd found himself a new place to stay for a while—he had left home determined to find one. And he wanted his jacket and gun back, naturally enough. So he came to the place where he knew he would be sure to meet Ken at the end of the day's run—the trucking office. And of course he got them. He looked surly and tough, D'Tela mentioned. Why wouldn't he—he was mad at Ken. And the—"

He had been about to say, "And the C-note I figure was in the jacket pocket. Or else maybe he borrowed money from Ken and got it that way." But he caught that before it got out. Instead, he said, "And the two brothers must have talked things over a little; for when we arrested him Harry showed from what he said that he knew an old woman had been robbed. He didn't know she was dead—maybe Ken himself didn't know or wasn't sure when they met. But that's why Harry was walking the streets so openly later on—he had no idea a murder rap was involved, or that he had been identified in it. He hadn't seen the early tabloids. When he found out, he clammed up to protect himself and his brother."

"Do you think he'd have gone to the chair for Ken?"

"I don't know. Maybe it sounds nuts, but if you'd talked to Harry in Sing Sing—well, he knew he was trapped one way or the other. And they sure were devoted, as Rosemary said. Look how fast Ken moved and the chances he took to frame Mackie, as soon as he learned about the cuff link. I should never have mentioned that to Rosemary but I guess Ken was so close to the whole thing I never dreamt... And Mackie looked hot."

"I'm sorry, sir," said the nurse firmly.

"Okay, Miss." Bauer got up. "One other thing. Ken said he knew that you could never be interested in his sister now, and he felt bad about it." Bauer looked down at Ryan. "Whatever that means. She told me she's taking a job out in Milwaukee next month. Well, don't worry about a thing."

Ryan grinned. "I don't. I'll be up in few days."

"Sure you will," said Bauer hastily. It was not until he left that Ryan realized Bauer had not been referring to his convalescence.

Next day his mother visited him, proudly bearing a new scrapbook, in which she had pasted the newspaper accounts of the gun battle at Mackie's. All the stories explained that even after Harry Derby's conviction Ryan had not been satisfied with the result and had continued working on the case in his spare time, with the result that Harry would now be tried for the drugstore robbery and Ken for the Connors murder. One of the most laudatory stories was bylined "By Jack Sandalwood." None of them mentioned anything about planted evidence.

One item in the scrapbook was a Walter Winchell gossip column, in which one line was ringed in ink:

> "Gee Gee Hawes, the star attraction, is holding hands with what star reporter?"

On his last day in the hospital Ryan received a new Faulkner novel in which was a note. "Good-by and thanks. I'm getting away from here. Too many people know too many things. And now there's only me left, anyway. A girl in Milwaukee has invited me to stay with her. I'm leaving the middle of next month." It was signed "R."

He returned to the precinct on an unseasonably warm afternoon that made people think of things to come, like flower peddlers' wagons and three weeks on the Cape, and cotton dresses and seersucker suits. He walked up the steps and inside the old, cool building, and Sergeant Weiner said, "How you feeling, boy?" and put out a hand of welcome. "Paul wants to see you when you got a moment."

"Thanks, Al."

Lee Lambert came down the stairs. "Hi, Lee," said Ryan, and Lambert looked at him and said, "Hi," and went on out. Lambert was in a hurry.

Ryan started up the stairs. He still had to take these easy. A young patrolman started down at the same time; Ryan recognized him as the rookie who had begun here about the same time he did. The rookie passed him without a glance and without even giving him half the stairs. Everyone seemed in a hurry.

Bauer and a stranger were going over papers at Bauer's desk. Bauer said, "Lieutenant Zimmer, this is Neill Ryan." Zimmer said, "Hello." Bauer shook hands and asked how he felt. Ryan said fine.

"Jerry and I are going over everything because I pull out next week, and he's taking over," said Bauer. "I'm going downtown."

"I'm glad for you," said Ryan. "But I'm sorry you're leaving, Lieutenant." Zimmer's presence made the formal salutation necessary.

"He's Acting Captain now, Ryan," said Zimmer, and added, "Don't feel too badly. You won't be here much longer either." For the first time Zimmer smiled.

So did Bauer, but his expression was pleasant. "It came through yesterday, Neill. You're going up to Harlem."

Ryan looked at them. Harlem?

"I never asked for duty there," he said. "Or even for a transfer. How come?"

"You've done a hell of a job, Neill," said Bauer. "Don't let anyone tell you different." He looked at Zimmer. "They need good men up there. You know what the Twenty-fifth is like. Something doing every minute. It's a compliment."

Ryan's knees felt shaky. Things were coming too fast. Three months ago he would have killed himself to win words like that from Paul Bauer. Now they didn't sit right. Maybe it was Zimmer, coldly watching him. Zimmer picked up a piece of paper from his desk and tossed it to him. "Here's something else." Ryan knew he would not like it.

It was a teletype. Patrolmen Arne Sieger and T. di Paolo at ten-twenty a.m. that day, driving a patrol car along Amsterdam Avenue, had seen a man run from a liquor store and had challenged him. The man ran and then fired back at the police car. One of his shots hit di Paolo's pistol, knocking it from his hand and spraining his wrist. Sieger had driven abreast of the gunman, called on him to drop his gun and then shot him through the head. The dead bandit had been identified as Harry Derby, thirty-seven years old, out on bail pending trial for a drugstore holdup.

"Your boy friend," said Zimmer. He rose suddenly as though he could stand this no longer. "I'll put these back in the file, Paul." He went out, walking on hard heels.

It had taken a while but Ryan got it now.

Bauer saw that in his face. "Relax," he said. "They'll get over this. You know how it is. Everyone gets edgy when a cop gets hit."

"Like hell," said Ryan. "The one thing everyone remembers is I sprung Derby. If he'd been in the death house he'd never have shot anyone."

"He didn't hurt anyone," said Bauer. "What's a sprained wrist?"

"Tell that to the guy he shot at," said Ryan. "And why am I being transferred?"

"Look, Neill. You couldn't expect to say here forever. You got to move around, see the job at different levels, in different areas. A year in Harlem, a year 'way downtown, a couple years with one of the specials—you'll be learning all the time. Don't think everyone feels like Zimmer. Most people feel like I do. You'll see."

Ryan's heart was pounding. What the hell were they doing to him?

"I mean it, Neill." Bauer spoke sharply, making Ryan look at him. "Any time I have a chance to have you working for me, I want you. Know why? Because you're level. I don't mean the others aren't. Zimmer's honest, too, according to his lights. But you've proven what you are by what you did for Derby, and his being killed has nothing to do with it. Zimmer don't understand that, but you do and you've got to allow for the Zimmers. If you don't like that, and can't stand it, this place isn't for you. Otherwise—get the hell up to Harlem."

Bauer had never raised his voice. But when he put out his hand. Ryan took it.

When Ryan went back downstairs a familiar figure—incredible!—was leaning against the desk, talking to Weiner with loud confidence. Time had turned backward.

"For the love of mike—Jabby!"

Jablonski swung around. His gray sports jacket had *Jabby* embroidered in white silk across the left pocket. "Neill! I was just askin' about you."

Ryan was genuinely glad to see Jablonski, and Jablonski was so stirred he replaced his half-smoked cigar with a new one.

"I dropped in to pick up a picture," he said. "How long you out of the hospital?"

"A week. A picture?"

"Yeah. One of the guys on the *Teley* got a good shot of us that night we came in with Derby. I thought I'd put it up in my joint. People are interested in things like that."

"Sure." Ryan looked at the photograph Jabby pulled from its envelope. It showed a confusion of uniforms and reporters in this very entrance. Jabby was a hat and a half-face in the background.

"If you're going uptown I'll give you a lift," said Jablonski. "I got the station wagon."

Weiner and Ryan looked at each other.

"Who drove in, Jab?" asked Al Weiner. "You or your man?"

"Oh, shut up," said Jablonski. "A secondhand station wagon don't cost no more than any other car. And it's handy for groceries and things."

The station wagon was in the parking lot next door. Jabby started it, relit his cigar, and said,

"Hey, you know something? That guy Sandalwood was around here earlier. I guess he doesn't know I'm retired." Jablonski swelled importantly. "He saw me and he says, 'Hey, give your partner Ryan a message for me.' So I say, 'What?' He says, 'Tell Ryan that Derby's getting killed this morning is the luckiest thing that ever happened—to Ryan. Now no one can bother him.' What do you suppose that meant?"

"I don't know. Nothing much."

Jablonski drew comfortably on the new cigar. "Well, I can tell you what it could have meant—if that jerk Sandalwood knew anything. It could mean that with Harry dead, no one in the department need ever find anything out at all. Eh, Neill? Whatever Ken could say would be only hearsay testimony, and from a confessed murderer at that. Eh?"

"I don't know," he said. He did not want to talk about it.

But Jabby was busy turning expertly in front of a cab. "The other night I pick up a little talk," he said. "One of the boys was out. He said you'd been playin' around with Derby's sister."

"Who was this?"

"Look, Neill. You know I've always figured you as my—what do you call at, prodigy? You've done great. I'm proud of you. But for God's sake get away from those Derbys. You mess with that dame, what'll they think of you downtown—a cop married to the sister of two heist guys? You fool around, you'll be transferred out of this precinct. And this is the place to be."

That decided Ryan.

* * * *

At ten o'clock next morning in the stiff-chaired anteroom to the chief inspector's office in New York's police headquarters a buzzer sounded. The uniformed sergeant at a desk told Ryan, "He'll see you now."

Patrick Pembroke's knobby face looked its usual angry inquiry. "I wanted to ask a question, sir," said Ryan.

"Go ahead."

"Before I arrested Ken Derby I saw a little bit of his sister. She's a decent girl. Not like her brothers. But I've been told if I continued to see her, or if by any chance I should marry her, it wouldn't sit well with the department."

Pembroke paused. "We don't usually tell a man whom he should marry."

"One other thing I'd like to ask, sir. I've been transferred from the Seventeenth to the Twenty-fifth Squad. I gather from hints various people have dropped that they feel I was demoted because I—I went out of my way to prove Harry Derby innocent. Which he was."

Pembroke leaned back and laced bony fingers over his midriff. "So that's it. Listen, Ryan. No man in my department ever has to be afraid of honesty. You're not being demoted. We're transferring four teams into Twenty-five—all of them picked for ability and guts. You were picked. Tell that to the first son of a bitch who suggests different. As for the girl, marry whoever you please. And if anyone doesn't like it, take a poke at him."

"Yes, sir. Thank you." He stood up.

Pembroke said, "By the way. What were you going to do if I had said anything else?"

"Well, sir, it was just that I had to get something straight. And I preferred to get it straight from the top."

"I asked, 'What were you going to do?'"

Ryan looked levelly at him. "I was going to send in my papers."

Red-lashed eyes stared unfriendliness at him. "You mind what I said about honesty before you think again of resigning," he said. "And remember me to your mother. I think I've not seen her since her wedding day."

* * * *

It was only an inexpensive ring but Ryan bought it in a Fifth Avenue store because he did not want her to be ashamed of it. Then he took a cab to the dingy building. It was warm and sunny; the front door was open. Ryan went slowly up the flights of stairs and when he got to her floor, he found the door open. She was sitting in a dark blue flannel dressing gown, sipping breakfast coffee and reading the *Mirror.*

She glanced up. "Look who's here!"

She was alone. He was glad of that. "Can I come in?"

"Why not?"

"Catch," he said and threw the little cube-shaped package.

"What's this?"

"I picked it up on my way. I had to go down to headquarters before— before buying it. I had to straighten something out. It's straightened out. I picked this up on my way back."

He looked at her a long moment. He had been deciding a lot of things, and he knew he had made the right decisions. "It's an engagement ring. Take it or leave it."

"An engagement—"

He knew that for once at least he had really surprised her. "Neill!"

"The last time I saw you," Ryan said, "I did a lot of talking about apartments in Queens and having babies and so on. I still think that's a good idea. But in the hospital I had time to do a lot more thinking. You were what I thought of most, Gee Gee. I want to marry you more than anything in the world. If you want to go on dancing and so on, I guess it'll have to be all right with me, at least for a while. But on the other hand, I've got to tell you that if another one of these Derby deals come up, I'll decide it the same way. Because that's the way I am. And also you better remember what I've told you about a cop's pay before you make any decisions and think of the things I won't be able to give you—"

She was bent over the ring, putting it on, the coppery hair hiding her face. Now she held her hand up for him and Ryan saw that there were tears on Gee Gee's cheeks.

"That's not much of a rock," he said. "It probably doesn't fit anyway."

"It fits perfectly," she said tremulously. "And now it's on, it's never coming off. Never."

Suddenly she was in his arms and their mouths found each other's. "You think I'm going to give up the only guy that's ever treated me like a—like a girl, instead of just something to grab?"

After a long time Ryan said huskily, "I think we better get married this afternoon."

www.ingramcontent.com/pod-product-compliance
Lightning Source LLC
Chambersburg PA
CBHW050729250626
47155CB00005B/1716